FOREVER

New York Boston

Forever
Hachette Book Group
1290 Avenue of the Americas, New York, NY 10104
read-forever.com
twitter.com/readforeverpub

First Edition: September 2022

Forever is an imprint of Grand Central Publishing. The Forever name and logo are trademarks of Hachette Book Group, Inc.

The publisher is not responsible for websites (or their content) that are not owned by the publisher.

The Hachette Speakers Bureau provides a wide range of authors for speaking events. To find out more, go to www.hachettespeakersbureau.com or call (866) 376-6591.

Print book interior design by Marie Mundaca

Library of Congress Cataloging-in-Publication Data

Names: Martin, Celestine, author.
Title: Witchful thinking / Celestine Martin.
Description: First edition. | New York : Forever, 2022. | Series: Elemental love ; 1
Identifiers: LCCN 2022005863 | ISBN 9781538738078 (trade paperback) | ISBN 9781538738054 (ebook)
Subjects: LCGFT: Romance fiction. | Paranormal fiction.
Classification: LCC PS3613.A77779 W58 2022 | DDC 813/.6--dc23/eng/20220216
LC record available at https://lccn.loc.gov/2022005863

ISBNs: 9781538738078 (trade paperback), 9781538738054 (ebook)

Printed in the United States of America

LSC-C

Printing 1, 2022

For Matthew
Thank you for being a wish come true.

Acknowledgments

I'm incredibly grateful to my agent, Lauren Bieker, who took a chance on my rough draft of a book many years ago. Thank you for helping make this dream come true.

To the team at Forever: Madeleine Colavita, Ambriah Underwood, the production team with a special shoutout to Penina Lopez and Anjuli Johnson for making this book sparkle and shine. Each of you is amazing at your job, and I thank you for helping make this book a reality.

This book would not have been possible without the support and nurturing of my family. Thank you to Mama, who gave me my first book; Papa, who took me to the library on the weekends; and Brother for buying my first creative writing book for my thirteenth birthday. I am who I am because of your love, strength, and joy. Love to my North and South Carolinas and Hawai'i families, who have always had a kind word or heart emoji for me no matter the time, day or night. Thank you to my aunts, uncles, and cousins, who have supported me in writing by giving me countless books, notebooks, and journals! You gave me the kindling to grow this fire to write, and I'm forever grateful for you all.

Thank you to my husband, Matt, who is sweeter than any

romantic hero I could ever imagine. You are wonderful, from listening to me talk out the beats, to ranting about sticking the landing, to caring for our baby so I could get in the early morning writing sprints. To our new addition, Poppyseed, you are a long-awaited wish, and you've brought immense joy into our lives. Thank you, my love.

I want to extend my sincere thanks to my Rutgers University/Douglass College crew, especially Emily and Patricia, and my mentor/professor and friend Susan Miller. I'm a better person for being blessed with your friendship.

To all my Creative Writing/CCNY colleagues who read the very beginnings of this book over a decade ago in our fiction workshop, thank you for your time and feedback. To Joe Okonkwo and Lisa Ko, thank you for reminding me to keep writing. To my day job coworkers who asked me during my lunch break whether I was still writing my novel. It's done! Thank you for asking after staff meetings and keeping me honest. I didn't quit my daydream because of your support.

To my professional and creative communities, including but not limited to RWA/NYC, NaNoWriMo, Library of Congress, and Romance Rogues, sincere thanks to every one of you who encouraged me to trust the process. I want to acknowledge the friendship and support of the following writers: Lucy Eden and Lori Wendy, for keeping me writing during the hard times, and Alexis Daria for telling me I had a good idea when this book was a scattered collection of scenes. To LaQuette, who answered my random texts and emojis and constantly gave me glitter and love.

ACKNOWLEDGMENTS

To Stacey Agdern, whose light and energy humble me all the time.

To my writing inspirations, Virginia Hamilton and Zora Neale Hurston, who published the myths, fairy tales, and traditions/customs that gave me the spark to write about everyday magic.

WITCHFUL THINKING

Caraway Notes on Herbs

Lavender *raises the spirits. This herb is used for relaxation, to calm nerves, and to treat burns. A few fresh or dried flowers added to tea will have a cheering effect on a person.*

Rosemary, *wonderful for remembrance, is often used to relieve cold headaches, tension, and forgetfulness.*

Rosebushes *produce fruit named the rosehip. It can boost the immune system.*

Passionflower *is used in sleeping blends and helps in addressing insomnia and restlessness. It will ease a racing mind.*

Honeysuckle *is used to protect homes from evil spirits and thieves. Keep it by your front door to guard your safe space.*

Black pepper *can be used to heat up any spell or root work. Be careful with this ingredient, as it can be used to make things hot and provoke change.*

Chamomile *can be used to ease a nervous stomach when made into tea. Place dried chamomile flowers in boiling water, let it steep for seven minutes, and add honey.*

A Brief History of Freya Grove

From the Freya Grove Historical Society website

The seaside town of Freya Grove, New Jersey, was founded in 1871 during the boom of the nationwide spiritualist movement. It is known to have mystical roots and supernatural connections to the spiritual underworld. Freya Grove, located on the Jersey Shore, is famously known as one of the Shore Point towns on the Garden State Parkway. The legend and lore of Freya Grove has attracted and brought tourists, writers, dreamers, and anyone interested in otherworldly affairs. Remember, you're only a stranger once in Freya Grove. The Grove always remembers.

May

lily of the valley and hawthorn

Chapter One

Whenever it rained in Freya Grove, New Jersey, Nana Ruth Naomi Caraway, the matriarch witch of the family, said the same proverb to her eldest granddaughter, Lucy.

"You don't know how deep a puddle is until you step in it."

With her plastic barrettes and baby teeth, Lucy had nodded, awed by Nana's never-ending words. They sounded so wise, but of course she, having only started kindergarten that year, didn't know what Nana was talking about at all. Nana leaned on her cane, squinted at the downpour from the warmth of their communal living room, and nudged little Lucy with her bony elbow. Her eyes twinkled with mischief as she opened the door and ushered Lucy outside into the rain. Together, they splashed around in the puddles on the sidewalk, their joyful laughs echoing out onto Summerfield Street. Afterward, they came back inside, dried off, and had cookies and hot mugs of loose tea. Nana showed Lucy how to read endless possibilities in the bottom of a porcelain cup through tea leaves.

That rainy afternoon was the first time Lucy learned that she, like everyone else in her family, was a very special person.

Plants bloomed and opened under Nana's attention and touch. Pots and pans bubbled with sweet and oily brews that were left to simmer for hours. Nana knew when the phone was about to ring before it made a sound and when visitors were coming over. Dressed in a pink calico house dress, she rolled the Mercury dime between her fingers while she scanned aged, stained pages of the ancestral spell book.

Nana was with the ancestors now, but the lessons remained rooted in every spell Lucy completed. Now when it rained, Lucy felt a grief so deep and swift it cut across her chest. She might have jumped in the puddles back then, but now Lucy avoided all big and small waters. What was the point of messing up her shoes? Her weather app alerted her to any surprising thunderstorms headed to the Jersey Shore. She had collapsible umbrellas in both her purse and desk at school. She didn't jump into bodies of water without looking, and she, as TLC warned years ago, didn't go chasing waterfalls. Lucy avoided surprises by keeping her behind home and staying away from places she had no business being.

No surprises. Just the way she liked it.

That's why she loved the Founders' Day Festival.

It took place the second week of May; it lasted for five days and was the unofficial start of the beach season in the Grove. All fun at the festival was structured and predictable. There was always the knockdown game, the Madame Zora fortune booth, funnel cake stands, and the Ferris wheel, which sparkled on the grounds. As she and her sisters drove to the festival from their family's house in their beat-up car, giddiness bubbled within her. Amusement rides, food trucks, and booths set up in Grove Park were illuminated in the near distance. Lucy parked the car and practically sprinted over to the festival, her sisters trailing two blocks behind her.

This event signaled the end of the school year and the beginning of summer vacation. She breathed in the fresh-cut grass and let out the stress of getting her final marking period grades in on time. The sun set, and the festival lights lit up the large park. Seagulls drifted on the thermals, searching for abandoned french fries. The ocean breeze, calm and inviting, wafted through the air. She stood at the edge of the fair-grounds, scanning the white and purple booths and smiling at the citizens—both human and non-human—who shared the same magic in their eyes. It was nice to see goblins and ghosts out on the prowl, rubbing shoulders with their fellow neighbors.

The Grove was out to play.

She smiled, but there was a sense of hesitancy inside that made her stand still. Tonight was her first time out in public since she and Marcus broke up over winter break. She'd used the cold season to recharge, drink huge cups of clove and cinnamon tea with honey, and prepare charms for the impending spring. But it was time. The seasons had changed, and she couldn't hide away at home any longer. Once spring bloomed, so did she, so she ventured out into the Grove. Her soul mate and destiny waited.

Cheers caught her attention like a forgotten song playing over the radio. Carnival barkers enticed people to try their luck. Squeals from passengers filled the air. The scent of delicious salty, buttery popcorn and fried dough eased her nerves. As a teacher, she wasn't running toward the end of the school year but rather throwing herself over the line like an Olympic racer trying for a photo finish. There were only so many times she could deal with that one colleague asking the unnecessary, long-winded question after every staff meeting and being asked to cover another class during her lunch break.

She wasn't burnt out; she was burnt to a crisp.

Summer was in her reach if she only held on for a little longer.

"Hey!" Callie walked up to her, knocking her out of her musings. "You didn't wait for us to pay the meter!"

A small wedge of guilt hit her stomach. She gave her youngest sister a weak smile. "I didn't want to miss anything."

"Were you trying to ditch us?" Callie looped an arm around Lucy's shoulder and pulled her in for a quick side hug.

"I thought about it." Lucy held back a laugh. "All's fair with festivals and funnel cake."

Callie pinched her arm. "Rude. Wait until I tell Sirena."

"Right." Lucy glanced around, found Sirena, and sighed. "I don't think she cares."

Sirena stood off on the sidewalk, catching up with a dapper-looking man.

"Welp. She's gone." Callie looked in Sirena's direction and let out a groan. "Is that Felix? Why am I not surprised?"

Lucy sighed sarcastically. "Of course. He probably wanted to talk about catering."

She eyed them for a long moment. Her senses tingled her neck. From the way Sirena laughed and played with her two-tone goddess locs and how Felix leaned into her space, it was apparent that she wasn't rushing to join them.

Callie lowered her voice and nodded over at Felix. "No one laughs that loud when they're talking about appetizers."

Lucy quietly agreed. Felix, with his constantly crooked smile, loved to talk to Sirena for "just a moment." Despite the obvious chemistry between the two friends, neither of them had made a move to go out on a real adult date. Nana had a saying when it came to matters of adult life and love: Fish or cut bait. You either made a move or you left a person alone. Felix did nothing, even though Sirena was tossing bait his way. Lucy hoped for her sister's sake that she'd stop chumming his waters.

"I guess it's just you and me tonight, kid," Lucy said.

She pulled Callie along to the ticket booth, where they stood in line for tickets. "Watch out for the satyrs. They always want to play you a song. Don't fall for it."

Just then, a pair of furry satyrs, bare chested and wearing crowns of grape leaves, passed by, openly assessing them with interested glances. It was as if she'd conjured them with her words. Lucy rolled her eyes. Callie winked.

"I can't make any promises," Callie said, giving the duo a flirty wave. "Can you imagine what you do with those horns?"

"Listen, I have no time for pan pipes and rolls in meadows."

"There's nothing wrong with having a friendly drink. That reminds me. Ursula's coming over tonight." Callie sighed. "She said she needed an emergency bridal party meeting."

"We just had a meeting on Tuesday," Lucy said, rubbing her forehead in frustration. *Everything is an emergency with Ursula.* "She called a Zoom meeting over ordering edible gold lollipops for wedding favors. I don't think she even ordered them!"

All three sisters were members of Ursula's bridal party, with Lucy being the maid of honor.

Callie pouted. "I can't believe she's getting married. Yesterday we were brewing potions and wearing black eyeliner."

"No, I tried to keep you from burning off your eyebrows with a glamour spell," Lucy said with a wince. Callie, with her penciled-in brows, had looked like Charlie Brown's long-lost sister for three weeks in high school. Lucy did her best to protect her sisters and fellow witches from reckless spells, but sometimes she missed the mark.

They moved up in the ticket line. "It would've worked if I hadn't mixed up the salt with sugar," Callie said. She grimaced in good humor. "Ursula finds the most interesting spells."

"You can't always trust spells from YouTube or Pinterest," Lucy warned.

"Listen, I found that feta and tomato recipe online, and you liked it," Callie pointed out. "Besides, whatever spell she cast on Lincoln got her a ring on her finger."

A feeling of melancholy flickered through Lucy. Ursula was the first of the Caraway cousins to get married. The unofficial fourth Caraway sister, Ursula, was the most polished of them all. She didn't go anywhere without wearing her strand of pearls, a cardigan sweater, and a pastel dress, always looking like an aspiring country club member.

"Dress for the life you want," Ursula had once told them over their monthly brunch. But behind that polish was a wild streak that came out whenever she got her hands on a root or a charm. Too many times, Lucy'd had to make sure Ursula didn't end up flashing half the town during the Siren Parade. They'd been there for each other no matter what, but their personal experiences and jobs had sent them in different directions. Soon Ursula would have her own home and children, and the growing gap of life would widen between them.

Soon magic would be the only thing they'd have in common.

Lucy brushed off her melancholy and greeted the ticket seller with a kind smile. "I'll take a hundred tickets, please."

"I don't think we'll need that many," Callie said with a laugh.

"These tickets are good for the whole week. I'm getting my money's worth."

Lucy paid for the tickets, then turned to Callie, who was busy scrolling on her phone. Ever since she was fourteen years old, she'd had the freaking thing in her hand, always illuminating her face like a makeup ring light.

"Sorry, I got a text. My mini mason jar shot glasses just shipped."

Lucy sighed loudly. Callie didn't look up from the screen. She kept typing, her thumbs flying over the phone. "This is my hustle. Don't make that annoyed-teacher sound. I have a business to run. I'm not one of your students."

"Then stop acting like one of my students," Lucy retorted. "Do you want to go on the Ferris wheel?"

"I don't like heights."

"Do you want to play the dart game?"

"The balloons don't pop! The game is rigged."

"Let's go get some kettle corn."

Callie dropped her phone into her back pocket. "Eh, the kernels get caught in my teeth."

Lucy groaned. Callie never made up her mind about

anything, which meant they did nothing when they were together. Well, she could make up her mind. She just didn't like any of Lucy's suggestions. It was her gift as the baby of the family to annoy her siblings with a smile. Sirena was usually the tiebreaker, but she wasn't here. Lucy had resigned herself to lusting over the kettle corn booth when Callie slapped her arm.

"Look." Callie slapped Lucy's arm again, excitedly.

Lucy pulled her arm away and rubbed the stinging skin. "Ouch. Stop hitting me!"

"There's Mayor Walker!"

"You know I can see her. I'm not blindfolded."

Mayor Walker stood over by the game with the stuffed animals. The mayor, the Honorable Des'ree Walker, dressed in a fashionable floral jumper, glanced around at the crowd with a superior air as if she were a queen visiting her lowly subjects. Her eyes flickered over the festival, and a pleased look flashed upon her face.

"She hasn't answered my email about the luncheon yet," Callie grumbled.

"Email her later. We're having fun."

"It can't wait. I'll be right back," Callie said. "Mayor Walker!"

Callie rushed over to the mayor without another look back. It was clear from her animated hand motions and lively discussion with the mayor that Cal wasn't coming back. Cal was a Boss Lady with a capital *B*, having started her own event planning business after dropping out of college. With her planning talent, she could even make a trip to the DMV something to look forward to by throwing glitter, giving out goody bags, and handing out flavored mocktails while drivers renewed their licenses.

Lucy was filled half with dread, half with anxiousness as she glanced over at Mayor Walker and Callie. If she was here, then Marcus was probably nearby. The dread went up a notch at that thought. Marcus Walker, the town's favorite son, was her ex and the mayor's elder son. All she had to do was think of Marcus and he popped up in front of her. They'd always bump into each other at town events and celebrations, and he'd sweet-talk her into another conversation about the good days.

He was comforting, like her favorite breakfast tea, which she drank every morning before work. Rich. Full-bodied. Basic. There wasn't anything wrong with Marcus, but there wasn't anything special about them being together. She'd seen the love between her grandparents. Their souls just clicked. Her parents, Vanessa and Isaac, married thirty-seven years, just fit together like missing puzzle pieces.

She and Marcus didn't click. She was searching for her soul mate, her personal click.

It didn't help that Marcus's twin brother, Lincoln, was engaged to Ursula, which meant she ran into Marcus all the time. Even though their breakup was amicable, Marcus was a typical Taurus man and didn't give up what he wanted— a second chance with her—without a fight. It'd gotten so awkward that she'd started finding silly-ass reasons not to go out with them for dinner, drinks, or happy hour. How many more times could she tell them she was cleaning her crystals and feeding their familiar, a gray cat named Shadow? She loved amethyst, but she needed to come up with another excuse. Oh well, at least the festival was a nice distraction from Marcus and everything else. Her phone buzzed. *Spoke too soon.* She glanced down at the incoming email. The subject line caught her attention, and she clicked it open with her thumb.

Subject: Alumni Class Note Deadline Tomorrow!

Hello Freya Grove Gladiators!

It's time to submit our class notes for the next edition of the *In the Grove* e-newsletter coming out this Sunday. Tell us what's going on with you! New job? New relationship? Recent travels? Exciting news?

It would be wonderful to hear from fellow alumni, even if not much is going on! Keep all class notes to ten sentences or less, and include your name!

As always, please pass this message forward if you know a classmate who is not getting this information, and please make sure I have your most up-to-date contact information.

If you have any questions, please do not hesitate to contact me!

Best wishes,
Quentin Jacobson
Class Secretary

PS. Mark your calendar for our reunion weekend during the last week of August. We'd love to celebrate this moment with you.

Well, that happened. All the funnel cake in the world couldn't change how crappy she felt after reading that email. Her mind answered the questions.

New job? She taught high school history and economics for the seventh year in a row, which was coming to an end soon.

New relationship? She was single again. No follow-up questions.

Recent travels? She hadn't left the state since Nana passed away two years ago.

Exciting news? Well, she'd inherited a hundred-year-old Victorian manor from Nana Ruth, along with a lot of spell books. That was nothing new. It happened a while ago...

She could cut, copy, and paste the same class notes from the last two years, and no one would notice. The only thing new about Lucy was the booty-enhancing boy shorts underwear she'd gotten on sale at Circe's Closet. A dull ache grew behind her eyes. Nana had trusted Lucy to watch over the Caraway witches' legacy. No one protected her family legacy like she could, but it gave her pause. Who in their right witchy mind could follow in Ruth Naomi Caraway's footsteps? No one. Ruth was a once-in-a-century witch who'd made an indelible mark on the Caraway family tree.

She'd be remembered generations from now. Who'd remember Lucy?

Her stomach churned. She was no longer in the mood

for carnival junk food. She'd just be another random face in the family album, her life forgotten to time. Years from now people would narrow their eyes and tilt their heads in memory and say, *Oh yes, Lucy, she drank a lot of tea, bathed in honeysuckle and vanilla oil, and she loved her crystals—a lot.*

Lucy toyed with the silver saint medallion on her charm bracelet, a sweet sixteen gift from Nana, while she gathered her thoughts. She racked her brain to come up with something—anything—special about her life. What was she going to talk to people about at the reunion? Her tea pantry? Her spell books? Her cat? She rubbed her temples gently with her fingers. All she could think of was she had a new tea blend—cucumber, mint, and melon—waiting to be tasted.

Ugh, an annoyed voice said. *Could you be any more boring?*

She wished she had a life worth writing about, worth being celebrated, but it was so ordinary. Her twenty-ninth birthday last month meant the return of Saturn, the time of great growth. Scrying into water bowls and reading tea leaves left her with more questions than answers. How was she going to grow where she was planted?

How was she going to create a life that made her excited? A lucky paper fortune from Madame Zora would give her the answers she sought. She walked over to the familiar burgundy booth by the Ferris wheel. The machine, wheeled in from the local arcade and hooked up to a small generator, was a popular attraction. Her heart lifted seeing the finely dressed fortune-teller figure with the painted smile.

It was magic time.

Madame Zora never let her down, and this machine was rumored to be blessed by her great-granddaughter. Lucy got in line behind two others, her foot mindlessly tapping as she waited for her turn. More people got in line behind her. It took five minutes before it was her turn. She stood in front of the electric light sign proclaiming MADAME ZORA'S MYSTIC FORTUNE BOOTH. If she didn't know what the future held, Madame Zora always had the answer for her.

She fed the money slot and pressed the button to start the reading. Bells chimed and the machine emitted an eerie light. Energy buzzed from inside and sparked against her skin. It was happening. The crystal ball glowed, and the robot-puppet waved her bejeweled hand over said ball. The machinery whirled. Lucy rubbed her hands together and cupped them to receive her fortune. *Come on, Madame Zora. Show me what you got.*

The machine grunted, then beeped. She watched the fortune dispenser slot for the yellow paper. Nothing appeared. Lucy took in a deep breath and calmed her nerves. It grunted and beeped twice again. No fortune popped out of the slot. She leaned down and reached into the slot with her fingers. The paper fortune was there—she could feel it with her fingertips—but it wasn't moving. *No. No. No.* Despite all the tugging, the fortune wasn't going anywhere.

A line was forming behind her. There were a few disappointed sighs.

She couldn't be the person who broke *the* Madame Zora machine!

Well, at least that would give her something to write about in the class notes.

"Is everything okay?" a male voice asked behind her.

She froze, her senses tingling. Why did that voice sound familiar?

"No." Lucy sighed. "My fortune got stuck."

"Hold on. I got you." The mystery man came to her rescue. Lucy stepped back as he stood in front of the machine. Whoa. He was a big, broad man who looked as if he could lift and shake the fortunes out of Madame Zora's machine without breaking a sweat. She studied his side profile. Her heart jumped in her throat. From where she was standing, with his high-top fade and strong chin, he looked a lot like Alex. Her spirit practically leaped out of her body.

She shoved away that idea. No, that wasn't possible. According to Alex's social media posts, he was cliff jumping into clear blue water with gorgeous models cheering him on from the sidelines. No one—absolutely no one—gave up Hawaii for the Jersey Shore. But with every passing moment, her tingling senses weren't tingling anymore. She had full-on goose bumps. Her eyes drank him in greedily, as if he were that last glass of iced tea and she'd just finished a long summer run. His presence cooled her inside. The thirsty parts of her rejoiced. She pressed her hand to her chest to make sure her heart hadn't floated away from her like a lost balloon.

Lucy stepped away. She was too close. The last time she'd seen Alex, he'd turned his back on the Grove and her. What in Earth's oceans could've possibly brought him home?

Chapter Two

☾

here was nothing in Freya Grove that surprised Alexander "Alex" Owen Dwyer anymore.

He'd been back in town less than two days, and nothing
had changed. As families *ooh*ed and *aah*ed at the electric
display, he merely blinked. A wave of recollection washed
over him as he watched neon make the air sizzle with light. It
was the same thing year in and year out. The tightness in his
chest eased a fraction. He reluctantly embraced this feeling,
as if he'd been given a heavy coat to wear in the middle of a
rainstorm, to shield him from the cold. The feeling kept him
in the moment. The town was predictable. Though a tiny
part of him was comforted by the ebb and flow of the Grove,
his family kept him checking his phone for random text
messages detailing another Dwyer misadventure. The Dwyer
merfolk were known for their...uh...interesting pursuits.
Some relatives blamed the merfolk blood in their veins for
influencing them to "go hard on all that weird whimsical
shit," as his college-age cousin Mariah would say in their
family text chain.

Alex thought it was just the risk merfolk took when they
made the journey from ocean to land. It was hard to be

human, and Dwyer folk were doing their best to find their rhythm on solid ground. If it wasn't his cousin Tony searching for lost treasure off the Florida Keys, it was his aunt Maggie investing her retirement money in a pirate-themed bed-and-breakfast. His parents, Kia and Nathan Dwyer, weren't immune to the Dwyer whims. His childhood, while stable in some parts, wasn't without the controlled chaotic moments.

It wasn't unusual to wake up and have Mom and Pop declare at breakfast that they were moving to Alaska, then at dinnertime decide that they didn't want to buy bear repellent. Their careers in the tourism and hospitality industry allowed them to move wherever the people and adventures were with ease. He'd lived in half of the country before his fourteenth birthday and had the T-shirts and mugs to prove it. Every school year, he was the new kid in town, until his family found a little bungalow apartment in Freya Grove. His last first day of school, he sat next to a girl wearing an overloaded charm bracelet, big brown eyes, and a sense of innate magic about her.

He shook off the memory, not wanting to go there yet.

Once he graduated from high school, he left Freya Grove and traveled the world, earning respect for his award-winning photography and social media posts. In the last decade, Alex made his biannual trip home like the good son he tried to be but then promptly left town before he could let the water dry off his scales. It wasn't good to get too invested. He really didn't want to get caught up in whatever his parents planned, but Mom could be very persistent. She used her exclamation key with reckless abandon. There wasn't an emoji Mom didn't use, conveying her bubbly personality through the phone. Mom kept sending cheerful messages closer to his birthday to get him to come home. With every incoming *ping-ping*, his nerves jumped up.

> It's your 29th birthday! Let's celebrate! 🎉

> It's the end of a great chapter in your life! We have to honor your Saturn year! 🪐

> We got you something special. It's too large to mail! You have to come home for it! 😌 ✉️

> It'll be fun! We'll go to Ad Astra. We'll order a cake, the fancy one with the chocolate ganache. 🧁 😊

He was here for chocolate cake.

Alex responded, I'll be there.

Mom immediately replied, Wooooo!! 😄

He'd be home for a few days in time for the festival. He drove into town just yesterday, the night before his birthday, treating himself to a long weekend stay at the Tides Hotel on Ocean Avenue. He celebrated his special day by taking a swim in the Atlantic, letting his home waters cleanse his scales. Alex planned a stroll around the grounds before heading over to Ad Astra for his birthday dinner and dessert.

Tomorrow morning he'd check out, birthday gift in hand, and head back on the road. The last year was...eventful. His apartment lease was up in less than a week, and whatever items he couldn't sell, he gave away or donated. On New

Year's Day, Nahla had promptly ended their engagement by leaving her princess-cut ring on the kitchen counter with a follow-up text to his phone.

Alex,

Hurting you is the last thing I want to do. There needs to be more to a relationship than having fun. Our connection seems so shallow. I need something deeper and real. I wish that the future holds something much better for both of us. I hope you find what you're searching for. I'm sorry.

XOXO Nahla

Damn. Those words haunted him, kept him up at night like a monster under his bed. She wanted to start the new year with a clean slate while cleaning him out of her life as well. He'd taken a sabbatical from photography, unable to find inspiration for his upcoming gallery showing. The potential of a good surprise, in the form of a gift from the parents, encouraged him to come home, if only for a few days. He'd be on a hunt for another apartment—or rather, another place to lay his head—soon enough. Once again, he was searching.

Standing under the light of the Ferris wheel, Alex snapped a few candids on his phone. He wanted good memories of this place when he left tomorrow. Maybe being back in the Grove would entice his missing photography muse to return to him. In his opinion, he hadn't snapped a good photo or image in months, unable to find that elusive perfect shot. Now, he couldn't put his phone down, trying to capture the images before him at the festival. Everything was touched with unspoken magic. Not every place in the world held the magic that the Grove did, so he reveled in the moment. Balloons that threatened to fly away stayed wrapped around small, eager hands.

Popcorn never spilled but stayed in its striped containers. Magic was an open secret in the Grove. Not everyone subscribed to the magic, but it was there in the atmosphere, ready for the picking like hanging flowers from a tree. He walked around, chuckling at the familiar entertainments. There was the knockdown game, the Madame Zora fortune booth, junk food stands, and the Ferris wheel, which had made the world glow and shine the same way so many years ago. This place had once been home but no longer. The Freya Grove Historical Society Founders' Day Festival was a popular Jersey Shore attraction every single year. Magazines and travel blogs he sometimes freelanced for repeatedly highlighted the event as a "must go" and "once-in-a-lifetime experience." Every late May, the Grove was descended upon by thousands of tourists who hoped to get a glimpse of a wayward witch or a ghoulish ghost. It was as if the town had been frozen by a timeless enchantment to remain changeless for years. The lights filled the darkening sky with animated colors. The Grove had once been his playground.

Gargoyles roaming around by the library. Okay.

Vampires bowling at the Grove Lanes at midnight? Fine.

Witches and fauns gathering around in the West Grove party wearing nothing but smiles and daisy crowns in their hair. Sure.

There was nothing exciting about the Grove. Period.

He scanned the festival and noted where he could take a quick picture. In addition to his photography career, he worked as a social media manager. Clients from all over the world hired him to dazzle and pull people onto the websites and social media feeds with images that incite the imagination. This town, as charming as it seemed, hid a dark side that he'd seen too many times. Behind the lace curtains and closed doors of the Grove, people gossiped and cast hexes against their neighbors.

Alex walked a few steps. The flash of a silver charm bracelet caught his attention and drew his focus. Like any merfolk, he loved shiny, beautiful things and often found himself coveting a vintage watch or an heirloom he spied on his adventures. His scales itched. *No way.* He knew that bracelet.

He'd seen that bracelet on his last first day of school and had met its owner.

He'd saved that bracelet from Grove Lake and been rewarded with the sweetest hug he'd ever been given. Years later, he still felt her soft body pressed against his—sending his thoughts spiraling out into the universe. He knew that wrist. He'd held that wrist and felt her pulse kick up under his palm when they danced under the tea lights on prom night.

He knew her. Lucinda Lucy Caraway. Lu.

He got in line behind her in the Madame Zora fortune booth line, where he stopped and studied her. Her hair, once long and braided, was short and natural, with ziggy curls that sprang out into the air. Her fitted pencil skirt showed off her thick, shapely legs, and her ballet flats tapped on the ground impatiently for the machine. He studied her full curves the way the first mapmakers did a map—with a sense of awe at the knowledge of a new world. The light-blue jean jacket she wore was covered in various pins and patches, including one circle patch that proudly said MY BROOMSTICK RUNS ON TEA.

She turned momentarily away from the booth. He caught her profile. *Hey now.* He breathed in shallow, quick gasps, as if he were prepping himself to submerge into an ice bath. She looked, with her touches of silver and gemstone jewelry, more ethereal than ever. Sheer magic glowed from her skin. A thrill of anticipation touched his spine. He leaned in as she stepped forward, fed the Madame Zora machine, and waited. He couldn't resist another glance. She'd starred in his dreams for so long, his brain didn't believe that she was close enough to touch. He kept himself from blinking in case she vanished from sight. A light breeze kicked up the festival, and her perfume, a mix of sweet, floral scents, tickled his nose. She bent over and fumbled with the paper slot, giving him a view of her round behind. *Hello.* He stared but shielded her from view so anyone else wouldn't get a look. He glanced over his shoulder. A line was forming behind them, and a few grumbles erupted from the growing crowd.

"What's the holdup?"

"You didn't break it, did you?"

When did people get so precious about the machine? For their senior prank, their class had dressed up Madame Zora and posed with it for picture day. Even the principal got in on the fun and took an ill-advised selfie with Zora. Alex chuckled at the long-forgotten moment, then returned his focus to Lucy, who yanked at the machine slot. Alex hesitated. This wasn't how he wanted to see her again—he hadn't planned on seeing her again at all, but fate was forcing him to play his hand.

"Is everything okay?" he asked.

She stilled for a moment. He held his breath. She didn't turn around.

"No." Lucy sighed. "My fortune got stuck."

"Hold on. I got you."

She moved back, and he stepped in. He knelt on the ground and reached into the dispensing slot. With a quick yank, he pulled the partially torn fortune out and then stood. He faced her, holding it in the palm of his hand. Their eyes connected. At that moment, everything crystallized. She'd grown into her beauty, her face rounded out by age and her curves lived in and fleshed out. Her charm bracelet jangled when she pressed a hand to her chest. Her open brown eyes were muted with distrust.

"Alex?" she asked. Her voice sounded unsteady. Uncertain. His stomach clenched. Yeah, he'd earned that hesitancy.

"Hey, Lucy."

She took the fortune from his hand, touching his scales with her fingertips. The brief contact sent an electric shock over his skin. It pulsed and charged every cell within him. Eleven years, eight months, three weeks, and twenty-seven days. That was how long it had been since he'd touched Lucy. And he'd sworn then that it would be the last time ever.

Chapter Three

𝒮hock hit Lucy like a quick, sharp pain when their eyes connected by the fortune-telling booth. It was like getting a paper cut, a quick slash to her senses, followed by a hurtful throbbing that kept her present. She'd accepted a long time ago that Alex Dwyer wasn't made for life in the Grove, and she wasn't seeing him again except for in her dreams. Once in a blue moon, she had one. She'd find herself magically transported into the middle of the ocean on a rowboat and surrounded by nothing but water and sky. There were no oars to help her row to shore. Just when she started to scream for help, Alex would pop up from under the surface. He'd peer at her, his face and chest covered in shimmering scales and shells. He'd look at her with a mixture of interest and wariness. It matched the look he was giving her right now, in real life. Unlike the dream, Lucy was very aware of the heat of his body and the subtle sea-salt scent of his skin. Stupid dream. She stepped to the side, away from the fortune-telling machine. Alex followed her.

"Thanks for helping me out," Lucy said. "I didn't want to be the person who broke Madame Zora."

"No problem." Alex waved her words away as if it were no

big deal. He considered the machine for a moment. "I'm sure she's seen worse."

She opened her mouth but then closed it. Her mind ping-ponged thoughts. *Is he talking about the senior prank? No, he probably doesn't ever think of the Grove.* Neither of them moved. Lucy came up with various dismissals. *It was nice seeing you. Have a good life. See you next lifetime.* She wanted to snap those words at him, but good manners and the thought of Nana coming back and haunting her for being rude kept her quiet. Even so, being near him reminded her of the hurt she'd felt when he'd left town mere minutes after graduation ended. She'd eaten a whole bag of fun-size peanut butter cups with Ursula and sang to some indie heartbreak songs she heard on MTV. How did the song go? *The first cut is the deepest.* She'd written countless pages in her note-book and knew there were many words to describe Alexander Owen Dwyer.

Social media demigod. Adventurer. *Merman.*

But the one she found most fitting was "heartbreaker."

They'd never officially dated. Being sweet naive teenagers at the time, they weren't brave enough to put out their bait. It was all the possibilities she saw in Alex that broke her heart. Much like the tea leaves in a cup, Lucy saw fluid visions of the romance that could have been if she had taken a risk with him. Sometimes, he stayed for a week. Other times he stayed until the end of the summer. She always ended up hurt when he left town, which he always did in the visions in her mind. What did Nana tell her constantly? *You can't keep a merman in a fishbowl.* This wasn't the night for regrets, so she pushed them out of her mind. She fixed a polite smile.

"How have you been?" she asked.

"Fine. How long has it been?"

"It's been a while."

Eleven years, but who was counting? Another silent, strained pause stretched on between them. They studied each other underneath the neon lights. His once boyish face was now rugged from being outside and in the sun chasing the perfect shot. Alex's hazel eyes were still piercing, but now they held the coldness of the ocean depths. There were crinkles around them from where he probably squinted behind a camera or into a lens.

His once-recognizable dark-green hair was now dyed black.

His summer suit outlined his solid form, a body that was carved by the ocean's waves.

Her mind spun in quiet concern. What brought the merman home after all this time?

The last news she'd heard about Alex—via a social media posting—a year ago, he was engaged to be married. The engagement photo had been the typical kiss and hug "she said yes" that populated her feed these days. Back then the news had shocked her. The merman who'd proudly declared to his entire senior class that he wasn't meant for an ordinary, boring life like everyone else got engaged. Just like everyone else. She scanned his hands, then snapped her eyes up to his face. There was no wedding ring. There wasn't even a tan line or indentation. Hmm. Apparently, no one had captured the slippery merman yet. He met her stare. Alex watched her carefully, as if he worried she'd disappear into thin air. Ha. She knew that he was probably the one who'd disappear. Mermen could swim an ocean's length in a matter of a day.

A flash of humor lit his eyes. "If you keep looking at me like that, I might think you like me," he drawled.

"Can't have that." Lucy waved her hand at his words. "Your ego is big enough. How many followers do you have now? Ten million?"

"If only. The last time I checked it was reaching one million."

Lucy held back a groan. She didn't have one million of anything—unless you were counting wishes. The gold flecks in his eyes caught the electric lights of the rides. He looked otherworldly, like a flashlight fish using bioluminescence to light its path in the darkness of the ocean. How had he grown more gorgeous over time? *Lucky merman.*

She must have made an odd expression because Alex asked, "What's going on in that mind of yours?"

"Nothing."

"For some reason, I don't believe you."

"Believe whatever you want," she said.

A strained pause went by. "So, how about this weather?" he asked.

What kind of weak sauce was that? Her eyes twitched. "Really, Dwyer? You can do better than that. I believe in you."

"So, what should we talk about?" Alex asked, his brow furrowed. It was clear from the annoyed vibe he gave off that he wasn't used to small talk.

"Are you going to the alumni reunion?" she asked.

His face went blank. His mouth opened and closed like a beached fish. He had no clue what the hell she was talking about. Lucy held up her phone, the alumni update email still open.

"Alumni reunion? Quentin's been sending, like, a dozen emails for the last two months about it." Alex barely scanned the screen, then looked back at her.

"Oh, those emails. I let those go to spam."

"You're gonna miss out on some good times," Lucy insisted, putting her phone away.

"If anyone wants to know how I'm doing, they can follow me online," Alex pointed out. "I don't need my business being shared in the *In the Grove* newsletter."

"You put your business out there anyway. Why not share it with the Grove?" Lucy retorted.

Alex gave her a "you got me there" single shoulder shrug. "I'm good. I'm honest with my followers. That's enough for me."

"Yes, because everyone is being honest online." There was defiance in her tone as well as subtle challenge. She saw him force his lips to part into a stiff curved smile. It seemed that she'd hit a nerve with that comment. Alex showed the merman he wanted the world to see, not necessarily who he was in reality. Once upon a time, she'd thought she'd seen a true glimpse of Alex. Maybe that glimpse of him was what her heart wanted to see.

"You know, people do lie to your face," he said sarcastically.

"You know I'm a terrible liar," Lucy said, mimicking his tone.

"I remember." He stuffed his hands in his pants pockets, looking away from her. She stared wordlessly at him, her heart picking up speed. Back in school, just before Valentine's Day, Alex had innocently asked Lucy if she had a crush on anyone in their class. Lucy had taken one look at his gorgeous grin and felt like her chest was going to burst open like in a horror sci-fi alien film. Then she started babbling on about love charms and spells. She had tried to assess his unreadable features, but he was called away for a swim team meeting.

He didn't ask her again, and she never brought it up.

Alex turned back to her. "Tell me what's going on with you."

The email flashed in her mind. Alex didn't want to hear about her job or...underwear. *Or did he?* Lucy batted that question down. "Nothing much has changed, really."

"I find that hard to believe." Alex tilted his head. "Nothing changed in all these years?"

Dissatisfaction flickered through her. Not everyone went cliff diving with swimsuit models in the summer. She had the Grove community pool and a thrift store coverall to keep her cool during their heat waves.

"I've had the same phone number since junior year. Nothing's changed," she said.

Alex pulled up his contacts on his phone and held it up. "Is this still yours?"

Lucy worked her mouth to answer him, but only one word fell out. "Yeah." He'd kept her number. The merman who didn't keep the same address for more than a year had kept her number. *Don't read into that,* a voice inside said. *He probably forgot to delete it when he crossed the town limits.*

Her high school nickname, Lu, and a photo of a witch's boots standing next to a pumpkin were displayed. *A pumpkin?* Lucy flicked a questioning glance at him.

"I didn't have a new picture, so I found a stock photo that

reminded me of you," he said, peering down at the phone. "Some things really don't change."

Lucy watched him. Did she hear wonder in his voice? Or pity? Through his feed she'd seen his life. Every year, there was a new home or a new job taking him all over the world. Only, this past year he'd stopped posting altogether. She hesitated to think what would happen if he was forced to stop in a place where he couldn't immediately leave. Things had changed, but he wasn't staying long enough to share himself with anyone, especially her.

He didn't get the emails, and he wouldn't reconnect with the Grove. It was nice that he'd kept her number, but he didn't text or call. Ever. He was still the vagabond, the roguish merman. Small-town rhythms couldn't compete with the lure of the many waters that appealed to Alex. When Nana taught her how to read tea leaves, she warned repeatedly, "Don't look for what's not there. Stop trying to shape the leaves to your will. Just read what's there. Read what you see, not what you feel." *Open your eyes.* He looked away toward the horizon, his lips drawn in and his shoulders tight. Lucy let out a small sigh. He wasn't staying in the Grove for long.

"It was great seeing you." She meant that.

"Same here," Alex said.

Lucy held her arms out, too wide for a handshake but big enough for a hug. He hesitated for an instant, then stepped into her arms, embracing her tightly. Every part of her body felt deliciously warm, as if she'd been dipped into a hot bath. Lucy closed her eyes and breathed in. The years between them went away. The mix of sea salt and a hint of mint permeated through his clothes. He'd probably taken a morning swim today; the ocean blessed his body with its essence. Alex had always smelled that way. Even back in school, when she spoke to him by the lockers, she always caught a hint of pure sea salt over her shoulder. And now, whenever she sprinkled it into a spell or mixture she was working on, she thought about Alex.

She hoped he was safe.

Her heart scooted closer to the edge of crushing on him—again. No.

She stepped out of his arms, the warmth of his touch dissipating automatically.

"I should go. I have a family dinner tonight," Alex said.

"I'm heading out, too. Give everyone my best."

"I will." He nodded. "I'll see you around. Good night, Lucy."

"Bye, Alex."

She lingered for a moment; her mind remembered today's date. She smiled to herself.

"Alex?" she asked.

He turned his head toward her, expectantly.

"Happy birthday."

Alex quirked a kind smile at her. "Thanks."

Lucy gave a one-handed wave and left. Everything made her skin feel too tight. After all this time, he was back, and she was still here. A memory came back to her in vivid color. He'd been the merman who'd transferred in, the new kid with green hair and scales on his palms that looked like chunky glitter. She'd been the baby witch drawing symbols on her notebook, desperate to finish high school without hexing anyone. The first day of sophomore year, in English class, he had sat down next to her, looked at her charm bracelet, then her, and said, "Pretty."

"Are you talking about the bracelet or me?" she'd asked slowly.

Alex had smiled, the type of smile that reached his eyes and hinted at fun trouble. He smiled at her as if he were a well-traveled sailor who saw home on the horizon. Her heart squeezed. The teacher started the class, ordering everyone to stop talking. Lucy, eager for an answer, started to speak. Alex pressed a finger to his lips and pointed forward for her to pay attention. From then on, Alex sat behind Lucy. Each day he picked out a charm and asked her about it. By the time it was winter, he had known about every single charm on her bracelet.

The day before winter break, he'd placed a small wrapped box on her desk, decorated with a bow.

She'd opened the gift. It was a silver seahorse charm with a red stone eye.

Dumbstruck by his thoughtfulness, she replied, "I didn't get you anything."

"No big deal. I thought it fit you."

Lucy touched the seahorse charm, still here after all this time. The red stone winked at her, reminding her of youthful memories. He'd probably leave town tomorrow. She knew he was going to leave because the Grove had never been enough for him. The tea leaves told no lies.

And she knew better than to crush on some merman who saw her only as a good friend and nothing more. It was a ticket straight to frustration.

He swam the ocean depths. She avoided puddles.

She lived life under one rule: You don't lose what you don't let go.

She didn't lose her heart because she never gave it away, not until she felt that soul mate click. Not to Marcus. Not to Alex. Not to the world. Life was better that way. No surprises.

Alex was a big, sparkly, sexy surprise.

There was no way she was going to have any fun with him roaming around here. Her subconscious would find a way to "bump" into him again and get to talking once more. The foolish heart she owned couldn't focus on the festival tonight when he was so close. He drew her in, the same way the moon influences the tides with an ancient force. She could try to ignore it, but no—she knew she wasn't strong enough to deny his aquatic magic. Lucy's phone buzzed in rapid succession. She checked it. Ursula had sent at least five texts to their group text chain:

Hey y'all hey!

Meet you at the house in ten!

At the house. Where's the blender?

NM found it under the sink.

Pick up lemons, limes, I forgot them! TY

Ursula was going to keep texting until they came back home. As she walked toward the car, she pulled the Madame

Zora fortune from her bag. Reluctantly, she pulled her thoughts away from Alex and read the card.

Madame Zora says:
Let go of what scares you.
Seek the life you desire.
Lucky numbers
1, 4, 3, 7, 10, 23

Chapter Four

*H*ow are you?" Ursula held the half-empty pitcher over her margarita glass. Lucy leaned back against the lumpy couch for a silent moment. Her mind replayed the evening with Alex. She had watched him under the light of the Ferris wheel, illuminated by the neon like an electric god. When she hugged him, a double current of want and warmth went through her and electrified parts of her that were once uncharged. She still had it bad for him and missed out on funnel cake. *Silly witch.*

She sat up and sighed. "There are several possible answers to that question."

"Let's keep drinking until we have a good answer." Ursula poured the remaining dregs of the drink mix into Lucy's glass on the coffee table.

Dinner had been cleaned up a while ago, and now the four witches were currently sipping their mixed drinks in their living room. Sirena was propped up against the hand-me-down fainting couch. Callie relaxed on the upholstered wood chair that was a flea market find. Lucy switched her focus between her drink and phone. She hadn't shared her sudden reunion with Alex. Her sisters would've grilled her for every single detail and demanded that she act on this decade-long obsession. Eh. "Obsession" was a bit dramatic. It was more like a "look him up on social media and analyze his posts with the focus of a codebreaker trying to uncover a spy ring" interest in Alex. If Callie and Sirena knew, they'd drag the drink from her hand and cast a spell to bring that merman right to her bedroom. Lucy shook her head. No way. If she and Alex were meant to be together, then it would've happened already.

"Does anyone want thirds?" Ursula asked.

Lucy waved her off. "I'm good."

"What did you put in this drink?" Sirena stared at her glass suspiciously. "I feel drunker than usual."

"Do you care?" Callie responded.

"I just want to know how hungover I'm going to be at brunch," Sirena said. "I don't want to burn anybody's eggs. I know a sous-chef who got fired because his bacon was too crispy."

"Stop. You're making me hungry." Callie flounced out of the room. "I'm getting snacks."

"Don't mess up my kitchen," Sirena called out. She worked as a chef at Ad Astra, the fanciest restaurant in town, a job that appealed to her potion making and brewing talents. There wasn't a day that Sirena didn't smell of some sprig of rosemary or lavender, a byproduct of her cooking experiments. She took a long sip of her drink but didn't move.

Lucy looked at Ursula. "Who's watching the shop tonight?"

"I hired Ernestine to do it," Ursula said. "She needs practice reading crystal balls for the weekly special. Two readings for the price of one."

Ernestine was their coven sister and a family friend. She was brand-new to the craft but eager to learn how to tap into her supernatural abilities. Ursula managed the local psychic and mystic shop Light as a Feather, which was owned by her mom, Aunt Niesha.

"You might need her to cover for me tomorrow, too. I'm tipsy." Lucy chuckled.

"You do know that *you* don't work at the shop. How drunk are you?" Sirena asked slowly.

"I'm drunk enough to tell this joke. Why is history like a fruitcake?"

"Why?" Ursula asked.

"It's full of dates!" Lucy cackled with glee.

Ursula groaned, amused.

Sirena reached for Lucy's glass. "That's it! I'm cutting you off."

"No, she'll get funnier if she drinks more. Have some more." Ursula waved Sirena away from Lucy's glass. Lucy spied that Ursula's drink was oddly empty. Hmm. Something was rotten in the Garden State. As with every monthly gathering, Ursula had made her infamous Bathwater Brew, a drink handed down from their great-auntie Lulu. It was a family favorite, a brew of rum, pineapple, and other deliciousness. As Lucy picked up the glass in her hands, the turquoise mixture shone. She drank, her eyes glancing around the living room at the collection of various-size bells, half-melted candles, and tattered leather-bound books. Their fluffy gray Chartreux cat, Shadow, flicked his tail, surveying the night with a passive interest. A handmade statue of Oshun, draped in a regal gown, stood with her arms outstretched in the air. The photos of their ancestors, hanging over the mantel, watched over them.

Lucy bowed her head and lifted her glass to those who had gone before her. *Rest easy.* No matter what, Caraways paid respect and honor to their ancestors in everything they did.

Honor the past. Protect your own. Use your power. This was the Caraway way.

Some of her relatives used their powers to enrich themselves and draw success into their lives. Other relatives worked their magic in secret and shadows, using their gifts only in the right time and situation. She sipped her drink again. The liquid flowed down her throat and hit her bloodstream, making everything from her hair to her toes loose and easy. The sparkle from Ursula's engagement ring caught her attention, causing waves of melancholy through her. Everyone—classmates, friends, random people at the grocery store—was moving on, getting married and finding out where they belonged. With her free hand, Lucy clicked open the class notes email again. She was right where she had been at eighteen—back in the Grove.

Ursula waved her bejeweled hand over Lucy's face. "Hey, don't do that. Don't get all sentimental. We're here to chill out, not to be all miserable."

Ursula, with her black-framed glasses and deep-set eyes, had her hair up in a fluffy pineapple style. She got up, teetering slightly to the left, her face flushed.

"We're not here to think, just drink. Si—help me distract Lucy."

Sirena crossed her fingers. "Well, I don't want to jinx it. I might have found an investor for my restaurant concept."

Lucy cheered. "It's about time." She'd been tending to her basil plant to bring success to Sirena's interpreter dreams. "I'm here to help you with a concept collage. My glue stick is ready."

"Thanks, sis," Sirena said warmly.

Sirena had spent the last three years trying to find a trustworthy investor to fund the restaurant concept close to her heart. When she wasn't working at Ad Astra, she cooked privately for the more well-off citizens of Freya Grove. Lucy considered herself blessed to be able to smell Sirena's cooking let alone taste anything she whipped up on their stove.

Callie came out of the kitchen, cradling her drink while holding a huge bowl of popcorn in the opposite hand.

"Cal, distract Lucy with good news," Ursula said.

"Nope. She's on her own. She did it to herself."

"Wait. What happened? What's wrong?" Sirena asked.

"She opened that silly class email again." Callie gave Lucy a pointed stare and dropped the bowl on the coffee table with a snap. Lucy guiltily turned her phone facedown. *Busted.* She had shared the email with Callie on the drive home.

"I told you to delete those class notes. Quentin's just finding a reason to be nosy," Sirena said, finishing off her drink.

"You do this every year. You ended up sending the same thing," Callie said.

"That's the problem. I send in the same paragraph. I don't need a paragraph. I could send in a sentence." Lucy pouted. She didn't want to be bratty, but damn she wanted some spark in her life.

"Don't be dramatic," Sirena said.

"Lucy still lives in Freya Grove. She teaches at the local high

school. She's single. She drinks tea and casts spells. Cut, copy, and paste. Nothing's changed," Lucy said.

"You left out your tea reading business," Sirena said. "Don't forget your side hustle."

Lucy twisted her lip to the side. Sirena wasn't wrong. During summer break, Lucy opened her doors and her tea pantry to interested customers who wanted their tea leaves read by a Caraway witch. Many times, the reading turned into a venting session for people who needed empathy and a big cup of tea.

She didn't charge money for the readings, feeling blessed to share her gift with those who needed advice. Lucy opted to barter goods in exchange for her tea reading services, which meant she always was paid with a diverse range of items. Customers paid her with everything from still delicious day-old croissants to fresh cucumbers from a personal garden.

"I don't really want to brag about that," Lucy said. "Everyone's auntie and uncle claims that they can read tea leaves in the Grove. That's not special."

"We got a cat." Callie pointed to Shadow. The cat meowed, making his presence known. Lucy blew a kiss at Shadow, who just yawned, then flicked his tail. Great, even her familiar thought she was boring. She cleaned out his litter box on a regular basis, and that was all the thanks she got.

"Name a witch who doesn't have a cat in their life," Lucy said.

"Well..." Ursula sat next to Lucy. "What if you wrote about the life you've wanted? Write the class note you wish were your life."

Lucy sat up, interested. "I'm listening."

"I'm not saying send it in. Write down your dream life. Manifest. Wish for all the things you want," Ursula said. Lucy bit her lip in thought. She took another big sip, then put her glass on a coaster. Her imagination went in different directions. Her mind spun with countless paths. Maybe another drink wasn't in her future.

"I'd love to learn how to bake something fancy," Lucy said. She wanted to make some pastry she had to spell-check.

Callie tapped the table. "Write that down. Keep going."

Lucy reclaimed her phone from the table and opened an email draft. Her thumbs went flying over the keyboard. The wishes came quick and immediate, popping up in her head like heated popcorn kernels. Apply for that teaching fellowship in Washington, DC. Train for a race. Save for that dream cottage. Use that designing passion for good. Making mood boards for projects. Stop waiting for that soul mate and freaking find him. Make that cake. Her fingers stopped typing. Lucy read over the paragraph, studying her closely held wishes. Here they were, the things she'd do if she had the money, time, and motivation. Everything within her yearned to make this hastily written paragraph the truth.

I wish this were my life. Lucy closed the email and dropped the phone. *No.*

To quote Nana Ruth, *If wishes were fishes, we'd all cast big nets.*

Lucy didn't want to cast her net wide and then deal with the failure of not catching anything. She'd just have to deal with the life she had. She sat up, refocused on the task at hand.

"You didn't come over here just to get us drunk. You called this meeting."

Sirena and Callie sat attentively, waiting for their cousin's next step. Ursula reached into her purse, took out her planner zip folio, and unzipped it. A collective groan erupted from the sisters. Ursula was unfazed. Whenever she brought out her monster planner, trouble soon followed. Ursula snapped it open to a stickered calendar layout.

"Mrs. Walker suggested we move up the wedding." She said it a little too sharply.

"Oh." Lucy blinked rapidly. The wedding was scheduled for next February. "When are you getting married now?"

Ursula scanned the calendar, then tapped her finger to the page. "Now we're getting married in August."

"This August?" Callie squeaked.

Lucy thought what she was too polite to say. *Is Ursula out of her French-pedicured mind?* It was late May, practically June. Callie said nothing but gave everyone a pained smile. For the last five months, since Lincoln proposed to Ursula last Christmas, the vision of Valentine's Day glamour, with a color scheme of ruby red and cream, was her goal. Now, with the sudden date change, there wasn't enough time to plan a themed birthday party, let alone redo an entire wedding. No one said anything, and the ticking of the grandfather clock against the wall filled the silence. Lucy looked to Sirena, then Callie. Was there another urgent reason for the rush?

"Why?" Sirena finally said.

Ursula rolled her eyes. "We're in love! People can't wait to get married and start their lives together."

"You don't have a little Caraway on the way, do you?" Sirena asked, eyeing Ursula's empty glass. Callie made a hopeful questioning sound.

"Not yet. That's planned for next year," Ursula said. "I'm getting married soon. I need to get on my grind and cut out alcohol now. Besides, our future babies will have their father's name."

"But summer? You hate hot weather," Callie said.

"No, I don't mind it."

"You buy box fans in March because you worry about getting hot," Lucy said.

"I like to be comfortable."

"You refrigerate your bedsheets to stay cool," Sirena said.

Ursula slammed the planner shut. "Fine. The Berkeley Hotel had a sudden cancellation since—"

"I knew it." Sirena sipped her drink with a triumphant slurp.

"A wedding fell through, and they told us the day was available." Ursula finished the sentence. "Lincoln said they offered us a steep discount. We'd be foolish to not take it. It's not that bad. I just need a new dress, change the date, pick out a cake, and redo the entire color scheme. I got this! We've got this! Mrs. Walker says the hotel needs an answer by tomorrow."

"You don't have to say yes," Sirena said tersely.

"Tell me how I should say no," Ursula countered. The Walker family was one of the most upstanding and well-respected members of Freya Grove. They got everything they wanted by either sheer force or some type of magic.

"Don't try to convince us. You'll have to tell Auntie Niesha," Callie reminded her.

Ursula frowned deeply. Niesha Caraway, Ursula's mom and their eldest aunt, didn't do well with surprises. She threatened to hex anyone who even said the words "surprise party" in her presence.

"How does Lincoln feel about the date change?" Lucy asked.

"He's fine, as long as he shows up on time," Ursula said, unbothered. "It's going to be okay. Mrs. Walker suggested that we'd take it and save some money."

"I didn't know *she* was getting married," Sirena said.

Lucy gave her a hard look. Sirena stared back without apology, slurping her drink to fill the tense silence. The middle sister did not, as Nana said, suffer fools gladly and didn't hold back on pointing out obvious issues.

Ursula made an exasperated sound. "I want my future in-laws to like me. What's wrong with that?"

Sirena made a doubtful face but kept her mouth shut. Lucy knew that sometimes people were determined not to like you no matter what you did.

She took Ursula's hand and squeezed. "Nothing. We just want you to enjoy *your* day."

"I'd like to break the tradition of Caraway women not being welcomed into new families," she reflected with some bitterness. They nodded, too aware of her family history. Ursula's parents divorced when she was young due to the meddling of her father's family, who had tried to make Aunt Niesha more, in their eyes, respectable as a society wife. He remarried and then had a new family one town away. Aunt Niesha didn't remarry, obviously soured on the whole marriage gamble. She'd been one of the cautionary tales that proved Caraway women weren't always lucky in love. Their aunts, cousins, and other female relatives didn't have the smoothest paths to their happily-ever-after or happy-for-now.

Even so, Ursula deserved her happy ending. It was her day.

"What's the new date?" Lucy asked.

Ursula made an embarrassed face. "It's August 28. It's not that busy, right?"

"Hey, that's right after the Freya Flea!" Callie said. "I can get your something-old gift then! Look at the stars align."

Sirena's jaw dropped. "You're getting married on the last weekend of the summer. People have vacation plans. Do you want anyone at this wedding?"

Lucy bit her lip. Their recently retired parents had just booked tickets for a Hawaiian cruise for late August. They'd be disappointed that they probably wouldn't be able to attend the wedding.

"All I'm asking for is one day." Ursula sighed, weary. "That's all I wish for."

Sirena slid Lucy a secret look. Sincere concern for their cousin was clear in her glance.

"There might be a spell for that," Lucy said. She went over to the bookshelf on the far wall. No one moved or spoke. She took out the thick tome with a brown leather cover, two ribbon markers, and their family symbol—four linked hearts in a circle pattern. It was the Caraway spell book. Her finger traced the symbol slowly, having drawn and redrawn this sign on every notebook she used since she was in grade school. It was their protection, a source of strength, and a connection to those who came before them and those who would follow their path. She brought the book over to the couch, cradling it in her lap. Ursula settled next to her on her left side, anticipation practically radiating from her. Callie sat on the right side.

"You've got a spell in mind," Ursula said.

"I'll know it when I see it," Lucy responded. She didn't raise her head while she spoke, keeping her attention on the current task. Lucy flipped through the well-worn and loved aged pages. Buzzy magic tickled her hands. Over the last hundred years, the Caraways had collected second-hand knowledge, rituals, and beliefs of mothers, aunts, and sisters to create their craft. Ursula nervously chatted on. Lucy only half listened as she struggled to locate the spell or root that might help them solve their current problem. Lucy read the titles as she flipped through the book. "Pay the Piper, Basic Care for Familiars, Key Work, Seeds and Garden."

"Maybe I can help." Ursula reached for the book, but Lucy slapped her hands away.

She was nearly at the book's end; the pages were getting sparse. Her mind was congested with doubt. *What if the spell she needs isn't here? What if you can't help her? What then?* Lucy searched on against those nagging questions. She reached the very last page.

It was written in Nana's spidery handwriting. *Wish Spell.*

Lucy leaned in to get a closer look, then pulled away. *No way.* This spell was a Caraway family legend, but she'd never seen it written down. Her heart lurched. There wasn't a Caraway witch who hadn't heard the bedtime story of the naive caster who used a wish spell and changed her life. It shouldn't even exist; it was only a story. She looked at her waiting family members.

Confusion crossed Sirena's face. Ursula's eyes widened. Callie brightened.

"I found it," Lucy said. It was *the* wish spell.

"It's a sign." Ursula pressed the page against her palm. The book appeared to glow from the touch. "I know it. Nana claimed Madame Zora gave her this spell."

"She also claimed that we're related to Pam Grier," Sirena said.

"It's real," Callie insisted.

"The wish spell is a fairy tale told to keep all Caraway witches from abusing their powers." Sirena studied the page with a critical squint.

"Well, this is meant to be," Ursula said. "It's Friday night. The moon is full—"

"We're drunk," Sirena interjected, raising her glass.

"It's the perfect time." Ursula chewed on her lip and stole a look at them. "I don't want to do this alone. You're my girls. You're my Caraway crew. So, what do you say?"

There was defiance in her words as well as a call to action. This was the point of no return. Nana used to call her four granddaughters the Four Musketeers because they were always looking after one another and the spells they cast. They conjured as a group, their power strengthened in their numbers. If they were going to do this spell, then they'd do it as one.

If wishes were fishes, they were going to cast their nets at the same time.

Caraways stuck together. That was the rule.

Sirena pushed up into a standing position. "I'm wishing for a sex god," she said.

"Wish for a million dollars. It will last longer than your sex god," Callie quipped.

Sirena stood, looking over the wish paper, and made a sound. "We need pomegranate seeds and hazelnuts."

Callie peeked at the paper. "We need paper and pens."

She and Callie went into the kitchen, talking about their future wishes.

Ursula turned to Lucy, eyes hopeful. "Do we have any candles?" Ursula asked.

"You already know it." Lucy laughed. She gestured over to the long row of pillar candles of every size, color, and shape on the mantel. "The candle shop sends me gift cards for my birthday. We'll need at least four of them."

While Ursula and Lucy went over to the mantel, Lucy glanced over at her cousin. Ursula rolled her pearls between her fingers as she scanned the row of options. Lucy's senses gave off a low vibration.

She lowered her voice. "Are you sure about this?"

Ursula's voice rose an octave. "I want this wedding more than anything."

"I know. I was talking about the wish spell," Lucy corrected.

"Don't worry." Ursula gave her a fragile smile. "I'm good. I just want my happy ending."

"Well, I have something that might help." Lucy reached behind the candles and took out a velvet jewelry pouch. She was saving this for the wedding, but Ursula clearly required a little luck on her side. Ursula held out her hands as Lucy slid the coin into her waiting palm. The bust of Mercury looking toward the future gave off a sense of hope and prosperity that made Lucy's heart joyful. It glinted under the overhead light.

"It's Nana's?" Ursula asked, her voice light.

Lucy nodded. "You should have it for your big day."

Nana Ruth swore that her lucky dime, minted on a leap year, was given to her by a kind woman with an angel's smile on her tenth birthday.

"Nana told me she wore this in her shoe on her wedding day."

"I know. She always had it when luck and fortune were needed." Ursula swallowed hard and bit back tears. "Sometimes I wish—" Her words failed her.

Lucy nodded, unable to speak, too, but she knew what Ursula was thinking without her saying a word. *I wish she were here, too.* She reached out and held Ursula, the two standing together, anchored by history. Callie and Sirena returned with their items. They gathered the candles and brought them over to the table. Callie held small jars filled with rattling hazelnuts and pomegranate seeds. Ursula placed the dime in the middle of their spell work.

"Light the candles. Write your wishes while the wax melts down our candle," Lucy read, her voice steady. Sirena lit the wicks with the matches. They each took a paper and pen.

"Write down your wish in complete detail," she instructed. Callie unscrewed the jars and sprinkled the seeds and hazelnuts over the table. They took a minute to consider their wishes. Then they lowered their heads to write. Lucy tapped the paper with the pen top. She scribbled, *I wish for excitement in my life.*

She glanced up to see Ursula quickly looking away from her.

"Keep your eyes on your own wish," Lucy teased.

Ursula lowered her head guiltily. Lucy cleared her throat

and read the next line. "Drip the candle wax over the most important words of the wish."

They each picked up a candle and dripped melting wax over their words. Lucy let it cover the first words of her wish. The words were swallowed up and encased.

"While the wax is warm, press your thumb into it."

They did as she instructed, pressing their thumbs into the warmth of the wax, leaving their imprint.

"Now fold the paper thrice while chanting these words: 'I wish, I wish, I wish.' On the final 'I wish,' extinguish the candle and let the smoke carry your wish out to the sky."

They chanted, their words echoing out into the air like a mystic chorus round. Magic hummed in their blood as the candle wax dripped on the table. It levitated, hovering as they chanted, their wishes crossing over one another and strengthening. Growing. Thriving.

Each Caraway paused on their last "I wish."

"I wish." Ursula stood and blew out her candle.

"I wish." Sirena blinked, and her flame disappeared.

"I wish." Callie waved her hand, and the candle died.

"I wish." Lucy cradled the candle in her hand, but she stopped, unsure.

It danced and dared her to act. There needed to be a sacrifice to the flame, a promise that she believed in the spell. She, unlike her sisters and cousin, felt compelled to give more, give a gift of credence because she'd turned away from magic since Nana's passing. She was the firstborn witch, a powerful and blessed position to have in the family, yet she used magic sparingly. Lucy fetched the Madame Zora fortune and a shallow glass bowl. *Let go of what scares you. Seek the life you desire.* She held the fortune over the candle until it caught on fire. It burned quickly, and she watched it as it was devoured by the flame. Then she let it drop to the bowl and burn, until nothing was left but smoldering ashes.

What do you want? Late-night calls. Kisses sweeter than honey. Someone that will stir my soul. Stupid inside jokes. Fun dates. Sharing hopes and fears. To feel safe and secure. A space of my own. In a long, steady breath, she smothered the flame until all that remained was a simmering curl of smoke that tickled her nose. Ursula tucked the dime away in her pocket. Lucy let out a long, audible breath. It felt as if a dimmer switch had turned on within, her inner light once dull, turned up. The net was thrown. The wish was cast.

Chapter Five

$\smile$

*A*d Astra was not the place to throw a tantrum. The upscale restaurant, voted one of the best places to dine in
Monmouth County, was the place to go for special events
and tastings for those who wanted a touch of elegance.
Countless anniversaries and engagements were celebrated at
Ad Astra, which promised customers a trip to the stars with
every dish. Alex felt like he was on the planet formerly known
as Pluto at this moment. He stared at the dish in front of
him, which wasn't the seaweed and kale wrap he'd ordered
but a pair of keys with an address tag attached.

"I don't think I ordered this."

"No, we did," Mom sang.

Alex glanced over at his brother, Horatio, who held up
his hands in confusion. From his wrinkled forehead, it was
clear he had no clue what was going on, either. Alex looked
to his mom. Her graying locs were pinned up with a seashell
clip. She wore a bright tropical-blue dress that reminded him
of the Caribbean Sea. Mom reached into her bra, where
she always kept her phone and mad money, and aimed the
camera at him.

"Happy birthday! We bought you a house!" Mom snapped

a few pictures. The flash made his brain hurt. "The look on your face is priceless! Nate, I knew he'd be so surprised!"

"You don't have to thank us, son," Pop said in a baritone that practically shook the water glasses at their table. Alex blinked, then clenched his jaw. An old joke repeated in his head, teasing from all the times he'd found himself the target of the class clown during his school days.

How did the mermaid get a loan for a new house? She went to the riverbank.

He didn't want his cursing to ruin anyone's romantic moment at Ad Astra. He scooped up the keys, trying to figure out whether they were real.

"Say something," Mom encouraged, snapping another picture.

"I don't—" He stammered to a stop, trying to figure out the rest of the sentence. *I don't want this*, his mind screamed, but he didn't say those words. He didn't want to ruin this day. "I don't know what to say."

"Ask us anything!"

"How did you afford this?" he asked, dread creeping up his spine. Mom and Pop did well for themselves, but they were close to retirement age. They needed to save money for future emergencies, not buy random stuff, like a whole house.

"That's not what you ask when you get a gift." Mom pouted. "We had money saved up, and well, we saw a property that we couldn't pass up."

"The bank was eager for a buyer, and the neighborhood is enchanting," Pop said with a wink. Alex held back a dubious cough. Everything in the Grove, even public dressing rooms on the boardwalk with painted suns and moons on the doors, was touted as an "enchanting experience." The word meant nothing to him anymore. He paused for a moment. That statement wasn't completely true. His mind flashed back to Lucy standing by the fortune-telling booth, covered in magical symbols. She had been enchanting as usual. It wasn't until he was back at his car did it occur to him to invite her to join his birthday dinner. He focused back on the gift in his hand.

Alex read the address tag: "1324 Summerfield Street."

Once Horatio heard the address, he visibly paled. He stared blankly at their parents. "Seriously, y'all?"

Alex sat back, watching the exchange.

"It's not a big deal," Pop said, without an ounce of apology. "It's one of those old houses. It's a good investment."

"It's more than that," Horatio responded. "You should've called me before you bought any house—especially this house. I would've inspected it for you."

"Sometimes you just have to move on a good deal."

"You know what also moves?" Horatio asked no one. "Termites. Water bugs. Ants."

"Please don't get so upset," Mom said. She reached for the saltshaker and sprinkled a generous amount into her water glass. Like most merfolk, they enjoyed a cold glass of salt-water with their meals. The couple across from their table watched her with interest. Alex let out an annoyed sigh. *Humans.*

"Can we discuss this later?" Alex asked in a low voice.

"Ants won't wait to damage your wood," Horatio said in a foreboding tone.

While Horatio outlined the horrors of not thoroughly

checking a property before purchasing it to Mom and Pop, Alex peered at the keys. The silver clashed against his scales, making for a disjointed image. No one in his family owned a house. Dwyers moved. Traveled. They didn't stay still. They did month-to-month leases just because it was easier than having to deal with the paperwork. Once Horatio brought up ideal weather conditions for water bugs in houses, Mom's face fell. Alex held up a hand. Horatio stopped talking. Pop remained silent.

"We didn't want to ruin the surprise." A slightly tentative look entered Mom's bright rust-brown eyes. "I hope you're not upset. We wanted you to have a special gift."

Horatio rubbed the nape of his neck. "It's really special," he muttered.

"A house is special," Mom said. "This house is more special than you can imagine. I saw it in a dream. I know I did."

Horatio pressed his hand to his forehead. "You saw it in a dream? Mom, did you fall asleep watching the home and garden channel again? You've done that before."

"I don't think so."

"Is it possessed?" Horatio asked.

"Mmm—I don't know," Mom said. "Maybe you can check for me."

Was there too much saltwater in his ears, or did he mishear Mom? They'd bought him a house. His parents, Mom and Pop—Nathan and Kia Dwyer to the rest of the Grove— were two eccentric and well-meaning, if not shortsighted, merfolk who wanted the best for their sons. He let himself look around Ad Astra. The people at the tables next to him glanced over with raised eyebrows and curious looks. Alex didn't want to embarrass himself after being in town for less than three days. The Grove gossip mill would be buzzing about this latest Dwyer mishap.

He focused back on Mom. "Anyway, I saw it. We saw it and thought of you," Mom said, shoulders lowered. Pop gave him a "you better fix this now" hard glare.

"We thought you'd love it," Mom said. "Do you love it?"

"I haven't seen it yet," Alex said slowly. This unseen house was already derailing his plans to keep moving. He didn't need this problem dropped on his lap, forcing him to make yet another huge decision. Why couldn't Mom and Pop give him a gift card or blanket sweatshirt like other parents gave their children?

The familiar frustration of being a Dwyer merperson bubbled up inside him.

A tense beat stretched on at the table. Horatio stood and slapped Alex on the shoulder, motioning to the bar.

"Come on, birthday boy," he said. "I owe you a drink. Mom. Pop. If you excuse us, we'll right be back."

Alex numbly got up and went to the bar with Horatio, taking a seat on a stool. The walls started to push in on him. He breathed deeply and glanced around the restaurant to ground himself. The rose-colored walls were decorated with brass mirrors and Tiffany stained glass murals. Reclaimed crystal chandeliers hung from the ceiling with an opulent shine. White tablecloths covered tables arranged with fresh flowers and water glasses. The polished bar felt cool against his scales. The keys bit into his palm as he clenched them. He, like always, looked to Horatio for advice. Horatio wore a crisp white dress shirt, beat-up jeans, and polished sneakers as confidently as a businessman wore thousand-dollar suits. After flagging down the bartender, Horatio ordered them Ad Astra's signature drink, the Stargazer. Horatio gave Alex a stiff smile.

"Happy birthday," Horatio sang weakly off-key.

Alex peered at Horatio. "Please tell me they didn't buy me anything else. I can't handle walking in my brand-new house and finding a unicorn."

"Hey, unicorns are useful. Their horns can fix anything," Horatio said sagely.

Alex shook his head. "Bro, please. I can't keep a houseplant alive. What am I going to do with a unicorn?"

Horatio straightened like a towering lighthouse scanning a far-off horizon for impending dangers. "Hold up. Take a moment. I'm joking."

Cold realization washed within him. "They really bought it."

Horatio nodded. "Mom and Pop do and buy whatever they want. You don't help them; you get out of the way and pray for a generous return policy."

"I thought Mom ordered me a seashell comforter or mother-of-pearl bed set. What am I going to do with a house?" Alex looked to his brother.

"Live in it," Horatio said.

"I'm not in the mood for jokes." Rising panic washed over him. They bought him a whole-ass *house*. Yeah, right. He'd probably lose his house like people lost expensive earbuds on the train. Life taught him to always pack what he could carry. He never wanted to get weighed down with anything that didn't matter. *How much is the mortgage? I need insurance. Where do you get house insurance?*

Alex took a deep breath and willed the panic rising with him to calm down.

Horatio's expression softened. He touched Alex's arm and patted it. Some of the panic that filled him ebbed away.

"Check out the house first before you freak out," Horatio suggested. "You might just like it—or at least not hate it."

"You said the same thing to me when you tricked me into eating broccoli." Alex eyed him. Back in kindergarten, Alex wanted nothing more than to be just like his wise fourth-grade big brother.

"It worked. You still love broccoli," Horatio reminded him.

Small touches of humor around the mouth and near his eyes hinted at the long-gone trickster he once was. Once upon a time, Horatio would've played this whole dinner and gift off as a joke. He wasn't laughing, but he'd turned thoughtful.

"You're on their side," Alex mused.

"They must've had a good reason to buy you a house." Horatio patted his arm one final time, then pulled his hand away. "I don't know why, but this gift came from the heart. Respect it, but be careful."

"What did they give you?" Alex asked cautiously.

Horatio blew out a sharp breath. "Oh, they gave me a hot air balloon ride."

"You hate heights."

"Don't tell them. I think they forgot."

Alex glanced around, making sure that no one could overhear them. Many a Grove citizen would love a chance to catch a merman and see if the myth was true. Legend claimed that if you caught a merman, you'd be granted your greatest wish. He didn't want to find out if it was real.

"The full moon is tonight. Are you going out for a swim?"

Horatio drew his lips in thoughtfully. "I wasn't planning on it. I'd figured I'd skip this time around."

Dwyer merfolk usually transformed with the phases of the moon. The fuller the moon, the greater his transformation, and his aquatic form resembled the classical storybook paintings.

The bartender delivered their drinks.

Horatio paid, took his drink into his hand, and made a pleased sound. "This looks good. Let's smile and finish out the night. We'll check out the house tomorrow." He directed Alex to his drink. "Take a sip of that, then come back to the table. We've got this."

What was there to get? No one had taken a picture of the house!

Alex held up a hand, the conversation at the table replaying in his brain.

"Hold up. You got upset about them buying a house—especially *this* house. What's up with it? It's not cursed, is it?"

Horatio studied Alex, a silent debate playing on his face. It seemed to Alex that he shook off whatever he wanted to say and instead said, "We'll deal with it tomorrow. Enjoy your day."

The two brothers took a moment, toasted, then tasted their Stargazers. Alex sampled the drink and nodded. It was soft and sweet, with hints of vanilla, pineapple, and rum. He especially liked the vanilla, which was warm and comforting. He brought the glass close and inhaled, the scent bringing back memories. The first time he'd tasted fresh vanilla had been with Lucy, who'd brought the bean to school for their cooking class. Years after, whenever he tasted sugar cookies, he thought of Lucy and sent good energy in her direction.

He breathed in again. The oil she wore had rubbed off on him. Her touch remained with him even hours after he'd seen her at the carnival. He'd broken his vow in less than twenty minutes with Lucy, allowing himself one touch for his birthday. Her proximity made every part of him tingle with inconvenient want. The panic lessened as the scent soothed him. He returned to the table. The rest of the meal was uneventful, pleasant but strained. Mom kept shooting him nervous glances, while Pop gave him a layered warning look.

Horatio tipped his tumbler to him.

Meanwhile, the keys now in his pocket held him down like a ship's anchor.

It seemed that wild seahorses couldn't make him stay in the Grove, but real estate kept him in town. This feeling—of being rooted in one place—made his heart pound in his ears and his knees lock. Merpeople didn't do this—they didn't stay in one place for a while. Even his parents had leaned into the nomad lifestyle until some mystic force had settled them here in Freya Grove. It was odd and even a little hypocritical. Mom and Pop had *literally* given him the keys to the domestic lifestyle they'd thoroughly avoided for most of their lives.

He'd check out the house, but that didn't mean he'd stay.

This place wasn't going to get in the way of his plans. Even if he was making these plans day by day. One waiter, flanked by two others, approached their table holding a silky chocolate ganache birthday cake, alight with a large striped candle. Alex sat up and faced them with a grin. The flame flickered as the cake was placed in front of him. Alex's family and a few diners sang the Stevie Wonder version of "Happy Birthday," rocking back and forth and clapping to the song's classic melody.

"Make a wish, Al," Mom said warmly.

His chest tightened and he paused. What did his heart wish for? That was a trick question, because the real question was how many hearts did a merman have? He believed he had two hearts. One heart was currently kicking in his chest like an eighties action star escaping an abandoned warehouse. His other heart had walked away from him at the festival. He'd messed up. He should've made things right between them before he left. Alex, for all his flirty, smooth charms, had never told Lucy why they couldn't be together. She needed someone reliable, dependable. He lacked the courage to be real with her.

Alex focused on the candle in front of him. He didn't make birthday wishes, believing that they were a waste of energy, wanting something that he'd never be able to get.

But tonight, surrounded by his family, he closed his eyes and wished.

I want another chance to make things right.

He inhaled, then exhaled, letting his wish out into the world.

Chapter Six

*L*ucy knew certain things.

Never run a broom across your feet. Carry coins in your pocket in case you need to pay a spirit. Always keep an eye out for future friends and lovers. And there was no way she was spending Sunday night grading exams, drinking chamomile tea, and grumbling over Instagram posts while the festival was in full swing. She still had a taste for funnel cake.

She waited for the universe to deliver a sign that their wishes were in motion. So far nothing had tipped her to their impending wish windfall. The Caraway house was alive and well with anxious waiting. Callie scrubbed out every iron cauldron in the kitchen. Sirena double-checked the pantry for herbs, charms, and potions that might have spoiled. Footsteps rattled the wooden floors. Curses echoed against the walls. Queen B blasted from their sound wave speakers. Even Shadow busied himself with yarn scraps. Everyone seemed jumpy after casting the wish spell, and nerves were tighter than Aunt Niesha in a pair of queen-size tights.

Lucy kept opening and closing her email in between sipping tea. All she could do was wait for the newsletter. What would the Grove think about her and her life? She had a sneaky feeling that everyone seemed so disappointed that she wasn't cursing her neighbors or dosing lovers with potions. All she wanted to do was to be worthy of the magic she'd been blessed with by blood.

After indulging in two—no, three—more servings of Bathwater Brew, she sent Quentin her class note.

He'd responded, saying the e-newsletter would be delivered Sunday night.

Lucy checked the inbox again. Nothing. She needed a distraction. She needed something fried on a stick.

"I'm headed out." Lucy snatched up her purse from the bench in the entryway.

There were three dozen festival tickets in her purse. Tonight was the last night she had time to use them, and she wasn't going to waste money.

"Buy me saltwater taffy," Sirena said from the couch.

"Stay away from the Ferris wheel!" Callie yelled from the kitchen.

Lucy laughed and closed the back door behind her with a snap. There was mischief to be made. Festival food solved all problems. The amusement rides and booths set up in the park twinkled in the near distance against the late afternoon sky. She parked and headed over to the festival. Tonight she was going to have fun, dammit—or at least she'd try. As she wandered the grounds, she noticed the sparks of small magic on the grass. Something special was happening tonight.

After thirty minutes or so, she'd ridden two rides and spent half her game tickets on trying to win a stuffed elephant. No luck. Couples cuddled up together, and gnomes roamed the grounds in pairs. The evening had been pleasant enough, but it would have been nice to share the night with a sister or a friend. *If Alex were here...* Lucy waved the thought away. He was probably cave dwelling in Mexico or had gotten an invitation to view volcanoes in Iceland. Alex had better things to do than to eat delicious fried dough with powdered sugar.

Oh well. More funnel cake for me. Lucy rubbed her hands in anticipation.

A group of her US History juniors and AP History seniors waved to her from the snack line. She was greeted with a chorus of shocked hellos. Lucy held back a smile and waved. Why did students act so surprised to see her out in the world? They probably half expected her to live in the school's book closet with the mice. One student, a junior named Asha, approached her with a wide-open smile. She was wearing a skater dress and her hair was dyed a neon pink that stood out against her dark-brown skin.

"Hey, Ms. C," Asha said. "What's good?"

"Hey, Asha. I'm just trying to decide between funnel cake or fried Oreos." Lucy gestured to the snack booth. The scent of frying sugar brought pure joy.

"Get both. You only live once. Live it up," Asha said.

Whenever Asha, a thoughtful student, had a question she wanted to ask, she scrunched up her face—just like she was doing right now.

"What's on your mind, Ash?"

Once the familiar nickname slipped out, Asha relaxed. She fumbled for her phone, pulling up a page and showing her an internship posting.

"I need a letter of recommendation. I know it's late, but I just heard about this cool internship!"

Lucy scanned it quickly, reading over the requirements. The letter needed to outline the specific skills and why the person was qualified for the position. A wave of nostalgia hit her. Just yesterday she was asking her teacher for a recommendation in her name.

"Should I go for it?" she asked nervously.

Lucy looked at Asha. Her lips were pressed shut tightly so no sound would burst out. Her entire being emanated possibilities that shimmered before Lucy's eyes. An acceptance. Job at the local museum. Next summer working at a museum in the city. Lucy blinked back at Asha.

"Absolutely." Lucy handed her phone back. "Send me an email reminder."

Asha's eyes softened in appreciation. "Thanks, Ms. C. I'll see you later."

Lucy ordered the jumbo funnel cake. She went around the booths, stuffing tasty pieces of powdered sugar dough into her mouth. Her blood hummed in delight as she sat at an empty picnic table. Between the spellcasting and all her teacher work, she'd earned the cake tonight. Her phone buzzed, but the sticky sugar kept her from reaching for her purse. It was probably the e-newsletter, but it could wait another ten minutes.

This cake was getting colder by the second. She had at least a wedge slice left to stuff in her mouth when she ran into Mayor Walker. She, in her belted dress, stared at Lucy with an odd expression. Was there powdered sugar on her face?

"I just read this week's *In the Grove*. I have to say I'm impressed. I didn't know you had so many hidden talents."

"Um...Thank you. I try to stay humble."

"I know you read tea leaves, but—wow. We just had an unexpected opening in the annual cakewalk fundraiser." Mayor Walker clicked a few buttons on her phone. She lifted a plucked eyebrow. "Would you like to submit a dessert?"

Lucy held back a squeal. "I'd be honored."

Mayor Walker cheered. Lucy basked in the sudden praise. She'd always wished that she had a dessert worthy of the Grove Cakewalk, but maybe her cowboy blondies would be good enough this year.

"I've never had croquembouche." Mayor Walker did an excited shimmy, attention focused on her phone. "I'm excited to see what you can do."

Hold up. Lucy leaned back. She'd seen an online video about the towering fancy French wedding cake covered in caramel, but she sure as Hecate didn't know how to make it. She opened her mouth to correct the mistake.

"I don't—I—" she stammered out. Lucy felt her tongue cramp and still, rendering her unable to speak. The sugar stuck like glue, holding her lips together. Maybe she should've splurged for that bottled water.

"What was that, dear?" Mayor Walker looked up at her. Lucy couldn't respond, so she grinned. Mayor Walker gave her a thumbs-up. "I'll get your contact information from Ursula. Enjoy your night."

Lucy returned the gesture, and Mayor Walker left without a second glance. She forced her mouth open. *Why would she think I could make croquembouche?* Suddenly it hit her. Lucy tossed her leftovers in the trash can and dug into her purse. She opened her email and clicked on the most recent edition of the *In the Grove* e-newsletter. Her eyes skimmed it until she came across the class notes. They were listed alphabetically so, surprise, surprise, her note was first.

A numbing sensation took over her body with each line.

The last ten years have been super busy for super home witch Lucy Caraway. In between perfecting her croquembouche recipe, training for her third marathon, finding her karaoke voice, and practicing interior design styling, Lucy continues to teach history to curious teens at Freya Grove High School. Recent travels include a wild high-roller weekend to Atlantic City and a campout under the stars at the Delaware Water Gap National Recreation Area. She plans to apply for a prestigious teaching program at the Library of Congress. Currently, she's decorating her HGTV dream home with her possible soul mate and planning for a bright future with her cat and a menagerie of plants.

She was so stunned, she checked to make sure her heart hadn't fallen out of her butt.

No, no, no. This wasn't real. None of this was real. This was the wrong class note. She needed to tell Quentin to retract it. He'd understand the error. She couldn't be blamed for what happened when she drank too much Bathwater

Brew. Her fingers flew, drafting out an email in less than a minute. Lucy hovered over the send button, but the email disappeared in a blink.

Wait, what? Lucy drafted out another one, but it was gone just as quickly.

It disappeared like magic. Her knees buckled.

Be careful what you wish for because you just might get it... The refrain played in her head, and she willed herself to stand up. She'd cast her net wide and pulled in a freaking giant squid. Spells didn't work that fast unless...Lucy struggled to finish that thought. She'd *never* had a spell work this fast. It had to be the Wish Spell at work. She needed to go home, make a massive pot of tea, and come up with a plan.

"Lucy!" a familiar voice called.

Her head snapped up from her thoughts. A flush crept across her cheeks.

Marcus Walker, as cute as he wanted to be with his Steven Q. Urkel–chic look, waved. She stumbled backward when he called out to her again. She knew from the curious light in his eyes and the way his head tilted to the side that he'd seen the email. Nope. He'd want to know about the soul mate. He'd want to know who she'd leave him for. Lucy didn't have a name. The lights on the giant Ferris wheel filled the darkening sky with animated colors that elicited delightful squeals from the crowd. All she saw was the empty passenger seat before her.

What's your escape plan?

Someone else was in that gondola, but she couldn't see their face.

Callie's warning rang in her head like a phone alarm. *Stay away from the Ferris wheel!*

Desperation pulled her toward the Ferris wheel stairs. She'd rather ride with a pillow stuffed with onions than talk to Marcus right now. She was in a tough spot. She didn't know the rules of this spell, but she knew she didn't have an answer for him.

Get on. Freya Grove was so small that she'd probably end up riding with her friend's sister's cousin's favorite barber for an uncomfortable five minutes. She jumped up the stairs leading to the boarding platform, ripped off half a dozen tickets from the strips in her purse, and thrust them at the operator. Out of the corner of her eye, she could see Marcus barreling forward. The ride operator, with his baby face, barely looked a year out of middle school, but he took the tickets.

"Close the door behind me," she begged him. "Please."

Lucy ducked inside the gondola. The operator waved off Marcus like a preschool bouncer. The door closed and locked behind her with an audible click. Safe. Dimly aware of the person across from her, she closed her eyes and relaxed against the stiff seat. *Thank you, universe.*

"Well, this is a ride we won't forget."

Her skin prickled at the sound of his bemused voice. Her eyes popped open. Familiar hazel eyes stared in her direction. Great.

"We have to stop meeting like this," Alex said slyly.

"You've got to be kidding me."

Lucy considered Alex. His dress shirt was wrinkled. His eyes looked unfocused and sleepy, as if he'd recently woken up from a nap. The image of Alex curled up in an unmade bed flashed before her, causing a thrill inside. *Look anywhere else.* Mermen could dazzle, but she wasn't going to be dazzled by him. She'd been there, done that, and written the vague Facebook message about heartbreak. She should've stayed home with Shadow. Her hand pressed against the cool mesh of the gondola ride. The sun was quickly setting over the ocean. For a moment it seemed like an illusion as if the sun was a swimmer going for a dip into the cool waves.

"How long is this ride?" she asked.

He rubbed his brow with his thumb. "I don't know."

"Make a guess. Please."

"Five minutes, give or take."

Just make it five minutes, and then you can go home, where you can drink your tea and cuddle with your grumpy cat. The Ferris wheel rocked and moved like a slow wave. It went around in one loop, dipping down and then rising into the sky. The gondola shook back and forth, forcing her to sit and face Alex. His attention remained on her, lingering on her eyes, then scanned all over her body. Had someone turned on the heat? She double-checked her outfit to make sure a button hadn't popped open, showing off the goods. Lucy threw a hand over herself. Four minutes left. Mentally, she listed her favorite herbs and plants and their uses. *A is for aloe vera, used for sunburn. B is for basil, great on a pizza—*

"I thought you liked it fast."

Say what? Lucy's eyebrows practically flew off. She peered at Alex expectantly.

"I thought you liked fast rides," Alex restated with a smirk. "You once told me that if you wanted to go slow, you'd get off and walk."

Lucy bit the inside of her cheek. Ugh. Of course he'd remember that little detail about her.

"I usually don't ride the Ferris wheel."

Alex stared at her, waiting for an explanation. Fine. Let him hear her tale of singledom.

"I'm a single rider," she explained. Alex nodded wisely. The ride attendant usually didn't let a single rider on without making a big fuss and screaming out for another passenger. Lucy looked at the empty seat next to him. Unless he was dating the Invisible Woman, it seemed that he was alone. Well, okay then.

"I guess they changed the rules."

Lucy folded her arms. "What level is your thrill ride?"

"I like fast, then slow," Alex said, a bit of bass in his voice. "I get a chance to catch my breath and feel it all. I like to take my time."

Lucy ran a hand over her outfit to quell the feeling. His words caused an excited shudder throughout her body. *I bet he does.* Everything felt a little tingly. Three minutes left.

"Good to know," she murmured. Silence stretched on between them. Back in high school, she would've given up peanut butter cups for a year just to get stuck in a gondola with Alex. Back then their future was as blank as pages in a new journal. Now time and distance had filled in those once-open pages and made them strangers to each other. The Ferris wheel came around again. It went for a third loop, but this time it went much, much slower. The gondola lurched forward, then back, and then it came to a sudden stop. Lucy held on to her seat, her heart hammering in her throat. She forced herself not to look down at the tiny people below. The entire ride didn't move. Lucy pressed her back against the seat, and her head moved back and forth. She didn't like heights. She sure didn't like being on malfunctioning rides. She was under a spell that she didn't yet know how to control.

The universe had answered.

You wanted excitement.

You got excitement.

Chapter Seven

If Alex's life were a movie, it would be a romantic comedy. He'd met the girl, lost the girl, and now he found himself right back in her life.

He'd watched enough rom-coms with previous girlfriends, friends, and female cousins that he knew how to recognize the beats. The lovelorn main character who almost had it all. The lovestruck love interest who wanted forever after. The wacky relative or friend who made obvious commentary. This moment, being trapped on a broken-down ride, had to be a meet-cute for the ages. Nancy Meyers couldn't have written a better meet-cute. Alex tried to imagine what pop song hit would play over this moment, the two romantic leads trapped together. All the Ferris wheels at the shore, and Lucy Caraway had gotten in his gondola. She, in a luscious tumble, had thrown herself onboard, and for one moment all he could do was watch Lucy. Sweet Atlantic Ocean. The sundress she wore, covered in moon phases, hugged her body. He even caught a glimpse of her cleavage before he snapped his attention back to her face. Still beautiful. Always lovely.

They made eye contact. He'd forced himself to say some clever wacky-ass line.

Play it cool. Freak out inside. The wiggle of her painted toes in old leather sandals completed the "witch at the fair" look. Once the ride got stuck and stopped, it was clear this night wouldn't end easily. If he knew the gods were suddenly granting wishes, he should've asked for the limited-edition sneakers he'd waited on line two hours for. That the coveted pair of medium gray-white and dark-gray shoes with a pigeon patch sold out the moment he got to the shop door proved only one thing: You can't always get what you want.

Flashing sirens pulled him back to here and now. A Freya Grove fire truck barreled down Main Street, turning in to the festival entrance, its lights and sirens squealing. Zeke was probably working the truck tonight. Guilt hit him right in the ribs. Maybe he should've gone out for a drink with Zeke. Alex let out a harsh laugh. *You weren't even supposed to be here tonight.* He recalled the events that had led him to the gondola. After eating two huge slices of birthday cake, he'd retreated to his hotel. He hadn't changed clothes, sleeping in them instead. He couldn't bring himself to go to 1324 Summerfield Street. The keys remained in his pocket. Horatio sent him a text message asking if he wanted to go over and check out the place, but he didn't respond. Just for one more day, he didn't want to deal with the house nightmare waiting for him. He scrolled his feed, stopping when he noticed Nahla had updated her profile with a new picture. She, in her baker's jacket, stood arms outstretched in front of a food truck decorated with dancing cartoon desserts. Nahla's face was split into a wide grin. He read the caption underneath.

Coming to a city near you! We're debuting Nahla's Nibbles truck this summer! Get a bite to eat of something sweet.

See, she seems happier without you. Alex tore his attention away from the picture. He had seen the carnival lights from his room. For one night he wanted to feel a little less alone.

He glanced over at Lucy. Her knee pressed against the gondola door. A crowd had gathered below. His overactive brain went into overdrive. *When was the last time this ride was serviced?* His chest tightened.

He forced a light tone into his voice. "Be careful. Those doors are tricky."

She said nothing but yanked back. The tightness eased a fraction within him. He avoided leaning on the door as well. Everything would be better if they were on the ground.

"Do you think they'll call another fire department?" She looked down at the commotion. Her face was pinched in with worry. "I do love a man with a nice big truck."

When he didn't say anything, Lucy added, "Don't even get me started on his hose." She waggled her brow.

Empathy washed through him. Some things never changed. Lucy always made terrible puns and jokes when she got nervous. If she was making dick jokes, then she was really freaking out on the inside. During their junior trip to Six Flags Great Adventure, while riding the gut-dropping Buccaneer Pirate Ship, she'd told more dirty jokes than a Netflix comedy special.

"It's going to be okay," he said gently.

Lucy exhaled, and her shoulders eased. "Do you think we'll make the evening news? The *Freya Grove Press* might show up."

They needed a distraction to pass the time since they didn't know when they'd be rescued. His mind rattled through a quick list of games. "Let's play a game."

"Like what?" she asked. "I left my Scrabble board at home."

One popped into his head. Alex snapped his fingers once he got it. "Two truths and a lie. Have you played before?"

Lucy gave Alex an "Are you kidding me?" face of disbelief. "I teach. Icebreakers are a job requirement. Don't get it twisted." She raised her brow questioningly, the same way she might have done with a smart-mouthed student who asked if they still had to do any homework for her class. He held back a smile. He liked getting a glimpse of the teacher she'd become. It wasn't too hard to imagine her standing in front of a classroom in a sweater covered in stars and wearing an eclectic dress that would make Lucy look like a much more fashionable Ms. Frizzle.

Admiration bloomed within him.

"Let's talk about rules. You share three facts about yourself. Two must be true, but one must be a lie," Lucy rattled off. Alex gave her a look. "Don't act surprised. I've played this game enough that people tell either all lies or all truths. Whoever finds the most lies wins. Let's talk about the prize. Winner takes all."

His attention dipped to her mouth. The merfolk in him dared him to be bold. "It depends on what you want."

"I know what I want." Her voice trailed off. She ran her tongue slowly over the line of her lips, then smiled fully.

Heat rose in his chest, and a soft ache stayed there. Damn, he forgot how her smile made him feel. It was as if the sun had popped out from behind gray clouds and warmed his skin. Her smile turned mischievous. "I want a large sausage and spinach pizza from Rapunzel's."

"Wow." Alex blinked, then laughed to himself. That pizza order was their usual pie—they'd shared it whenever they were studying for an important test. "I didn't know Rapunzel's was still around. Do they still have their Tower special? With the lemonade and iced tea drink?"

"Of course." Lucy held out her hand. "Bet?"

Alex took it and held her hand. "Bet."

For the second time in twenty-four hours, he'd touched Lucy. Each time he touched her, it felt like pure sweetness was being shot into his veins, making him feel like he was on a sugar high. He understood, just from her touch, why candy was so addictive. It made you instantly blissful. When he left this town, he was going to leave craving every part of her.

He noticed a smudge of powdered sugar on her lips and clenched his fists to keep from cleaning it off with his thumb. Yup, he was in his own personal romantic comedy hell. He pulled back, then gestured to his mouth. "You've got some sugar here."

It was better to remove temptation.

"Oh." Lucy wiped it off, then licked her fingers clean. Alex watched, dazed, heat rising in his chest. *Too late*, he thought. *She is the temptation.*

"Okay. You start," Alex said.

Lucy tapped her chin. "My mom and I have the same

middle name. My uncle taught me how to drive. My parents didn't let me date until I was seventeen."

"The second one is a lie," he said after a short pause.

Lucy laughed. "You're good. *Dad* taught me how to drive. Mom and I both share a middle name."

"Ruth?" he blurted out.

Lucy tilted her head. Her face lit up. "I told you?"

"You told me during that econ assignment. We had to fill out that fake paperwork for our fake house."

"I forgot about that." Lucy chuckled. "What did we call our fake bungalow?"

"Shore Thing," Alex said without missing a beat. She responded with a smile. His heart ached. "I thought Mr. Clarke was going to spit out his coffee at that joke."

To teach life skills, their high school economics teacher, Mr. Clarke, had made them team up, build a life together, and create a household on paper. The memory of the project washed over him. They played house for two weeks, creating the Caraway-Dwyer household, then were tasked with presenting their findings to the class. They picked out a house, selected careers, and figured out mortgage payments on their imaginary salaries. In that imaginary life, she'd worked as a first-grade teacher at the local elementary school, while he taught photography classes at the local community college while submitting grants for his art projects. During those two weeks, he'd seen what would happen if he'd stayed in the Grove for good.

He'd gotten a glimpse of the future and had honestly gotten spooked at the idea of domestic life. He liked the fantasy a little too much. But it was just that, a dream of a teenager who wanted a place to call home. Everything looked good on paper, but real life didn't work out that way. He'd learned with Nahla that making a home wasn't as simple as putting your name on an address. It took effort. He just didn't have it.

"We got an A-, though," Lucy whispered, interrupting his thoughts.

"What about the whole dating thing? Could you date or— were you locked up in a tower like a princess?"

"No. My parents weren't worried about me dating." Lucy lifted and then dropped a shoulder. "Unless a boyfriend fell out of my spell book, then I wasn't doing any dating."

Alex leaned forward. "I thought you had a protection charm on your head."

She gave him a guarded look. "No. Nothing like that."

"How come you never had a serious relationship?"

Lucy lifted a brow. "Why? Are you writing a book?"

He held her stare. "I'm curious."

"You know, curiosity killed the cat." She lifted her chin, meeting his stare.

"Well, satisfaction brought him back," he said.

The air charged when the word "satisfaction" came up. Neon light shone brightly in her eyes, sparking something within him. *When was the last time you were satisfied?* Suddenly, he became aware of how small this gondola was and how good she smelled. He was a merman with a serious sweet tooth. Here she was smelling like an entire plate of fresh-baked sprinkle cookies right out the oven. His stomach churned. Yeah. He was screwed.

"I never clicked with anyone back then," Lucy said casually.

"I hung out with guys, but nothing serious. Besides, you and I were cool. That was enough back then."

She motioned between them, obviously talking about their teenage friendship. Alex relaxed against the seat trying to ease his stomach. It was true. Their friendship, those half-spinach-and-half-sausage pizzas, cream-soda-can weekdays, and arcade weekends had been enough to satiate his desire for something more. He thought that he had found that "something more" with Nahla, but he was mistaken. Maybe he wasn't meant to have anything beyond a casual relationship.

"Alex? Everything okay?" Lucy's question rocked him out of his musings.

"Yeah." A chill came over Alex. He rubbed his arms to get warmed up, but he still felt cold.

"Your turn, Dwyer," she said, rubbing her legs. There wasn't much room in the gondola, but he shifted so she could stretch out. Every time they touched, his senses short-circuited. Her scent spun around his head.

"I only have one cousin. I used to live in Colorado. I like iced coffee," he rattled off.

"The first one is the lie," she guessed. "I remember the family tree you drew out. I thought my family was big."

"Like Pop says, Dwyers don't die—we multiply," Alex said. Lucy chuckled at the familiar saying. He'd always liked her laugh. "Pop is one of thirteen merchildren. I have at least twenty first cousins, or some ridiculous number like that."

"Family reunions must be insane." Lucy rested her chin in her hand with an amused grin. "You've been to Colorado. I've always wanted to go, have a Denver omelet, and see the Rocky Mountains."

"Yes, we lived in Denver for a while. Mom didn't like being so far from the ocean, so we moved," Alex said. "That's where we moved before we came here."

"How many times did you move?" Lucy asked.

Alex made an uncertain sound. He'd lost count around St. Louis and San Francisco. The number was low enough that it wasn't too unusual but high enough that he'd stopped telling people because of the shocked responses he got.

"Your turn."

Lucy tapped her chin. "I'm allergic to strawberries. I take a bubble bath every night. I think lavender smells strange."

"You're making this too easy. The second one is such a lie."

"How do you know?" Lucy squawked, mock offended. "I could totally take a bubble bath every night. I like bubbles."

"I can't see you taking a bubble bath."

A beat passed. She stared at him, that spark reignited in her eyes. "What do you see me doing instead?"

Alex raised a brow. He had a vision of her covered in rain, caught in a summer storm, her skin glistening. She had water in her soul. He held his breath as the image played out before his eyes. Her head was thrown back as she sang into the storm.

"I bet you sing."

"I do," Lucy said, looking away. "I don't sing well, but I sing."

"I remember you have a pretty voice."

Lucy thought for a moment, as if she wanted to respond to his compliment, but shook her head. "Your turn, Alex."

"One of my videos went viral. I have been trapped inside an elevator. I own a home."

"Come on. You're not playing fair. The last one's the lie."

"I wish," he said with light bitterness. Lucy watched him with a cautious glance. "Guess what I got for my birthday?"

"Your parents got you a house," Lucy said, in a joking tone. "All I got were unicorn slippers. Where is it?"

Alex fished the keys out of his pocket. He read off the address on the tag. Lucy laughed without humor. He bristled, feeling left out of a joke the universe seemed to be playing on him. Realization dawned on her, and a cascade of emotions flickered in her eyes.

"*You* own the Fortunato Cottage," she said in a disbelieving tone.

"You know where it is?" Alex's stomach bottomed out.

"It's across the street from me."

Neither of them said anything. Mutual shock had stolen their voices. He watched as a question lingered in her eyes. *Will you stay?* They'd been friends, but there was an invisible line they'd never crossed. Her heart had been the undiscovered country he'd yearned to explore but was terrified of spoiling and ruining with his actions. He'd left his sticky fingerprints all over the Grove, and he didn't want to do the same with her.

For the time being, he would be right across the street. Close enough to touch. Close enough to hurt. The Ferris wheel shifted, then groaned to life. It creaked, the lights blinked, and their gondola lurched forward. They were descending back to the ground, but everything was up in the air.

Chapter Eight

☾

$\mathcal{F}$ ields of Enchantment, in Downtown Freya Grove, provided every witch and caster within the tri-county area with all their magic-making needs. Cone incense burned in a red stone container and filled the space with the scent of earthy sage and sweet blessings. Copious amounts of glitter had been trodden into the wood floor over the last thirty years. Half a dozen wind chimes dangled above and sang every time the door opened or a random spirit came through the shop. An altar situated in the corner of the shop with unlit and half-melted green and white candles nestled between necklaces, saints' medals, and seagull feathers gave the store an unspoken reverence.

It sold everything from oil-dipped candles, to blessed herbs, to various items for enchantments. There was also a lending library, which was used by those who wanted to share their mystical knowledge with anyone who needed help with pesky spells or hexes. On Wednesday afternoon, Lucy ran her fingers over the spines of the well-worn and loved books borrowed by many casters looking for answers. According to family folklore, the trouble with the day Wednesday was that you could never spread rumors or speak ill of other people.

If you did, the words would come back and haunt you. Lucy did her best to keep her mouth shut, especially when the rumor of the day was that Alexander Dwyer had bought the infamous Fortunato Cottage. At least three of her neighbors had texted her, asking about whether she'd talked to the new owner. *Yeah*, she thought, *we've talked*. She'd spoken to Alex once since the Ferris wheel incident, but she didn't want to get too involved.

Yesterday as she headed to school, she saw him outside on the sidewalk in front of the cottage. He didn't go in, but he seemed transfixed by the house. Alex stood, his hands on his hips, his head tilted to the side.

It was clear that this gift was a temporary problem for him.

"It has to be the wish." Callie shook her head, amazed. "Your high school crush buys your dream house right across the street. This is fate."

"No, it's real estate market," Lucy quipped, running her fingers down book spines. "It's not my dream house."

"Please. Don't try to fool me. Every time we play the lotto, you start talking about how you'd buy the whole thing, including the honeysuckle bushes. You said you'd even hire the gnomes to landscape the place," Callie said.

"Okay, so I like the Fortunato Cottage. It's no big deal Alex owns it," Lucy admitted, a thread of jealousy bleeding into her words.

Lucy scanned the bookshelf until she came to a book spine that read *Cottage Style*. The gods were just rubbing Alex's good fortune all in her face.

She didn't just like the cottage; she yearned for it. She followed Instagram pages like *Old House Lust* and *Old*

Homes, New Life and marathon-watched house and garden shows on weekends. Whenever she came home after a long day of teaching, she'd stop and stare at the For Sale sign on Fortunato Cottage and wish. She'd wanted the money to buy it, the time to decorate it, and the will to leave the Caraway house behind to make a space of her own. The problem with inheriting a home filled with so much life was that there was little room for hers. Lucy carved out enough space in her large bedroom, but she yearned for a true home. A place where she'd make her tea blends, have stacks of books and design magazines, and fall in love. A place where she could plant her herbs instead of leaving them on the porch. Once Alex told her he'd been gifted the property, she'd been stunned into complete silence. From the disappointed look on his face, it was a gift he didn't want. She wanted to be angry, but instead, she was gripped with sadness and envy that she'd lost out on another dream.

Callie, face buried in her smartphone, spoke up first. "What's got you all upset?"

"I'm feeling a little overwhelmed," Lucy admitted.

"Your wish came true."

"That's the problem. I don't know how to control it." Lucy kept searching for the book. She stopped on a book spine. *Caring for Your Familiar.* She owed Shadow some prime cuddle and treat time. Lucy dropped the book on top of the steady pile of items she was buying from the shop.

Callie looked up from her phone. "It's a wish, not a hot air balloon. Just go with it."

"Are you just going with it? You've said that before—

you know, about school," Lucy asked carefully. Callie looked back down at her phone, her brow furrowed in thought. A strained silence stretched between them.

Whenever the family brought up the topic of college or going back to school, they treaded carefully around Callie. It was a bit of a sore subject since both Mom and Dad had been full-time professors at both Meadowdale College and Pennbrook University. She, for an unknown reason, had dropped out of college at twenty and instead started her event-planning business. Lucy trusted that Callie, with her prophetic dreams and cryptic statements alluding the future, knew the path before her and stood by her sister's decision.

Just then, Callie's eyes snapped up from the screen. An excited light entered her eyes.

"Well, good news. My credits transferred over to Meadowdale College," Callie said. "I have a nontraditional student meeting next Tuesday."

Lucy clapped her hands together in surprise. "I'm so proud of you."

Callie squirmed uncomfortably under her praise, then, with a shy smile, snapped her head back to her phone. "I'm just checking my phone for any updates."

"That's great."

"It's nothing. I figured I needed to help the wish along," Callie said. "Wishes don't work unless you do. That's why I'm repeating to myself—just go with it."

"I can't go with it if I don't know what it can do." Lucy glanced around. "It's been three days. So far, I got asked to run in a 10K, bake for the cakewalk, and sing in the karaoke contest."

Callie gave her a surprised look. "Wow, that sounds exciting."

Lucy's shoulders slumped. It sounded exhausting. She hadn't run in over a year. She only designed houses in *Dream Home* phone games, and she sang mostly in the shower. Each exciting opportunity was a chance to fall flat on her face and fail with the entire Grove watching her. If she could make the wish give her less excitement, then maybe she could get a handle on it. Lucy scanned the books again.

"Tell me what you're looking for." Callie came over to the bookshelf, phone in hand.

"It's a blue and gold book called *Wishcraft Made Simple*."

"You want to call off the wish."

"I'd rather slow it down—at least for me," Lucy clarified.

Callie opened a new browser on her phone and began typing. She hummed to herself before clicking her back teeth. "Well, it's out of print online. There are a few copies being sold, but they're super expensive."

"That's why we're here," Lucy said. "This store always has copies on hand."

"I'll ask up front," Callie volunteered. She left Lucy and went up front to the counter, speaking to the store employee. The front doorbell chimed, and Ursula came in, wearing her typical pink pastel outfit, her designer bag nestled in the crook of her arm. She joined Lucy by the books, pressing a hand to her slicked-up hairdo.

"Sorry I'm late. I just got your text," Ursula said.

"No problem. I wanted to know which herbs and flowers you wanted for your bridal comb."

Ursula wrinkled her nose. "Oh, I didn't know we're still doing that tradition."

"Absolutely. Nana would haunt me if I didn't," Lucy said with a firm shake of her head. Since the first Caraway wedding, it was tradition for the bride to wear a hair comb or fastener with protective flowers and herbs to bless her marriage. Lucy had already gone to the farmers' market, prepping for this event. She'd gotten a great deal on lavender and sunflowers. Ursula would look lovely with a crown of flowers.

"I'll let you know," Ursula said. "I'll see which herbs go with the dress. We just had the fitting."

"Today?" Lucy peered at Ursula. "Um—I thought we were going on Saturday."

"Mrs. Walker thought it would be better if we just got it done now. We're on such a tight deadline that we couldn't push it back. We did have to tweak the color scheme a bit, so your dress color might change. Schedule your own fitting appointment when you can. Today's super busy." Ursula flashed her a stressed grin.

"I will. I don't think you want me wearing a bedsheet at the altar," Lucy quipped.

"No, of course not. Um...can we talk for a second?"

"Sure." Lucy fully faced Ursula. Her manicured fingers picked at the dangling charm from her designer bag. Ursula didn't fidget unless she was super nervous about something. Lucy swallowed hard and straightened up. She silently pleaded that she wouldn't have to wear a school-bus-yellow bridesmaid dress down the aisle. Even so, Lucy would sashay and strut her stuff if Ursula needed her to step up for her special day.

"Mrs. Walker brought up a few things," Ursula said in a cautious tone. "You signed up for the cakewalk. You're making a...uh...croquembouche?"

Lucy's throat started tingling. "I guess so."

Ursula stared at her as if trying to divine whether she was lying. Lucy had learned through her last few encounters that if she tried to deny the opportunity, she'd be rendered voiceless. If she made a neutral statement, she'd be able to respond. She was basically living out the real-life version of that Jim Carrey movie where he couldn't say no. It was a hot mess, and she'd been under this spell for less than a week. She'd be lucky if she didn't end up running down Main Street in her underwear, screaming, because of her inability to lie.

"A French cream-puff tower? That sounds difficult for a home baker like you." Ursula winced.

Lucy narrowed her eyes. *Why did she say "home baker" with the same disdain one said "amateur gold miner"? I know how to read a recipe.*

"It's not impossible," Lucy said.

"Professional bakers have failed making this dessert. You've never made anything other than brownies and blondies," Ursula said, her tone hardened.

"That's true." Lucy had never pushed herself to bake anything more complicated because she was scared to fail. The spell wouldn't let her fail, right? Right?

"I'm running the cakewalk fundraiser," Ursula said with a hint of boastfulness. "Mrs. Walker trusted me to organize all the bakers and donations. I'm responsible for making sure that we don't have a single empty table. I'm going to crush this fundraiser. I have to crush it."

Lucy watched Ursula. Her desire to impress the Walkers was stamped in gold on her forehead. Empathy for her cousin washed over her heart. This wedding had to go off without a problem, so Lucy needed to get this wish under control. She tried to assure Ursula that she wasn't going to let her down, but she couldn't work her mouth open. Instead, Lucy nodded and smiled. It seemed to work, since Ursula gave a relaxed smirk.

Callie returned from the counter. "So, bad news. All the copies are rented out. Good news is, once a copy is available, they'll call us. We're on the waiting list."

"Which book are you looking for?" Ursula looked at Lucy, then Callie.

"It's nothing, just a book about tea blends," Lucy said quickly. She didn't want to alarm Ursula with her wayward wish. She wouldn't want anything to ruin the wedding or stress out her already high-strung cousin.

"How's your spell going, cuz?" Callie asked Ursula. She gave Lucy one last glance, then looked over at her cousin.

Ursula's face brightened. "Oh, yes. Everything's going great. I picked out a new dress, we're working on a new color scheme, and we have a cake tasting."

"What's the new theme?"

"Boho." Ursula's smile seemed slightly strained. "It's the perfect time for a boho beach wedding."

"You don't like sand," Callie said. "You legit called Grove Beach a massive litter box for people."

"I was joking," Ursula said, a little too brightly. "We're having the ceremony on the boardwalk."

Lucy leaned against the bookcase, getting mental whip-lash from all the changes being made within a single week.

"We're having the rehearsal dinner and drinks at Berkeley."

Lucy looked closely at Ursula. She appeared dazed, as if she had just had too much sugar or rosé.

"This can't be what you wished for," Lucy said. *Was this her or the spell?*

Something furious and a bit desperate flashed in Ursula's face, then vanished. She took a steady breath, then exhaled. Her features schooled into a posh mask, and then she said, "This is what I want. Everyone's coming together to help make this wedding happen. It's going to happen. Okay. Marcus has been great. He's helped me with getting favors and the guest list reorganized. You don't have to be rude to him."

She ended her rant panting. A chill filled the store at her words. A nearby customer, noticing the vibe, moved away from them, to the other side of the store.

"This convo is getting awkward." Callie focused on her phone.

Lucy blinked rapidly to control her rising annoyance. "Hold up. When was I rude to him?"

"Marcus said you ran away from him at the festival," Ursula said.

A stab of guilt hit Lucy's gut, but she pushed on. She still had no regrets about running away, especially when there was a spell involved. "I really wanted to ride the Ferris wheel," Lucy said.

Callie squeaked, offended that Lucy hadn't heeded her

warning, but she didn't look up from her phone. Lucy went to apologize but then stopped.

Why was Marcus putting her name in his mouth? He could've called her instead of bothering Ursula with his problem.

"He just wanted to say hi. You're both in our wedding party."

"When did you talk to Marcus?" Lucy asked.

"He texted me. You got off the ride with Alex. Marcus also said you found your soul mate," Ursula said in an astounded tone. Her eyes narrowed. "Is that true? Alex is your soul mate."

No. No. No. Lucy's mouth didn't open despite her best efforts. Where was a purse-size crowbar when you needed it? She dipped her head in reluctant acknowledgment. The wish was completely out of hand.

Callie whipped her head up, invested now. "Lucy, you wicked witch."

"You've been dreaming about him forever." There was a slight tinge of wonder in Ursula's voice. "It's about time this happened for you."

Defeated by the wish, Lucy couldn't say anything negative but just pressed herself against the books. For a moment back in high school, she thought she might have felt that telltale click inside. If only Alex had been her true match. But he hadn't felt anything other than friendship toward her.

"So, I assume he's going to be your wedding date," Ursula drawled.

"Maybe," Lucy eked out, unable to scream the words "No way, baby."

It took her an entire month to ask him to senior prom. How was she going to ask him to Ursula's wedding? Ugh.

"That's perfect. You don't have to go far to pick up your date," Callie said with a grin.

Ursula threw a questioning glance at Callie, and Callie told her, "Alex bought the Fortunato Cottage."

Ursula clucked happily at this sudden news. Lucy gave Callie a pointed glare, but Callie was unfazed. "There are no secrets in the Grove. You should know that by now."

"Perfect. I was just about to ask you about your plus one," Ursula said. "We're updating the guest list. The caterer needs a final head count for the menu."

"Oh, okay now. What's on the menu?" Callie asked.

"Um...it's going to be a buffet. We've decided on a menu called King Triton's Feast."

Callie nodded automatedly like a bobblehead doll on a car dashboard. *What the what?* Lucy turned toward the bookshelf so Ursula wouldn't see her stunned look. Ursula, the woman who hated sand with a passion and once tried to free the live lobsters at Uncle Mac's Seafood Shack in Cape May, was having a beach-themed wedding. It appeared that Lucy wasn't the only one whose wish seemed to be going out of control. A voice in her head warned her, *If Ursula's wish is acting up, what's going to happen to you?*

"Lucy?" Ursula's voice interrupted her private freak-out.

She blinked her thoughts away and faced Ursula. "Hm?"

"Confirm if Alex is coming to the wedding. We need a final head count by mid-August."

A rapid beeping sounded off. Ursula searched frantically

for her phone in her bag. "That's my alarm. We have the cake tasting at four. I'm heading out."

"I thought you decided to serve red velvet cake."

"No. It doesn't fit the new theme. We're thinking mango or pineapple-cherry sponge cake." Ursula found her phone and swiped off the alarm.

"Are you serious about the pineapple sponge?" Lucy asked.

"This is my wedding cake! It's not like we're picking out something simple like a tea blend."

Lucy glared at her. *You wish.*

Ursula blew a kiss. "Text me later. Love y'all."

Callie waved weakly while Ursula rushed out of the store. She whipped her head toward Lucy. "She's been replaced with an evil twin."

"Callie. You can't be serious."

"If she's not an evil twin, then she's a changeling! Don't be fooled by the fae! There's no way Ursula would willingly have mango in a cake. Think about it. We have to find that book."

"You just said just go—"

"I know what I said," Callie interrupted with a frantic hand wave. "We can't let her plan this wedding, sprung out on magic. That's no good for anyone. Let's make a plan to talk to her soon."

"What about Alex?" Lucy asked.

Callie gave her a saucy look. "You're going to sashay over there and tell that merman to show his tail."

"Callie," Lucy warned once again. It seemed her upcoming college life was making her sister go a little wild.

"I'm playing. Ask him to the wedding. He can either say

yes or no," Callie said. She scratched her cheek in thought, then frowned. "He might feel a little odd eating seafood."

Lucy groaned, not trusting herself to use words. If she was going to ask her new neighbor for a favor, then she was going to appeal to his stomach. One could catch flies with honey, but how did you catch a merman?

Chapter Nine

☾

*A*lex looked at his house. His house. His cottage. This storybook-looking cottage, with overgrown honeysuckle bushes flanking the blue front door and a stone path that wound its way from the door to the sidewalk. He glared at the bugs and butterflies that fluttered by in the sunshine. *Whimsical jerks*, he thought, shaking his head as he walked up the stone path. Even his scales itched to photograph this place, despite the fact that he didn't want to be here. A sense of reluctant awe came over him. This place was, for lack of a better term, picture-perfect. Alex, inspired by his encounter with Lucy, decided to give the cottage a chance. He couldn't walk away without seeing it, especially after the flicker of interest he'd seen in her eyes when he'd told her he owned this place. Alex could only avoid the whole house problem for so long. Mom kept texting asking questions about the cottage that left him fumbling for answers. By Thursday afternoon, he couldn't avoid his house any longer. It was time that he faced this problem. Besides, what was the point of paying for a hotel when he had a place to stay? He'd miss the room service, but it was time to see this gift.

As he surveyed the cottage, Alex reflected on his breakfast

meeting with Horatio at Mimi's Diner earlier that morning. He had picked at his pancakes while Horatio talked to him. Chocolate-chip pancakes couldn't fix his mood as he learned about his new digs. His so-called home sweet home was a hot mess, emotionally speaking.

"I know how Mom and Pop got the place for so cheap. No one wants it. It's jinxed," Horatio said, sitting in their diner booth.

"You mean it's cursed."

"No. A jinx brings someone bad luck. A curse invokes a supernatural power to bring harm to a person or place," Horatio corrected without missing a beat.

"Don't tell me how you know that." Alex sighed. Keeping track of all this magic was exhausting.

"Listen, I've renovated enough houses and homes in the Grove. I have to know the difference. Family curses and ghosts will drive down your property value in an instant," Horatio said. "I'm glad you're still here. I thought you'd run out of town by now."

Alex shrugged. He had nowhere to go, a merman without a place to rest his tail. His apartment with Nahla was gone. The truth was that his family didn't even know that he had been engaged. Horatio didn't feel comfortable using social media save for a business page he updated once every six months. Mom and Pop thought a digital footprint was the name of his favorite band. The life he posted and shared online was gone as if someone hit the refresh button on his entire life.

"I have to settle this issue first," Alex said simply. "Let's swing by the cottage. Maybe we can grab some sea salt to cleanse everything just in case."

Horatio sighed. "I can't do today. I have a job in the West Grove."

"Really?" Alex asked curiously. The West Grove, the spookier neighborhood in Freya Grove, was known for the more gothic beings and creatures who went bump in the night. Alex had known a few goblins and ghouls in high school who called West Grove home.

"Yes. Vampires need remodeling services, too," Horatio said. "I'll come over next week to inspect everything. If you're serious about selling the house, I can get you a spot on the Open House New Jersey Tour."

"Okay." Alex leaned back.

"Hear me out," Horatio said. "The cottage will be placed on a list. People from all over the state will get a chance to visit and put in their offer."

Alex rubbed his jaw. "Does it work?"

"Last year, every single house was sold. If you're looking to sell, this is the best way to do it."

"Tell me what I need to do."

"Have the cottage ready by August," Horatio said. "I'll personally get you on the list."

After Horatio paid the check, he reached into his pocket and placed a four-leaf-clover key chain charm on the table. The green enamel clover glinted under the overhead light.

Alex tried to give it back to him, but he pressed it firmly into his hand.

"Take all the luck you can get," Horatio said. He slid it over to Alex.

He attached the keys to the charm. Maybe, luck would be on his side.

Alex shook off the conversation. Focus up. The Fortunato Cottage was simple, symmetrical, and rectangular—orderly and straightforward. Alex ambled up the path and touched the front door, placing a hand on the knob. The brass doorknob felt real and solid underneath his scales. *I'm here.* He turned the knob and walked inside.

The door opened directly onto a polished wood staircase squarely in the center of the house. He studied the entryway, impressed. The wood floors, scuffed and slightly worn, sounded solid under his feet. He walked through the first floor, strolling through each area—living room, kitchen, family room, and dining room. The place didn't seem jinxed. However, he got an odd feeling standing alone inside the house. He didn't feel alone. It felt like when you were standing in line at a checkout counter and you feel someone behind you but you can't see their face. He shuddered all over. Battling voices warred within him.

Just leave. Apologize later. But if you leave, where would you go? You don't have a fishbowl to live in, a voice sneered in his head. *Eventually you're going to run out of ocean to explore.*

As of Friday, the apartment lease was up, and he'd given away or sold everything that he owned. He had to deal with this house and find a way to get out of this situation.

His agent had left a message for him about an upcoming photography showcase if he was interested. Alex hadn't returned the phone call but rather kept that nugget in his back pocket. He placed his hands on the walls, letting the weight finally hit him. The Fortunato Cottage was one of the oldest houses in the Grove. It was sturdy, dependable—it was exactly what he didn't need in his life.

Three words chimed through him like warning bells.

Responsibility. Liability. Burden.

His friends and cousins shared wedding photos and baby announcements on their social media profiles. Alex switched his profile picture from him and Nahla hugging to a solo picture of him standing on the horizon alone. Make no promises, break no hearts, put down no roots. It was better that way. It had to be better that way. Now he had the Fortunato Cottage to tend to for the foreseeable future. The warning bells sounded again.

Responsibility Liability. Burden.

No more rented spaces and tiny apartments that he couldn't call home.

He didn't own a lawn mower, but now he had a whole lawn.

He lived under one rule: If you don't keep anything, you can't lose it.

When he was a kid, he'd felt like a goldfish dropped into an aquarium with plastic palm trees and stone castles. The Grove had been his aquarium. Everything used to be exciting, but he always bumped up against the walls and limits of that world. As Alex grew, he'd felt like an overgrown fish in a bowl, flopping out tail first and wanting to see the world. By the time he turned eighteen, he'd completely outgrown the Grove. Even after more than ten years away from home, being back here made him feel like he had when he was eighteen, right back in the proverbial fishbowl. He was trying to make his way. He pulled away from the walls that seemed to close in and steal his air and walked out of the cottage.

Alex took in a deep breath, forcing air into his lungs.

This house was just another adventure. Another project

he could post to his feed. He crushed adventures on a regular basis, and this house would be no different. He'd get the cottage ready for the open house, decorate, then sell it. Until then, he was here in the Grove for good. He scrubbed his hands over his hair and groaned. *Just my freaking luck.*

He hadn't left the Grove on the best terms—having not only burned bridges but torched everything with his words. He didn't regret leaving, but he regretted who he'd hurt on his way out. The flash of hurt on Lucy's face when he tossed a careless goodbye over his shoulder, turned away from her, and drove off immediately after graduation haunted him even now. The very people he'd never thought he'd see again were now his new neighbors. Those same ones hiding in their homes but watching his every step. Alex glanced around Summerfield Street. Lace curtains fluttered as people peeked out their windows at him. His next-door neighbor, Ms. Shirley, lingered on her porch, cradling a cup of coffee, while glancing over at his house.

Alex raised his hand and waved. "Good morning," he called out.

Ms. Shirley sheepishly smiled, then went back inside the house without another word. Okay. Irritation needled its way into his chest and stayed there. That's what he got for trying to be friendly. Alex went to the sidewalk and turned to the house. Cars slowed down as they passed. Dog walkers slowed their pace. He was the freak at the freak show. He heard approaching footsteps coming up behind him. Her oil—a mixture of something peppery and sweet—wafted in the air.

"The whole damn neighborhood's out here," he said under his breath.

"Not the whole neighborhood," her voice said over his shoulder. "The gnomes are busy stashing their treasure."

Alex faced Lucy and put his hands together in a prayer motion. *What were what?* "Please tell me you're kidding about the gnomes."

Lucy shook her head sagely. "I never kid about them. Watch your silver and gold."

Alex rubbed his eyes in a motion of annoyance and frustration. He forced his hands down to his side. Gnomes. Witches. Hexed house. He looked at Lucy. She wore a crocheted shawl over her shoulders, hiding her Freya Grove High School T-shirt and jeans covering a shapely bottom.

Lucy held out a tinfoil-covered plate to Alex. He eyed it warily. Wasn't he warned in fairy tales not to take treats from witches, especially the ones that were beautiful?

"I figured you needed something sweet," she said, waving the plate at him.

"Something sweet other than you?" Alex took the plate from her. He noticed the blush cross her cheeks. A ripple of pleasure went through him. He liked making her blush.

"You mermen are too much," Lucy said, waving his compliment away.

Alex lifted the plate. He held back a gasp. "Cowboy blondies."

His mouth watered at the sight of the chewy chocolate-chip, coconut, and brown-sugar treat cut into neat squares.

"Is that sea salt on top?" he asked. Of course, there was

sea salt on top. She wasn't playing fair. These treats would be gone by the end of the day.

"Nana always made a plate for new neighbors." Lucy tapped the plate lovingly. "I guess that means you."

"Thanks, Lu."

The old nickname slipped out. She swallowed and gave him a small grin. "No problem."

Alex gestured to the house. "I'd invite you in, but I have nothing to sit on."

"If you're looking for cheap chairs, the Freya Flea Market is in August," Lucy said. "I know a few vendors who'd love to decorate this place. We can make a deal."

Alex hesitated. When he was furnishing his old place with his ex, he'd gone to the Bushwick Market and rummaged through unfinished chairs and macramé plant holders to find treasures to decorate their home. He'd been covered in dust and cobwebs, but he'd been happy at the time. His chest ached. There were too many memories about that space that he didn't want to think about now. This house wasn't going to be a home for him. It was a project.

"I don't know if I'm going to keep it." He didn't want to waste her time and energy.

Lucy's shoulders dropped a fraction. Displeasure flickered for a second in her eyes. "But it was a gift."

"It's a huge-ass, pricey gift."

"The mortgage can't be more than rent on an apartment in the city," Lucy pointed out with a knowing grin. Alex huffed at her words. She wasn't wrong. He'd gone to the bank, spoken to the home lending advisor, and seen the monthly payment amount for himself. It would be cheaper just to stay here than to rent a temporary place elsewhere.

"Give it a chance. If you don't like it, sell it at the end of the summer," Lucy said.

"You make it sound easy," Alex said. "I can't just post this house on social media and sell it."

"People sell everything on the internet. I just saw someone try to sell a haunted doll." Lucy visibly shuddered. "You do not need that supernatural drama."

"What about a jinxed house?"

"It's not the house's fault. Wouldn't you be mad if people kept falling in and out of love with you?" Lucy rolled her eyes at that phrase. Alex gave a ragged sigh. She softened when she looked him over. "The house isn't jinxed; it just needs love. If someone invested in it, rather than run away when things got tough, it wouldn't be for sale every six months."

Alex froze when he heard this news. "How many people have owned this place?"

Lucy frowned. "Let's just say I've perfected making my cowboy blondies for all our new neighbors. The last time I counted, it was fifteen owners in the past five years."

"Yikes," Alex groaned. "That makes me lucky owner number sixteen."

"You might be what this house needs. I have a good feeling," Lucy said.

"I can't just sell an empty house," Alex said. "I need to stage it. I have to show the possibilities."

"I like possibilities," Lucy said, rubbing her palms together, excitement vibrating from her entire being. She lit up from the inside out. "What are you thinking style and decor wise? Seaside? Countryside? Hollywood bungalow?"

A familiar sensation of sinking hit his stomach. He held the plate close to his chest. "I don't know."

"What's the vibe you're getting from the house?"

"It's giving me a haunted hideaway feeling," Alex said.

Lucy held up a hand. "Have you seen or heard a ghost?"

"Not yet."

"Don't claim it. Get paint samples from the hardware store downtown. Start getting a real feel for the place. Get a cat. Buy a plant." Lucy placed a hand on his shoulder. It was a simple gesture. He felt her warmth through the shirt. It felt nice to be this close to someone even for a moment. A small, enchanting smile touched her lips. He was spellbound.

"Do something that scares you," she said.

Alex froze. A splash of apprehension hit him like a wave of icy water. He'd done that by moving in with Nahla and asking her to marry him, and it didn't work out. From now on, he was sticking with what he knew, and that was to keep moving on. A moving merman never got caught.

"I hope you're taking your own advice."

She scanned his face, and her hand dropped away. Something like frustration flashed in her eyes. "I'm trying. Enjoy the blondies. Keep the plate. Save some for the gnomes."

Lucy gave a salute, looked both ways, then walked back across the street.

"Hey, Lu."

Lucy stopped on the sidewalk in front of her mailbox. She waited.

"I still owe you a pizza with iced tea and lemonade."

He hadn't forgotten their bet. A momentary look of delight crossed her face.

"Don't tempt me with a good time, Dwyer," she said over her shoulder, walking back up to her house.

Her words kicked his heart rate up a notch. Fun had been in short supply for Alex after his engagement ended and the loss of his apartment. He'd like nothing more than to have a good time with Lucy.

He waited until his quickened pulse subsided before he went back into the cottage.

Many neighbors had watched him from the safety of their porches and windows, but none of them had come over to say hello. Except Lucy. She'd chatted with him, made him laugh, and given him some comfort food. She never seemed to be scared to walk up and introduce herself to a new person when they were young. Having her as a temporary neighbor seemed like it was going to be a quite an adventure. His chest eased, and he felt a little less alone.

May 31

Dear Freya Grove Gladiators,

It is incredible that we are now only a few months away from celebrating our 10th reunion. If you have not marked your calendar yet, please do so now.

Reunion Weekend is August 27–30, and we are counting on you to be a part of this celebration.

If you have any questions, please do not hesitate to contact me!

Best,
Quentin Jacobson
Class Secretary

June

rose and honeysuckle

Chapter Ten

*L*ucy wore emerald earrings on Fridays—the best day to wear the gemstone. There was only one week of school left, but so much work remained. The emeralds helped her hold on to what eloquence she had on hand. Graduation speeches, classroom cleaning, and ending the school year pushed her to the limit. She delivered Asha's recommendation letter before the deadline and signed dozens of yearbooks with heartfelt memories and best wishes to the departing seniors. She needed a nap, but she settled for caffeine. There was only one place she wanted to go. It was fitting that she celebrated another day closer to vacation at the Little Red Hen Bakery Café.

Barn-red walls were decorated with silhouettes of hens and framed photos of barnyard animals scratching the dirt. The counter was lined with polished chrome espresso and frothing machines. Behind the cashier was the illustrated outlined story of the Little Red Hen, who managed to grow wheat, cut wheat, and bake bread without the help of her barnyard friends. Indeed, the Little Red Hen was Lucy's role model.

Lucy also didn't ask for help, and she loved her carbs.

She shifted her tote bag from one shoulder to the other, trying not to strain her neck. She'd earned her tea today. Ursula had texted her every morning this week, updating her on the wedding changes, but didn't hint about her bridal flowers and herbs. The Valentine's Glamour Amor wedding was now a Boho Beach–theme wedding at the Jersey Shore. Lucy rented as many pastry and baking books as possible. Their *Wishcraft Made Simple* book still hadn't come, but she managed to find a used copy on a used-book website. It hurt her wallet, but she needed the book like yesterday. She smothered a huge yawn behind her hand, trying not to show off her back teeth to the hardworking barista. The wish wouldn't leave her alone. She'd started training for the charity 10K race in Grove Park. She got pop-up notifications to "Get That Booty in Gear," courtesy of her running app, which she couldn't turn off or uninstall. She got scared and didn't ask Alex to the wedding. She'd get her life in order tomorrow; today she had sugar. The glass case held a selection of muffins, sandwiches, and cookies. Lucy eyed the chocolate-chip muffin in the front row. She wandered over to the case.

"Hello there, my pretties. If I get a blueberry muffin, that'll be my fruit for the day," Lucy muttered to herself.

She paused the fantasy of impending summer days and focused on her afternoon snack.

"Go ahead and treat yo'self," said a voice behind her.

She bit back a yelp and faced him. "Marcus."

"Hey, Caraway."

His large eyes the color of coffee without cream were hidden behind ombre sunglasses. His shaved head was shorn down with hair fuzz growing back. She'd loved touching his head whenever it was buzzed down like it was now. He was tall with a slender build and was outfitted in a plaid shirt, dark jeans, and boots. A backpack was slung over one shoulder. There was never a good time to run into an ex-boyfriend. The man looked like he was about to head back to his cabin in the woods. The whole lumberjack-by-the-shore look used to be her catnip. Now she leaned toward more seaside sexiness. Like merman sexiness.

He tucked his hands into his pockets. "How are you?"

"I'm good. Just getting myself a little snack."

"I know you deserve it." Marcus popped his lips into his mouth and licked them. She gave a small grin. Oh. Yeah. Those lips were once her ultimate kryptonite.

They asked her a question. She tuned in. "Did you hear about the wedding date change?"

Lucy nodded. "Ursula told me."

"I think they might be rushing this whole thing." Marcus scanned her face, as if looking for permission to share his thoughts with her. She wasn't going there with Marcus, especially since Ursula was her cousin and best friend. Caraways stuck together, no matter what.

Lucy held on to her poker face. "The heart wants what it wants."

"Really?" Marcus nodded. "What does your heart want?"

Alex. Her heart shrieked like a tipsy college student ordering fries from a late-night food truck.

She absolutely wasn't going there with her ex, so she pivoted. "I'd really like carbs."

Marcus took the bait and laughed. "I hear that. Ursula told you about the Atlantic City weekend, right?" Marcus asked.

"We're thinking about having a joint bachelor/bachelorette party. I figured she'd tell her maid of honor."

"She did. It sounds like a fun time."

"That's a whole lie. You've never liked AC." Marcus laughed, using the nickname for America's playground.

"I never had a reason for not liking AC. I never really gave it a chance."

"Maybe we could find a reason," Marcus said gently.

In another life, they could've been talking about their wedding party weekend, but she and Marcus hadn't worked out, despite their best efforts. They just didn't click. It was like trying to force a USB port into the wrong slot and blaming the computer for not changing. He wanted to solve every little problem instead of just listening to her sometimes. They would make each other terribly unhappy if they settled for their relationship and not for the true love they deserved. She'd sincerely loved Marcus, but she hadn't fallen for him like one would fall for a soul mate.

She gave herself a mental shake. Marcus watched her, waiting for a response.

"Sorry. I blanked out for a moment. It was a long day."

"No worries. We should catch up. What are you doing now?" He looked at her hopefully. "Let's get some coffee."

Uh-oh. That was his code for "let's get naked." A shimmery vision of a possible future clouded her eyes. If she hooked up with Marcus, they'd inevitably get back together. Then they'd go to the wedding together and then...they'd be stuck again as a couple. She'd give up on finding her click and then—no, she had to act fast.

"I'm meeting someone," Lucy blurted out.

Marcus blinked, stunned. He narrowed his eyes. "You came in alone."

"He's not here yet." Now she had to pull a random name out of the sky and pray to the Goddess they'd magically appear somehow. "I'm just having…tea with…"

Think, witch, think. The doorbell jingled as another customer came in. She saw his suit and tie before she saw his face. He was going to be so smug. She'd deal with him later.

"Alex." Her voice rose in relief. "You made it."

He gave her a small, uncertain smile. She willed him to go along with her ruse.

His smile widened. "Yes, I did. That'd be me." He stepped over to her and Marcus.

Alex leaned over to Lucy. He brushed a gentle kiss across her cheek. He'd done it countless times before back in high school, but back then he gave her a quick peck. No. This was different, more intimate. This kiss felt like a homecoming. A knot rose in her throat once she realized he didn't immediately move away. He hovered near her as if he were a cold traveler trying to warm himself by a fire. She pressed a hand to where his lips touched her skin. His touch felt like a cool wave, reviving her senses into waking up.

His sea brine cologne touched her nose. A part of her soul sighed; the brine made her feel at ease. Alex swung an arm around her shoulder and pulled her in close. Now her soul purred. He made sure to keep an inch or two between them, respecting her space.

"I'm sorry I'm late. There was a water break on Main."

"I thought mermen like getting wet," Marcus joked lightly.

A tense beat went by. Ugh. She knew—based on all

the shouting matches he'd gotten into in high school—how much he disliked merperson jokes. Alex assessed Marcus with a quick gaze and then blinked.

"We usually don't mind it, but the outfit is new," Alex responded evenly.

A mischievous glint entered Marcus's eyes. He leaned back in understanding. "I get it. So, he's your long-lost soul mate."

Alex's hazel eyes widened in astonishment. Lucy fought the urge to break off the nearest table leg and jab it at Marcus. He gave a fake friendly smile that glowed with superiority. He was always stirring up trouble. "I read the e-newsletter and wondered who'd captured our Goosey Lucy. I'm stunned."

She was going to pinch Ursula for sharing her camp nickname with the Walkers.

Lucy and Alex locked eyes, and Alex gave her a small nod, a motion for permission to play into this misunderstanding. She nodded back. He eased his arm from her shoulder and down to her waist, pulling her flush against his body. He held her tight, closing the inches and feeling solidness. The man was a rock. Strong. Hard. Probably fun to sit on.

"Soul mate? Is that your secret nickname for me, Lu?" Alex murmured.

"No, you know what I call you," she said, giving him a playful grin.

"I don't think I can say those words out loud." He gave her a heated look that sent her thoughts screaming like die-hard fans at a boy-band concert. His eyes darkened. The air around them caught on fire. A mixture of shock and heat caused her response to wedge in her throat. What would she call him behind closed doors? She'd probably be too busy moaning while he pleasured her with his fingers, which were currently drawing lazy circles on her hip. Yikes. She didn't break the stare, not wanting to let this moment pass.

"Well, of course you're coming to the wedding," Marcus said, a little brittle.

Alex kept his attention on Lucy. "Absolutely. I wouldn't miss it for the world."

Lucy's heart jolted in anticipation. He sounded like he was sincerely excited to be her wedding date. Inconvenient truths bubbled up inside her brain. He was leaving town soon.

Lucy wrenched her attention away from Alex. "We'll be there."

"I'm all yours, Lucinda," Alex said in her ear. She tingled all over at the sound of him saying her full name. Why did he have to say it like that with all the regalities? Like a knight kneeling before her, ready to serve. He said her name with the power that it was imbued with. If he said her full name like he did, she might do something stupid. Sexy, but stupid.

Like ask him to kiss her again, you know, to fool Marcus.

Lucy said goodbye to Marcus and went with Alex to the back booth, weaving between the tables. Even though she didn't see it, the sensation of his hand directing her to their table made her trill with anticipation. Her heart pounded. She swallowed tightly as she took the seat across from him in the booth, missing his heat immediately. They had a bit of privacy back here, so she could explain to him what the hell had just happened. She also wanted to talk to him about his plans for the house and didn't want an audience to overhear her. The Grove had been abuzz with Alex owning the Fortunato Cottage, and she'd done her best not to jump in.

"Lucinda."

"Lucy," she gently corrected. Her heart couldn't stand him calling her by her full name. It was a bit too intimate. That was an intimacy she'd reserve for someone who would commit to her.

He held up a hand. "Right. My fault. How are you, Lucy?"

"I'm better. Thanks for helping me out back there."

"If it wasn't me, it was going to be someone else."

"Right." *No*, her soul stated, it wasn't going to be . . . someone else. A moment passed between them. They hadn't talked much since the cottage incident, but they'd waved to each other from across their porches. Over the last few weeks they'd become friendly yet distant neighbors, which was fine. He'd even returned her plate, loading it with her favorite rainbow sprinkle cookies from the local bakery. They'd gone perfectly with her honey, vanilla, and chamomile tea blend.

"How long should we fake this meeting?" Lucy gestured between the two of them.

He looked her over, then grinned. "As long as you want."

She swallowed a sigh. It was too easy to get lost in the way he looked at her like she was a lake he wanted to dip his toe and whole body into. Everything fluttered. *Think of something else.*

"What's been going on with you?" Lucy asked.

"I had a conversation with my agent."

"Okay now, look at you, Mr. Fancy," Lucy said. "I didn't know that you were that in demand. Should I pay for your time? I don't want to mess up your hustle."

Alex looked at her; a flash of humor crossed his face at her teasing.

"It's not even like that. I had to settle a few things." The humor faded away from him and was quickly replaced with disappointment.

"Like what?"

"I pushed back my gallery showing. I'm not going to be ready in time. I don't like the photos I've been taking lately. I feel so—" He interrupted himself with a groan.

"Uninspired? Uncertain?" Lucy suggested.

"Yes, to both of those words. My agent's great, but I can't ask her to delay. I have to get my spark back." Alex gave her a smile that didn't quite reach his eyes.

"Maybe being back in the Grove might spark something in you," Lucy said hopefully.

Her heart went out to him. She knew what it was like to lose that creative spark and feel that everything you made or did wasn't good enough to show the world. Currently, she felt that way about her teaching and was struggling to get that creativity back. There were a few professional learning programs she could apply for that might get her groove on, but she'd delayed putting in her applications.

"I'm definitely going to need some caffeine," Alex said. "You didn't get anything to drink."

Lucy clicked her teeth in displeasure. "I know. I got distracted." *By your hands on my body. By your body hugged up on me.*

"I heard their coffee is great."

"I'm more of a tea person," Lucy said.

Alex nodded, stood up, and went over to the counter.

This accidental meeting didn't need to be long at all. She just needed to hang out here until Marcus left, and then she'd be on her way—without her muffin or caffeine. Meanwhile, her attention darted over to the door, where Marcus moved to claim a single tabletop. Was he sitting down and taking out his laptop? Come on. What was she going to do? Rush out and go home? No, she couldn't keep doing this.

She saw the possible path before her. Marcus would grab her hand as she left and look at her with those big eyes that were like hypnosis wheels, weakening her defenses until she was exhausted waiting for her soul to click. He'd croon and talk her into one coffee. Then that afternoon coffee would turn into evening drinks, and those drinks would turn into coffee...at his apartment after they spent the night together. She didn't even like coffee!

Lather. Rinse. Repeat.

Marcus was familiar, just like the festival and just like everything else in the Grove.

He didn't push. He didn't demand anything from her. He didn't click.

Marcus was there. She was there. It was easy. It was comfortable. She blinked back to the table and the present. She wanted more. She wanted excitement. She wanted...tea?

Alex placed a brewed iced tea on the table. He also placed a few honey packets next to the drink. He clutched his own coffee cup, saucer, and spoon as he sat down with her.

"It's called Meadow Dew. It sounded refreshing."

"Thanks," Lucy said, cradling the cup in her hand. "How much do I owe you?"

Alex waved her off. "Consider it a thank-you. I finished those welcome-to-the-block blondies in a day."

Pleasure sparked within her. "I can make you more if you like."

"I don't know. Hansel and Gretel would warn me about taking extra treats from a kindhearted witch," he said in a husky whisper.

"I have other ways of fattening you up," she joked.

"You are dangerous," he said. His eyes dipped to her lips. He absentmindedly ran his thumb over his lips, as if pretending he was touching hers. Oh, sweet Atlantic. Lucy undid the lid of the iced tea to give her hands something to do other than touch Alex. She added honey to the drink, twirled her finger, and sent the ice cubes spinning with her thoughts. They fell into a companionable silence, with only the sounds of baristas calling out drink orders and the muted conversation in the café space in the background.

"So, soul mate?" Alex asked, stirring his coffee. His spoon clicked against the cup. He removed the spoon and cleaned it with a long, lazy lick. His darkened eyes never left hers for an instant. He should get an award for what he did to that utensil. Mercy.

He hadn't seen the email; she might as well rip off the bandage. Alex dropped the spoon, his brow raised in question.

"Let me have my tea first before I get into this."

She took a long sip of her drink. The calming tea blend of chamomile flowers, rooibos, and lemon peels alleviated her fraught nerves. *No guts, no glory.* Lucy showed him the e-newsletter with that class note. Alex gave it a critical squint, his brows lifted in surprise as he read it.

"So, you've been busy," Alex said, his voice resigned. "I didn't know you were dating someone." His eyes dipped down to his coffee cup.

Lucy lurched forward. No. Not like this. She pushed the words out. She didn't want to lie to him, not over this wish. She touched her emerald earrings, remembering the lore. *Emeralds aid you in having an honest tongue and open heart. Hold fast and speak true.*

"It's a spell," she blurted out, shocked by the truth in her voice.

"What?"

Lucy lowered her head. "It's a spell," she repeated. Relief rushed through her body, causing her hands to shake. It felt good to be real. "I made a wish, and—oh man—it's gotten out of hand."

"So, there's no soul mate?"

Did she detect a note of hope? Relief? Was this just wishful thinking?

"He's out there somewhere." *I wish*, she added silently.

Her senses pricked her sides like an itchy sweater. He stared into his coffee as if he were searching the foam for a secret message. His face tensed and his brow furrowed. She knew that look from all the times they had lunch after science class and he'd searched his juice bottle for answers to the upcoming test.

"What's on your mind, Alex?"

"What did you wish for?" His expression became hungry, interested.

"Excitement. I wanted excitement in my life."

"You teach high school. That sounds exciting enough to me."

"Says the merman who cliff dives."

"I'll tell you a secret." Alex motioned for her to come over. She leaned over the table; he moved in close enough that his breath tickled her ear. He was near enough that he would have kissed her cheek or neck or mouth just by moving in a few inches.

Shivers went down her back and settled in her stomach.

"I had to be pushed off that cliff," Alex said.

"Of course." Lucy laughed, forcing herself to lean back from him. If she was going to give in to her teenage dream, she'd rather wait for the right moment. There was a brief pause in the conversation. A small flash of wonder shone in his eyes as he watched her.

"How do you do it?" Alex asked quietly. "How do you stay still?"

A tight knot formed in her throat. Most days, she held on to the Grove with both hands, but on some days she held on by her fingernails. She'd sought excitement before, back in college, and her family had been worse off for it. While studying abroad in East Africa, she and her friends had gotten into a terrible accident. Everyone, thankfully, ended up with only bumps and bruises. Lucy never forgot the fear she heard in Mama's voice when she called to tell her what happened. She'd been a heartbeat away from changing her family forever. She wanted excitement, but there was a cost. Lucy wouldn't seek it again.

She became aware of the questioning gaze Alex gave her

and took a deep breath, then said, "You make it work. You hold on to—something solid."

"What makes you hold on?"

"It depends," Lucy said honestly. "My job. My family. Having a home helps keep you grounded."

"I'll figure it out," Alex said forcefully. "Horatio said he might be able to help me sell this house. I don't know."

Alex briefly explained the open house to Lucy. To her, it sounded like a good option for him. He wanted to travel, and having a home didn't fit into his plans.

"Maybe you should sell." It hurt Lucy to say it, but there was no reason for him to be miserable. She'd seen him many times over the last week, standing on the sidewalk facing the cottage with a blank stare. He and the house might be better off apart.

"It won't be easy. It was on the market ten months before Mom and Pop bought it," Alex said. Lucy groaned. Most houses in the Grove were sold in less than a month. "No one's eager to move into the Funny House."

"Ugh, you found the Reddit page." Lucy made a face. The Fortunato House was nicknamed by the ghost-hunting community as the Funny House. People got strange vibes from the house or funny feelings, which caused owners and guests to get out within days, if not hours.

"You didn't tell me a two-part *Ghost Chaser* episode was filmed there," Alex muttered. "I mean, they didn't even stay the whole night!"

"Well, you'll change that."

"How?"

"Turn that house into a home," Lucy said. "Show people what it could be rather than what it is."

She reached for her tote and yanked out her notebook and a pen. Her brain went wild with ideas. She opened to a fresh page and wrote *Alex's Fix-It Plan* at the top.

"Pick two colors that you like, then list the different shades. Let's create a color list, so we can narrow it down."

"Blue and orange."

Lucy wrote that down. "Blue and orange. Let's think. Let's go with cobalt and tangerine."

"So dark blue and dark orange," Alex said coyly.

"Don't start. Trust me. List off all the shades of blue you see in your life."

Alex did. Lucy wrote them down. *Sapphire. Ocean. Navy. Cerulean. Denim. Sky.*

Her pen jumped to the next list. "Now list the shades of orange you see."

"I don't know about that. Can goldfish be a shade?"

Lucy scribbled it down. "It's on the list. Let's keep the party going."

They went back and forth, listing shades of orange. *Goldfish. Rust. Carrot. Tangerine. Marigold.* Lucy jotted them down, putting them into two separate columns.

"Now we write down neutral colors that can help tie these colors together. White. Cream. Beige."

"Black. Brown."

Visions of blood-orange accent pillows, bright white and blue toile wallpaper, and cream-colored rugs came to mind as she scribbled down these notes. The cottage was coming into shape before her on this paper. She felt Alex lean over the table. He made an amused sound. Her heart sped up the closer he got to her.

"How many interior design classes have you taken?"

"None. I've earned four and a half stars on my *Dream Home* game app." Lucy tried to suppress a laugh but failed. "I've designed apartments in Monte Carlo, homes in Alberta, and living rooms in León without leaving my bed. It's a hobby."

"That sounds awesome. Why don't you try it for real?"

Lucy ducked her head so she didn't meet his inquisitive yet admiring stare. This merman was going to be terrible for her ego. The typical reasons began to roll off her tongue. Not enough money. Not enough time. She went with the truth.

"What if I'm terrible?"

"What advice would you tell your students?"

"I'd tell them to try." Alex gave her a grin. *Clever merman.* Using her own advice against her. Lucy finished writing. She neatly tore the paper from the notebook. "There's your color scheme. I'd make a mood board with all these colors if I were you. Make a collage of everything that inspires you. Start looking for items that fit the style of the house. Go slow. Find pieces that speak to you for each room."

Alex peered at the list. A small light of hope lit his face. He shook his head and folded the paper.

He slid it back to Lucy. "I don't even have a bed."

"Where do you sleep?"

"I have an inflatable mattress. It's fine," Alex said. "I need to sell this house, but a color scheme isn't going to solve this jinx."

"It's not a jinx. Trust me, we would've heard about it. If a house is around long enough, then it gains an essence," Lucy said. "Fortunato has a special essence. People have tried for years to get rid of it, but it's like cutting out the heart."

"If this were your house, what would you do?" Alex asked earnestly.

Lucy put the pen down on the paper. "Let the heart live. Make people fall in love with it. How do you make someone fall in love with you?"

Alex stared at her. He studied her face as if trying to commit her to memory.

"You make them feel appreciated and special. Embrace what makes them passionate."

She flushed but remained silent. He was good at that. He'd brought balloons to school on her birthday and tied them in her locker.

"I'll make you a deal. I'll help you with your soul mate search if you help me design and sell this house."

"You don't like the neighborhood," she said lightly.

"The neighborhood is lovely."

Lucy stilled. Something in the way he said that sentence so endearingly made her seriously doubt that he was talking about the neighborhood. She shifted uncomfortably. Alex blinked, then lifted a single eyebrow. "I'm just looking for a place that fits my lifestyle."

Ah. Of course. "Same. I'm looking for a soul mate who fits."

He gave a measured, self-conscious smile. "Okay. Let's see what we can do."

That was fair. Lucy considered spell work. A candle dipped in tangerine oil might help him with decorating skills. Maybe a root would boost his self-esteem to get the house sold.

"So, you need me to fix a spell for you? Give you a

confidence boost? Get you an interested buyer? Help you get your groove back?"

There was a note of disbelief in his voice. "You have a spell for that?"

"Alexander, there's a spell for *everything*."

His gaze lowered, as did his voice. "Everything?"

With his attention focused on her mouth, her lady parts perked up. *Hello there.* She sipped on her iced tea, the cool, sweet liquid quenching her thirst. Well, one thirst was quenched. He turned his smile up a notch.

She put her drink down. "Yes. So, tell me what you need."

His words were as soft as a caress. "I need to unjinx this house. I need you."

Once upon a time, she would've loved to hear him say those words, thrilled that he finally, finally needed her. But it wasn't real. He needed her now—for a purpose. What about later? What was she going to do? Crawl through his window and hang up a few charms? Or sprinkle pixie dust to bring in prospective buyers? She was being offered the chance to design her dream home for someone else. What would happen at the end of the summer, when he sold his house and left town again?

She shook her head. "You need an interior designer, not a teacher with a home design hobby."

"If you say so."

Alex kept his face deceptively composed. He had one hell of a poker face. She promised herself not to play strip poker with him because she'd lose her panties to him. *Don't think of him holding your panties. Wait, too late.* Lucy added more honey to her tea. They said nothing else but enjoyed their drinks together. His kiss hello still burned her cheek. Alex had grown from a gangly boy with a constant goofy grin to a tall man with broad shoulders, sculpted arms, and a chest visible under his fitted polo. His physique matched that of world-ranked Olympic swimmers. This distance between her and Alex seemed vast. It felt as if she and Alex were on opposite shores, separated by an invisible storm-tossed ocean; she couldn't navigate the water alone, and he couldn't cross over it to meet her.

Chapter Eleven

☾

The waters of the Atlantic Ocean, murky and deep, called Alex that next week. The early hours, when the stars disappeared from the sky, were the best time for a merman to get in a good swim. The full moon was approaching, which meant his transformation was at hand.

For now he'd keep his legs, but soon the water would bring forth his tail.

Alex missed being able to sleep in on Saturday mornings. He loved being able to watch the sky lighten through the apartment windows and bring the day to him. His automatic coffee maker would click on and percolate his brew to help him start the morning.

This Saturday morning he couldn't sleep. If it wasn't the phantom touch of Lucy lingering in his mind, the conversation played on repeat in his mind. It was a little too easy to slip into the role of Lucy's soul mate. He could give two clamshells about Marcus's feelings, but when Lucy looked at him with a hungry heat, he let himself pretend for that instant. He pretended that this cottage was theirs and that they were working together to fix it up. She'd move in and then—what—make a home together. How long would he stay before that ancient call pulled him away from the Grove? Nahla was smart. She had left before he did.

The inflatable bed Horatio lent him had deflated in the middle of the night. He'd lain there, counting the stripes on the wallpaper and listening to the creaking and groaning of the house. His house. He had to get used to saying that fact. His phone beeped. It was Horatio checking in with him with a quick text. He'd graciously inspected the house while Alex was handling business with his agent. Apparently, Horatio wanted to speak to him face-to-face. Alex texted his early morning plans.

He was going for a swim. The ocean called to him.

Alex drove his car to the boardwalk and parked. Seagulls cried overhead, swooping and diving around seeking abandoned meals. He yanked his knapsack from the backseat and slung it on his shoulder. Alex walked on to the path of wooden boards built along Grove Beach. The saline of the Atlantic Ocean touched his lungs and made all the muscles in his body relax.

Horatio sat on one of the benches facing the beach. He waved Alex over to him.

They greeted each other with a brotherly hug and pat.

Horatio tossed a towel over Alex's shoulder. "I knew you didn't have one."

"Thanks for that. Tell me something good," Alex said.

"There's nothing wrong with the house," Horatio replied. "I checked it twice. Other than a few squeaky floorboards, it has good bones."

That was unexpected. He figured that maybe Horatio

would either find a secret door to another world or closet filled with random doll heads.

"Oh, okay."

Horatio cocked his head to the side. "You sound disappointed."

"It's not that," Alex said. He looked to the waves, trying to collect his thoughts. There was no point lying. "I can feel there's something strange about this place."

"Hmm, you sound like Mom," Horatio said. "Well, back when she had her visions."

"Yeah, I know. You're sure you didn't feel anything... spooky?"

Doubts whipped around his brain. If so many other people ditched this property, what's going to happen with him?

Horatio gave him a once-over. "I can almost hear you thinking."

"Please, I can't handle if you magically became telepathic. I'd have to leave town."

"No. It's a good space. It'll be perfect for the open house. I know a cottage just like it went for a half a million last year."

"That would buy a lot of towels," Alex joked. "I don't have much of anything right now."

Whatever large items he couldn't sell or donate, he'd left for Nahla to have. He left his apartment with a few toiletry items and what clothes he could carry in his duffel bag. You only kept what you could carry.

"I'm going to need to go shopping," Alex said.

Horatio spoke in a casual, jesting way. "So, you've decided to stay."

This statement was made with no hint of sarcasm or smugness. Did Horatio sound happy? The only things that made Horatio happy were sweet potato fries and hardware stores.

"Just until the end of the summer. Maybe I can find a better buyer in the fall," Alex explained. He didn't want to give anyone any false hope of him coming back to the Grove. It was nice to be home for a while, but eventually he'd grow bored and move on.

"Well, good news," Horatio said. "I got you a spot on the open house tour. You're scheduled to show off the cottage at the end of August."

"Thanks," Alex said. He ignored the sudden twitch of hesitance in his gut. There was no way he'd gotten attached to this place already. He didn't do instant lust when it came to things and places. However, there was something about this house that seemed special. Man, he really needed to find another word to describe it.

Horatio glanced over Alex. "You'll be ready by August. You've got this."

He said these words with a faith that Alex didn't feel yet.

"I'd better be ready." He didn't even want to think about what would happen if he didn't sell this house. There was no other option. He'd sell the house, repay Mom and Dad, and take what was left and live somewhere else.

"If you design it right, you could sell it by the end of the open house. They might take the whole thing as is. You've got an interior designer in mind?"

"Yeah. I do."

Lucy had the passion for this project. He recalled Lucy's

class notes. He was charmed by it. They were harmless white lies, an embellishment of a life that was perfectly ordinary. The last sentence sent a chill through his veins. It came back to him in fragments. *She's decorating... dream home with her... soul mate and planning for a bright future.*

He'd been shocked by the word "soul mate." It was bad enough that he couldn't forget the feeling of her lush body pressed up against his at the bakery. He'd fought the temptation to bury his face behind her ear and breathe in that special scent—fresh honeysuckle, tea leaves, and something spicy like pepper. Would she smell like that all over? He imagined running his nose over the dips and valleys of her body, to elicit squeals and sighs from her.

Gods, he needed a swim to clear his head.

"I'm going out," Alex said, pointing to the ocean.

He paused, looking at Horatio. As they grew older Alex had embraced the ocean. Horatio had turned away from the water. They hadn't swum together since high school. They'd been two young mermen, eagerly exploring the ocean bed, finding shipwreck debris and floating messages in bottles. Back then the Grove had been enough. Now he didn't know what was enough for him. What would quell this restlessness that kept him unable to commit to anything for more than a season?

Horatio waved to him. "We'll go out next time."

Alex nodded. Next time. He liked that plan. He tossed off his shirt and stripped down to his swim trunks.

"Let's make time to hit up the hardware store."

"I also need a bed and dresser." His back would thank him for getting off the floor and onto a real mattress.

"We'll go to Furniture Depot," Horatio said. "I got a hookup with a complete living and dining room set."

"I'm good if you have to go. Leave my knapsack and towel under the boardwalk." Horatio gave him a thumbs-up. Alex ambled down the stairs to the beach. Alex dug his toes in the cold sand, pushing stones and mussel shells out of the way. The ocean beckoned him forth with its spell like a drunk firefly buzzing toward blinking twinkle lights. His thoughts went to the water. He watched the waves bend and twist, suddenly filled with a sense of dread and destiny. Alex went to the ocean's edge. He dipped his toes into the sea-foam. It rushed toward him, hissing as it ate up the space between him and the sand. He had left the Grove, but it had never left him. He was no different from the people in his family, descendants of a long line of headstrong merfolk who took and did whatever they wanted without question or consequences. It wasn't uncommon to hear a story of a Dwyer merperson stealing away a bride on the day of her wedding or seducing an innocent person with a promise of pleasure.

Instead of causing chaos, Alex used this single-mindedness to propel him forward in his career and his life. He went after what he wanted and got what he wanted without question.

He'd wanted to start his social media platform—he did. He'd planned to sell it for ten times more than it was worth—it was done. He wanted to win every major photography award. His professional résumé was longer than a Trader Joe's store receipt after a marathon shopping session.

For a time, he'd desired Lucy. He'd wanted everything she had to offer—attention, laughter, and smiles. She'd asked him to be her prom date, and he felt like a king of the ocean. The instant he got everything he wanted, the responsibility followed soon after. He had to prove he'd earned that award. He had to show that his company was worth the price tag. He had to prove that he deserved her. He wavered with Lucy. There was too much responsibility in loving someone the way she deserved to be loved—he didn't have it back then.

He didn't know if he had it now. There was an unspoken rule in the Dwyer family: *Don't keep anything that you don't want to lose.*

He didn't want to lose Lucy, so he'd left. Her cousin, Ursula, was right to warn him away from Lucy. He didn't want to be the one to break Lucy's heart. It had been the right thing to do for him to turn down her graduation party invitation. She was tough. She'd be fine. However, staring at her face in the bakery, regret had filled his chest and made him feel like he was treading water. Once he made things right between them, they'd be able to move on from their teenage infatuation. She'd meet her soul mate, the one who could give her the life she desired and fully deserved. He'd probably see her again in another ten years.

The next time she'd probably have a ring on her finger and a young baby witch looking up to her like she was their universe. A sudden sadness hit him at that thought, so he pushed it away. He still had this summer to enjoy her company before her soul mate would come to claim a place in her life. He felt the faraway rain and distant thunder on his skin. Storms brewed and churned a world away on unseen seas and oceans. He breathed in deep and walked into the water. Broken seashells. Seaweed clumps. Tension washed away with each rolling wave that hit his body, until he effectively became boneless. With each wave that washed over him, her scent was dulled, and his senses returned. If he was going to get this house in shape, he had to get his head on straight.

He lowered himself until the coolness lapped at his collarbone. He went under the surface and swam out past the sandbar. He sent out a prayer for the souls who survived the Middle Passage and for those whose souls remained with the water. Their names may be forgotten, but their ancestors of the land and sea continued to honor their strength. His skin shimmered underneath the early-morning light. The moon and sun for a moment shared the sky, the blending of blue and orange. The blue was light, like dull sapphire stones in an old ring. The orange was burnt like apple cider in a mug. He paused, stunned by the poetry conjured in his soul. This town was doing strange things to him. Fish swam up to him and poked at the scales on his palms, his brethren welcoming him home.

You didn't keep anything that you didn't want to lose.

He'd let Nahla go. He'd let his apartment go. He'd let jobs go.

During his travels around the world, he didn't speak about the Grove, but he dreamed of it all the time. In his dreams, he ate countless slices at Rapunzel's Pizza. He raced Horatio up and down the boardwalk while trying not to trip and fall over the crooked planks. He especially dreamed of Lucy wading into the water, smiling up at him before he left for good. His gut ached. He could go where he wanted, see who he wanted, and feed his every craving without issue. He was a gentleman when it came to women, but he hadn't been a saint. Yes, he was free, but was he satisfied? No. He was scared. He went under the water.

Once he removed the fear, he'd get back to the life he wanted.

✳

The water didn't let Lucy rest. Dreams of the ocean invading her bedroom and shaking the walls shook her awake just before dawn. School was officially out for summer, but she was still on teacher time and woke up as if she were still going in early to make copies. The phantom touch of the waves pulled her out of sleep. She got dressed in her comic-book-print leggings, fitted black sweatshirt, and running shoes. She planned for only a quick run through the neighborhood to clear her head but ended up running all the way to the ocean.

The boardwalk was deserted save for a few stragglers and early-bird joggers clustered together like seagulls hunting for snacks. The ocean breeze washed across her chest, reminding her of last night's dreams. She wasn't going into the ocean; she didn't have a bathing suit, and no lifeguard was on duty. Maybe a walk would ease her mind. She descended the stairs until she hit the sand, where she toed off her shoes, balled up her socks, and buried her toes in the sand. *Nice.* The cool sand felt like a mini massage. Lucy took a few steps forward, until she could see the crash and surf of the wave. She heard behind her the hiss and burble of the public shower.

Lucy turned around, and her thoughts stammered to a stop. Three words came to her mind. *Oh, my ocean.* Alex. Was. Here.

His eyes were pinched closed. He was rinsing off the sand from his skin using the shower. The showerhead doused his golden skin with rivulets. Beads of water collected on his hair and ran down his back and past his ass. Whoa. It sloshed down his broad chest and defined arms and legs, washing away grit and sand and making him clean. His board shorts were plastered to his thighs, showing off *everything*. He'd been gifted generously by the ocean in more ways than one. Craving clawed at her chest, and her body throbbed as she watched him glistening in the water and sunshine. How divine. She bit down a smile. Heat raced over her skin. She should be ashamed of herself, but she couldn't look away. He stilled, and his eyes snapped open. Embarrassment filled her, but she didn't break the stare. She couldn't look away. His steady gaze bored into her with expectation. Water hung off his long eyelashes, and his eyes flashed with liquid fire.

A silent wish whispered from her heart. *Let me be the water on his skin.*

"Take a picture. It'll last longer," Alex said, his voice seeming to simmer with barely restrained control. *What would make him lose that restraint? Do you want to find out?* That picture he suggested might last, but she wouldn't. In five seconds, Alex single-handedly provided five months of late-night fantasy material.

"I wasn't staring." Lucy lowered her eyes to the sand. She wasn't staring *now*.

"You weren't looking away," he retorted playfully. "Hand me my towel, please."

Lucy noticed the towel hanging out of the sports knapsack by the stairs. When she brought the towel over to him, he shook the water off his body like an old-style shampoo commercial. She squealed as fat drops of water landed on her face, neck, and chest.

He took the towel, dried off his face, and flashed her a lopsided smile. "Sorry. Did I get you wet?"

Lucy bit back a sharp response. *Don't. Fall. For. It.*

"I have to check."

"You let me know." Alex toweled off until he was dry. He dressed and slipped on his shower slides.

"What's good with you?" Lucy asked. She kicked a few seashells and pebbles with her foot, unable to stand still. Being around Alex made her restless.

"I just went for a swim."

"How's the ocean today?" Lucy peered up into his eyes.

Alex nodded. "She's good. How are you?"

"I'm on summer break. I have time to drink my tea while it's hot."

"You've got any plans? I wanted to check out the stores." Alex motioned over to the shops that lined the boardwalk.

"I've got some time," Lucy said. Her morning was free for her to do as she wished. There was a bridesmaid fitting scheduled for later this afternoon, but for now she was just relaxing. As for the fitting, Ursula gave her a choice of wearing either pale yellow or a sea blue. Lucy still hadn't made her choice.

"Care to join me?" Alex gestured to the boardwalk. Lucy nodded. She brushed off as much sand as she could and slipped on her shoes. They went for a stroll on the boardwalk, their footsteps echoing on the planks. The oceanfront walkway was filled with colorful murals, sea-themed eateries, and beach bars. Alex's face furrowed at the various storefronts.

"What happened to Bruce's Arcade?"

"It moved a block to Ocean Ave."

"I don't see Yesteryear. Did it move, too?"

Lucy frowned. Yesteryear was a secondhand shop she and Alex frequented after school looking for hidden gems. She, like every Caraway witch, loved getting a bargain and didn't hesitate to buy Pinterest-worthy outfits to supplement her professional work clothes from vintage shops.

"It closed this past winter. Ms. Lofton moved down South to be closer to her grandkids."

"I'm happy for her, but I'll miss the shop. I bought the best cameras there."

"Well, there's plenty of places to search for treasure in Freya Grove," Lucy said. "The Freya Flea Market is coming. Not all treasure is silver and gold."

Alex said nothing. Instead, he offered her a sudden, arresting smile that made her insides feel all glittery.

"How's the soul mate search going?" Alex asked.

She might as well be real with him. "Uh, I signed up for a dating app."

He slid an unreadable look toward her. "Oh, okay. I see my services are no longer needed."

"No. Your services were great. I—I promised myself I

wouldn't, but I can't keep you on the hook." Lucy winced, mad that she'd made an obvious fish pun.

"I like being on the hook." Alex winked at her.

"What happens when you start dating again? What are you going to say? *Hello, this is Lucy. She's my soul mate. Pass the seaweed.*"

"Pass the—" Alex blinked at her, amused. "I don't eat seaweed for dinner."

"You know what I mean."

Lucy felt her cheeks burn. She'd spent last night filling out her profile, trying hard not to scare off potential dates with her witchy wiles. There'd been a few interested messages in her inbox, but no one really interested her. She really wanted to date Alex, but he didn't fit her life. The moment Alex had a Sold sign on his front lawn and the payment hit his account, he'd leave town. She didn't want to accidentally slip her heart in his back pocket when he walked away.

"You helped me out with Marcus. Don't feel obligated to keep helping me."

Alex placed a hand on her shoulder. "You're never an obligation. I should be lucky to be considered a candidate for your soul mate."

Her heart *squee*d for a long second. *Shut it down.* She needed to keep her head on straight. The most she could do was invite him to indulge in his sweet tooth.

"Well, then, I'd like to invite you to the cakewalk."

"I'd love to go. When is it again?"

"Next week Sunday. I know I have time to prepare but I'm still freaking out."

"You entered the cakewalk. Are you making your cowboy blondies?" His eyes lit up. "Can I come over and lick your spoon?"

The thought of Alex licking any of her spoons in her kitchen made her knees buckle. Lucy bit her lip in regret.

"No. Sorry. I'm making a croquembouche."

Alex went stock-still. His eyes widened. "You're making a cream-puff tower?"

Lucy leaned back at his shocked tone. "Is that too hard for a home baker like me?"

"Can I give you some advice? I don't want to give you advice you didn't ask for."

"Talk to me, Dwyer."

"This dessert doesn't complement your skills," Alex said, appearing to be carefully considering her feelings. Lucy bristled slightly, but she listened. "So much can go wrong with croquembouche. You can burn the caramel. The cream puffs can slide down. You can over-pipe the balls— it's rough."

He sounded like he had firsthand experience with this dessert.

"Did you date a baker?" she asked.

"I was engaged to one," Alex said softly. "She wanted it to be our wedding cake. I said I'd like cake slices, but she said it would be more elegant."

"I didn't know." Lucy's shoulders drooped a fraction. The last thing she wanted to do was to bring up a past heartache. Alex held up a hand, waving off her worry.

"It's okay. I'm fine. I'm worried about you. Have you ever made a cream puff?"

"Once," Lucy said. Doubt crept up her neck. She tried to divine how her baking experience would go, but all she could see was lots and lots of used mixing bowls piled up in the sink.

"Try making sixty cream puffs at once," Alex said. "Then you lose half of those puffs because you stuff them with too much cream. The cream will get all over you. Sorry, that sounded dirty."

Lucy bit the side of her cheek. Sirena would ban her from the kitchen if she left anything out of order or a mess. This cake of her dreams was quickly turning into a possible nightmare. Maybe it wouldn't be as bad as she feared.

She faced Alex, trying to project confidence that she didn't feel. "I can handle dirty."

"I never said you couldn't."

The flirtatious glow in his eyes gave Lucy pause. Okay. Was he talking about erasing-your-search-history dirty or putting-your-headphones-on-because-of-the-NSFW-sounds dirty? Never assume. She shook her head. Her imagination was completely out of control.

"What made you pick such a complicated dish?" Alex asked.

"It looked impressive. I figured go big or go home. What did you mean that this dish didn't complement my skills?"

"I've photographed a lot of food. I bet your croquembouche tastes wonderful, but if it doesn't look professional, you're going to get dismissed. People eat with their eyes before their mouths." Alex shrugged.

"I have to try," Lucy said. "Last year I heard an argument broke out over Mr. Clarke's lemon bars recipe. A few hexes were placed on one unfortunate chiffon cake. People were undermining bids and knocking over tables. I heard pixie dust got involved."

"What? This is a literal cakewalk. Shouldn't this be easy?" Alex raised a brow.

"Not with this crowd. You are volunteered to bake," Lucy said. "It's an honor. I've always wished to be asked, and I was."

"I'll forward you some recipes," Alex said. "If you're going to go big, have a good cream-puff recipe."

"You're not trying to change my mind?" Lucy asked.

"I know better than to do that," Alex said. "Once a Caraway decides, all conversation is done."

"Am I really that hardheaded?"

"No, you're just that determined. If you need a taste tester, I'm available," Alex said. "My mouth is at your service."

Lucy forced herself not to leap at his offer. She'd love to put his mouth to work if he was willing. "Good to know."

"Also, I'm still your date for the wedding."

"It's not too late to back out."

"Are you kidding me? I can't pass up the chance to do the Cupid Shuffle and the Electric Slide." Alex did a few dance moves on the boardwalk, throwing in a few hip thrusts for good measure. Lucy laughed.

"I'll make sure to RSVP for both of us. Are you going to the alumni reunion?"

Alex slowed his steps. "I probably won't. I don't have a good reason to go. I follow half our classmates online, so I don't see the point in seeing them in person."

"Rethink the old you and introduce the new," Lucy said.

"Is that a special Caraway incantation?" Alex asked playfully.

"No, it's a helpful mantra from my monthly therapy group. I'm pretty much the same person, but I'm still going," Lucy said. Alex gave her a questioning glance. "I don't know. Maybe I need to be reminded of who I used to be." She wanted to go back to a time when she was braver and took more chances.

"Nostalgia is one hell of a drug," Alex said.

"True. I think this whole email thing got me thinking about the last ten years," Lucy said wistfully. "I should've done more. I should be better."

Alex stopped. He peered at her. "What's better than who you are now?"

Lucy studied him. Drops of moisture clung to his forehead and his hair curled. His outfit clung to his sturdy frame. She absentmindedly stroked her arm. The mere sight of him made her long for Sunday-morning breakfasts and cozy conversations over tea. He was a man who, with a single lifted brow, caused waves to jump, and with a smile, sent women trembling with want. Desire zipped down her spine and lodged in her core, where it throbbed. How she throbbed. She dug her nails into her palms. She wanted to reach up, bury her nose in the crook of his neck, and nip the salt from him. How was she going to survive the wedding without wanting to climb him like a tree? If she was able to hold out for that long. She might end up dragging him into her bed by the Fourth of July. There would be more than just fireworks going off if she had her way.

Alex looked her over. "What's on your mind?"

Lucy mentally shoved those freaky thoughts away for another day. "Nothing much. I was thinking about the wedding."

"I didn't even ask who's getting married."

"My cousin Ursula's getting hitched."

Alex stopped. He turned to Lucy. "Wait. The same Ursula who threatened to hex me with chunky glitter is getting married."

"Hold up. When and why did she threaten you?" Lucy asked. Nana had a strict rule about hexing people. You didn't hex or harm anyone because that negative energy just might come back on you.

"She wanted to make sure that I didn't get too friendly with you at prom," Alex said. "I guess my reputation worried her."

"I didn't know. I'm sorry, she shouldn't have done that."

Prom night wasn't anything special. They went together as friends, dancing in a circle with their classmates and filling up on food from the open buffet. Alex was a gentleman, asking her to dance but kept his hands to himself. He went to the after-party at the lake. She went home resigned to the fact that Alex only saw her as a good friend and nothing more.

"I'm glad she did," Alex said quietly. "I was so careless. Who knows what would've happened if she hadn't said anything?"

Who knows? She could find out once and for all. She reached out and took his hand.

Alex didn't move, but he faced her. She closed her eyes. A vision shimmered before her. He stood on the decorated dock of Grove Lake on prom night in a borrowed suit and dress shoes while he watched Lucy. He was eighteen again, his face fresh and glowing with hope. She, in a dress the color of ocean foam, swayed and mouthed the words to the slow-burn eighties pop song. He approached her and took her into his arms. They pressed their foreheads together and swayed to the song being played on a distant radio on the shore. He leaned down and he pressed his lips to hers. Lucy did a double take at the scene before her. Whoa. In all her previous visions, there never was a kiss on prom night. They flirted and teased each other, but they hadn't kissed. Euphoria shot through her veins at the sight of this tender embrace worthy of a movie screen.

Her phone trilled. The vision fizzled away leaving her bereft. Her eyes snapped open. Alex stood there watching her. She dropped his hand, breaking the connection.

She checked her phone. It was Ursula texting her an update. "The bridesmaid dress fitting got moved up. I have to go."

"Sure. I'll see you around the neighborhood."

Lucy walked away, but he called to her. "Hey, Lu."

She turned to him. "Yes?"

"Do you know what color your dress is? I want to match you."

"I don't know yet." Lucy quickly explained to him her color choices. Alex listened. He looked her over deliberately slowly, practically drank her in like an icy glass of water on a humid day. One corner of his mouth quirked up.

"Pick blue," Alex suggested. "You'll look gorgeous, no matter what you're wearing, but blue is made for you."

Everything within her felt light. She knew merfolk were charming, but—*Mercy*. She stood a little taller, buoyed by his words. Alex looked down at his shoes, and Lucy noticed his ears were turning a little red. He waved and turned away from her. Lucy watched him head toward the parking lot. He had been in the zip code for less than three weeks and she wanted to take a few laps with him. She usually wasn't so bold with such thoughts, but being around him made her feel a bit bolder. Maybe it was the spell.

Chapter Twelve

The Freya Grove Annual Cakewalk Fundraiser was being held in the Grove Park, underneath the wooden picnic shelter, safe from the sun. It was a lovely summer Sunday with a wide blue sky and bright sunshine, a good day for cake. A mobile DJ table complete with large speakers, adjustable monitors, and gear was set up next to a speaker's podium. Alex stood around with the prospective buyers, who pointed and schemed on which dessert they were going to bid on. The place was an open-space area with twenty tables set up in a horseshoe pattern. Each baker was allotted a table for their dessert. The more ambitious bakers not only had their dessert set up but had themed decorations and signs to draw attention to their treat. Colorful plates of confetti cake, chocolate-dipped sponge, and other tempting treats were a few of the items on display. He nodded his head, impressed with the setup. This wasn't his mom's cakewalk, which consisted of people walking around, musical-chairs style, hoping to get a chance to get their favorite dessert. Every table was taken but one. Lucy's table was empty—she wasn't there yet. Alex glanced at his watch. She'd texted him that she'd meet him bright and early. The cakewalk was starting soon. A woman with the same big brown eyes he'd been staring into for the last month, wearing a pink floral dress, came up to him.

She clutched a clipboard to her side tightly. "Hey, Alex. I don't know if you remember me, but I'm Ursula. Lucy's cousin."

"Oh. Yes, of course. It's not every day someone threatens me with glitter."

"Well, yes." Ursula gave him a sharp smile. "It's nice to see you again."

Alex extended his hand to her. She briefly took it, then let it go.

"Have you heard from Lucy? We're going to start in about twenty minutes, and well—" Ursula motioned over to the empty table with a raised brow. Disappointment seemed to radiate off her in waves.

"I'm sure she'll be here."

"Do me a favor. Remind Lucy. Let her know we're really looking forward to having a peek at her—um…creation."

Something about her bemused tone brushed him the wrong way. Ursula seemed a little intense about this event. She nodded, then left Alex alone. He watched as she triple-checked with every single baker about their cake table and straightened out anything that was crooked.

Ten minutes before the start time, Lucy appeared from the parking lot. She wore a blue watercolor dress that hit her knee, ballooned out, and made her look like an elegant jellyfish. A tote bag swung from her elbow. Her ballet flats shuffled on the ground as she walked slowly, holding her container. It was clear she was making sure to watch out for sticks and rocks that might trip her and send the cake flying out of her hands. The thought made him nervous, and he raced over. Alex met her halfway, taking the cake stand from her and bringing it to her table. She thanked him.

Lucy gestured to her dessert. "Meet Claude."

"You named your cake Claude."

"Yes, I named Claude after the Impressionist painter."

"Why?" Alex asked, worried. She looked very flushed. Maybe she needed some cold water.

"Because it's French, and some people will think it looks like a whole mess."

Alex truly looked at the croquembouche. Words failed him, but then he decided on the truth. "Your croquembouche looks—"

"Eh, don't lie," Lucy interrupted him. "It's not a croquembouche; it's a pile of crooked cream puffs and tears."

"It's okay. The tower's there."

"It's not a tower. It's more like a three-story oceanfront condo." Lucy huffed. She cradled her face, a large bandage apparent on her right hand.

Alarm raced through Alex. He took her hand in his and lightly examined it. "Lu, what happened?"

"Sugar burns like hot glue. I learned that at three this morning." There was a thread of hurt in her voice. He didn't let go of her hand, wishing he could take away some of the pain. He could get used to holding her and not letting go. Her eyes were rimmed with exhaustion. Concern bounced inside him.

"You haven't slept."

"I haven't slept. I haven't eaten. I don't know if I have a bra on."

His eyes dipped down to her chest, then snapped up to her face. "I don't know how to answer that."

"This is my third cake; my kitchen is wrecked, Shadow hates me, and I have cream everywhere."

"Everywhere?" he asked in an interested tone.

"Every. Where," she said pointedly, a note of heat in her voice.

Alex held her stare. Suddenly, he didn't care about cake, pie, or cookies. Lucy blinked, the heat ebbed, and the moment passed. She took in the space, the other bakers, then removed her hand from Alex's. He tucked his hands into his pockets to keep from missing her touch.

"I—don't . . . I don't know what's going on anymore," Lucy said tiredly. "I just want to get this over with."

It bothered him. All the joy she'd had for the cakewalk when they'd spoken at the beach seemed to have been drained from her. He wanted to bring back that joy somehow.

"I'll set up your table," he offered.

She glanced around at the other tables, horror-struck. "I forgot my design bag at home. I was worried about getting here on time," she said in a whisper.

"Is there anything in your car you can use?"

"Maybe." Lucy went to her car and returned with an overstuffed trick-or-treat bag.

"I found Halloween classroom decor in my trunk," Lucy said, a little breathless. Alex dug into the bag, pulling out the black and gray spiderweb-printed tablecloth. She lifted the cake while Alex put down the cloth, straightening it out. They worked together in perfect harmony to arrange the table. No one else helped, but they watched with amused, haughty looks. The baker next to Lucy watched the arrangement with a curious stare. They were short and lithe, with dark-brown skin, and wore a dark gray jumper. Their hair was neatly clipped down to show off the shape of their head.

"What's your table's theme?" they asked.

Lucy scattered a handful of plastic spiders on the cloth. She thought for a second, then said, "Tower of Scream Puffs."

Their face lit up. "I like it."

"You do have an eye for design," Alex said.

Lucy stopped and graced them both with a bright smile. "Thank you."

She came around, stood next to Alex, and faced the table. He took out a garland of pumpkins connected by vines from the bag.

"Too much?" He held it up.

"Just enough," Lucy said.

He handed her the garland, which she took from him. "It won't stay without tape. We might need scissors."

The baker next to her reached into their pocket and pulled out a roll of tape and craft scissors. They handed them to her.

"Thank you—"

"Poe. Call me Poe."

"Thank you, Poe. I'm Lucy. This is Alex."

"Don't mention it," Poe said. "We're all here for a good cause."

Poe returned to their table to make last-minute changes. It seemed that Poe had made a classic birthday cake completely covered in multicolored sprinkles. Lucy measured the garland twice, then snipped it to make sure the length was correct.

"I didn't ask. What does the cakewalk raise money for?" Alex asked.

Lucy kept taping up the garland on her table as she said, "We're raising money for the Jersey Shore University Hospital Fund. I wanted to bake something that would pull in a generous donation. The hospital took great care of Nana. Even if I don't get any bids, I'll bid on myself."

"Same here," Poe said. "I'll make you a deal. I'll bid on yours if you bid on mine."

"Deal." Lucy returned the tape and scissors to Poe. Alex gave Poe a fist bump, which they reciprocated. It was nice to know that Lucy had someone here on her side with the cakewalk.

She looked at Poe's rainbow confection and gave a deep sigh. "Your cake is a technicolor delight."

"You're too kind. I think your table's perfect," Poe said. "The spiders really tie the table together. Halloween's my favorite holiday."

Lucy faced Poe. "It's my favorite, too. I wish my cake looked as good as the decorations."

"Looks can't make up for flavor. I bet your cake is probably just as good as the lopsided carrot cake from that baking show," Alex said.

"He's right. I saw that episode of *Baking Battles*," Poe said. "The judges thought the cake looked terrible, but they couldn't stop ranting about the taste."

"You're a fan of *Baking Battles*," Lucy said to Alex.

"I never miss an episode," he responded without missing a beat.

He admired those talented people who took raw

ingredients, mixed them together, and made food that defied logic. Alex must have angered the kitchen gods in another life because he couldn't toast a bagel without burning it.

Poe's phone rang. They went to answer it. Lucy returned her attention back to her cake.

"I see you picked the stacking method," Alex pointed out.

"I couldn't attach the puffs to that Styrofoam tower. They kept sliding down like contestants on an obstacle course. I added more and more caramel, but—ack." Lucy stopped, her face twisting in the memory. "Nothing went right."

"At least you know for next time," Alex said. He hoped she didn't give up.

"Tell me. How does it really look?" Her voice had softened. She stared down at her ballet flats. Alex gave her cake a closer once-over. The cream puffs were arranged in a sticky pyramid of spun sugar and caramel. It was a little crooked, but there was a homemade feel that made it more meaningful. He rubbed his thumb with his forefinger, the fingers he used as a kid when he'd sneak a cookie out of the porcelain goldfish jar that used to be in his kitchen. He'd forgotten about that memory, but looking at the cake, a feeling of want came over him. Alex took out his phone and snapped a few shots of her croquembouche.

He moved around, getting different angles of it, then turned his screen to Lucy to show his pictures.

She peered at them; her eyes sparkled with delight.

He leaned in next to her. "See? It looks good. I really want a bite."

Lucy looked up at him. "Go ahead and take a bite. I won't tell," she said in a teasing whisper. He didn't move. Neither did she, and they stared at each other. Something shifted between them in that moment. They weren't just friends from high school anymore, instead they'd become adult friends who were building their secret history of inside jokes, private looks, and smiles. There was an undercurrent of yearning in him that filled him from head to toe.

"Good afternoon! May I have your attention!" a voice called out.

They broke off their heated stare and turned to the front. Poe hung up their phone. It was Ursula waving her clipboard at the podium.

"Hello, all. Welcome to the annual Freya Grove Cakewalk. My name is Ursula Caraway, soon to be Walker. I'm the head of the cakewalk committee for this year."

She waited for applause, which was low but enthusiastic. Lucy gave a loud cheer for Ursula.

"Before we get started with the rules, we have an announcement. After last year's...um...issues, we've made a new rule: Bakers can't bid on their own desserts. Bakers also cannot bid on each other's desserts."

A rumble of terse comments and conversation went through the crowd. Poe gave Alex and Lucy a pointed look. From what Lucy told him via text, it wasn't uncommon for a partner or a fellow baker to bid on a cake, but it looked like things had changed. Ursula held up the clipboard, quieting everyone.

"The committee came to a unanimous decision that we want to level the playing field and get generous, honest bids. We want to reward the work of our bakers."

"Yeah, sure," Poe said, under their breath. "That's what they want us to think."

"When the cakewalk starts, DJ Ghost Sounds will play our cakewalk playlist. While the music plays, you are free to walk around and visit the tables. All official bids must be written on the cakewalk clipboard sheet we're leaving at your table right now. Write down your bids on the paper using dollars and cents. Once the music stops, then bidding is over. Does anyone have any concerns?"

Ursula glanced around the crowd. No one rose their hands or asked any follow-up questions.

"Great! We'll start the cakewalk in two minutes," Ursula said, slapping her hands to the clipboard. Alex really wanted to hide the clipboard for a moment.

Poe made a face. They leaned over to Lucy's table. "The reason that rule was made was because barely anyone bid on Ursula's angel cake last year," Poe said in a low voice. "She didn't act like an angel at all."

"That doesn't sound like my cousin," Lucy said slowly. Alex stood at the table, minding his own business.

Poe looked over at Lucy and lifted a brow. "You and Bougie Barbie are related?"

"We are." Alex heard the note of pride in Lucy's voice. "Don't let her catch you calling her that. She'll change her Twitter handle and make a T-shirt because she loves being called bougie."

"You're a Caraway," Poe said with awe. "I should've known. You've got the same eyes."

"I'm sorry about the whole bid rule thing," Lucy said. "I know we wanted to bring in big money."

"Don't worry about it," Poe said. "There's plenty of folks here. I'm sure we'll get enough bids. I invited all my coworkers and friends. Besides, the Delectables will be here to buy any leftover cake, so no one has to take their goodies home."

"Who are the Delectables?" Alex asked.

Poe lifted a brow. "It's our small group of home bakers who hang out. We make magic in and out of the kitchen."

"Really?" Lucy asked.

Alex saw her face light up with interest. Was she always this beautiful or had he really been so ignorant not to see it?

"Well, we watch baking shows and try to replicate what we see," Poe clarified. "Even if we fail, we have a great time eating our mistakes."

"That sounds like the greatest club ever. Text me everything about it."

"Absolutely. We love fresh blood. Our text chains do get a little wild," Poe said. Lucy and Poe quickly exchanged numbers. Alex nodded. He knew this fact was true from firsthand experience watching Nahla defend her love of buttercream icing against her fondant-loving friends. He looked to Lucy. He had a feeling that she could hold her own among the Delectables.

Poe looked to Alex. "Your boyfriend's invited, too. Anyone who likes *Baking Battles* is alright with me."

"Thanks. He's not my— He's my neighbor," Lucy corrected. Hm. He didn't like the twinge of displeasure in his chest at hearing her perfectly fine but incomplete explanation. She helped him pick out colors. They pretended to be soul mates. They were more than just neighbors. Right?

Poe slid a look to Alex. He quickly schooled his face to hide his feelings, but Poe gave a knowing grin.

A clipboard was placed on each baker's table by a cakewalk

volunteer. Poe grumbled. Lucy made a low dismayed sound. Alex opened his contact list. Everyone got their game faces on.

"Good. Who can I call?" Lucy took out her phone, scrolling through her contacts.

"I'll make a bid." Alex wanted to fix this, to make this right for her in any way he could.

"Don't bid on my cake," Lucy said to Alex. Her eyes went over to the charity committee, standing off to the side. "They'll think it's out of pity."

He bristled. He couldn't give a flying fish—his uncle Delmar's favorite expression—what anyone thought. He was helping a friend.

"No one cares," he said gruffly.

"I do," Lucy said gently. Pride shone in those big brown eyes of hers. "I made this cake by myself. I can get a few bids. Give it time. Don't feel like you have to rescue me."

"What about your sisters?"

"Sirena's at work. Callie's at school." Lucy scrolled through her phone. "Aunt Niesha doesn't like sweets. Uncle Leo—I don't know."

"Bidding starts now! Bidding will be open for an hour. Buyers, you may make your bids," Ursula called out. "DJ, turn up the music."

DJ Ghost Sounds nodded, put on her headphones, and started the music. Cameo's classic funk song "Candy" came over the speakers. Interested buyers bopped to the beat as they entered the cakewalk space, scanning the tables and looking through the selections.

"Your parents would bid."

"They would if they were here." Lucy kept scrolling.

Apprehension filled Alex. He liked the Caraways and hoped nothing awful had happened to them in his absence.

"Um, are they retired?" Alex asked.

"Yes." Lucy looked up from her phone, and her face softened. "Mom and Dad Caraway are living their best lives traveling around the world. I got an email from them the other day."

"How are they doing?"

Lucy gave him an exasperated sigh. "They keep *gently* reminding me I could be teaching college instead. They forward me job listings from Meadowdale all the time. I told them I'm just fine."

"I'd glad they're good. Give them my best."

"I will." Lucy tucked her phone away. She scanned the crowd for possible customers.

"I'll call Mom and Pop Dwyer," Alex said. "They've always liked you. I'm sure they can help."

"I didn't think they'd remember me. I haven't talked to them much since you moved away," Lucy said, smiling at a few buyers who gave her cake a hard glance, then moved away. Her smile fell. This happened three more times. Each time her smile dimmed a bit. The song ended and transitioned smoothly into another classic song about sweet treats and sugar.

Alex's face grew hot. Enough was enough. It was time to call in reinforcements.

"I'll be right back," he said, touching a hand to her arm. Alex stepped away from the tables and dialed his mom. She picked up. He explained the situation, to which Mom responded with an understanding sigh.

"Those cakewalk people are worse than the bingo-hall-raffle people. We'll put in a bid. Write us down. Anything to help your girlfriend!" Mom said in a cheerful tone. "You'll have to invite her over for tea."

"She's not my girlfriend. She's my friend," Alex said, a little too quickly.

There was a significant pause. "We're talking about Lucy," his mom said, uncertain. "Lucy Caraway?"

"Yes."

"Okay."

That one word from his mom had at least a dozen meanings to Alex. *Okay, go ahead and climb that tree, but I'm not taking you to the hospital* to *Okay, don't study and see what happens to your grades.* This "Okay" from Mom sounded way too different, too hopeful. His scales itched. Mom Dwyer had something to say.

"Mom." Alex rubbed his forehead. "What do you mean by 'okay'?"

"Well, consider this," Mom said slowly. "Why aren't you bidding?"

"She doesn't want it to be a pity bid."

"Well, do you pity her?" Mom asked.

"No," Alex said forcefully. "She worked so hard. She deserves to get a bid. It makes me upset to see her...upset."

He let those words linger.

"Al, do something about it," Mom said. Alex nodded even though his mother couldn't see. She ended the call with a promise that he'd visit soon. Alex walked the grounds, watching Lucy in the park doing her best to get bids. Old concerns bubbled up from the depths. Everyone from Horatio to his former swim teammates had constantly told him to "just go for it" when it came to Lucy.

People in the Grove kept asking how he could be just friends with her. She had this effortless girl-across-the-street beauty—or rather, witch across the street who never failed to stun him with her enchanting beauty and everyday magic. Even now, as she chatted with Poe and greeted every buyer with a graceful smile, she radiated complete joy. He'd been careful hiding behind the shield of friendship, not crossing the line or doing anything to overtly show how much he cared about her.

Alex stuck to the "we're better as friends" line because he knew relationships between humans and merfolk were destined for disaster. Fate was rarely kind to those who loved each other in the space where the ocean met the land. Even the happily-ever-after ending of the classic cartoon *The Little Mermaid* was problematic for Alex. What human was worth giving up the ocean for?

He noticed that the fairy tale ended with complete sacrifice.

Just then a man with neatly clipped hair and wearing wire-rimmed glasses approached Poe and Lucy. Poe gave him a big hug and then made introductions. Alex watched from a respectable distance. He looked like a character from a Dark Academia inspiration board, dressed in a white button-down shirt, slacks, and dress shoes, with a tweed jacket slung over his arm. Lucy brightened and greeted him. Poe spoke animatedly to him, pointing at Lucy's table.

Then Tweed Jacket leaned over and wrote a bid on Lucy's paper.

Envy, sharp and ragged, splintered inside him. He'd asked

for a second chance to make it right, but he was going back to bad habits. *Show her you care, but don't show too much.* Low expectations meant low disappointment. He couldn't disappoint her if she didn't know how much he cared. Lucy had crushed on and flirted with boys throughout their high school years, but she'd never had a serious boyfriend. He'd worked under the assumption that a magical force kept them apart, but it had been him. He'd planned to ask her out once the assignment was over, but he'd never gotten the chance. Or rather, fate kept stepping in his way.

She had a crush on a vampire. He dated a fae. He missed a window or lacked the courage to risk his heart. It went on that way until they graduated. Their dreams were pulling them in different directions. He didn't want their friendship to dissolve into a memory, the way of many childhood and teenage connections. So, he'd told her immediately after their commencement ceremony that they should go their own ways. She'd invited him to the graduation party at her house and he turned her down. A clean break would be better for them in the long run. Pain now rather than disappointment later, because he'd disappoint her somehow, and he hated to see that emotion in her eyes. The minutes ticked on; Alex watched as two more bids came in for Lucy. Songs played on the speakers as buyers made their final bids. She clapped her hands together and chatted excitedly with Poe. Tweed Jacket added another bid, canceling out the previous ones. Realization rippled through Alex like a stone dropped in a pond. He didn't have to bid on her cake to make her feel better. He wanted to because he cared. He wanted her to know how proud he was of her for trying a difficult cake. For wanting to be a part of the Grove community. For standing here and fighting for every single donation. He wanted her to know he saw her.

"Three minutes left. This is our last song of the cakewalk."

The song came over the speakers. Alex knew it immediately from the first opening notes. He hadn't heard it in years, but he remembered the last time he heard it.

Prom night. Their last dance together. The last time he was brave with her.

Alex returned to Lucy's table. Tweed Jacket stayed there, his attention still on Lucy. Mermen weren't known to be possessive, but he was learning there was a first time for everything.

"Alex, I got bids!" Lucy trilled happily. She gestured over to Tweed Jacket, who had the nerve to duck his head and try to look humble. "Theo was kind enough to be my first bid."

Tweed Jacket had a name: Theo.

"I just got the ball rolling," Theo said casually, but he shot a warm smile in Lucy's direction. He might have bid on the cake, but he wanted something sweeter. Lucy blushed. Alex's stomach grumbled. He had no one to blame but himself. The song egged him on, encouraged him to act while there was still time.

"Two minutes," Ursula said, making a lap around the pavilion.

Alex glanced down at the bids. Theo's bid was generous, but it could be outdone. Alex checked his wallet. He didn't have enough on him, but he had enough in the bank. He called out to Ursula, and she came over, clutching her clipboard, a professional smile on her face.

"You have a question?"

"Do you take mobile payments? Cash App? PayPal? Venmo?" Alex rattled off.

"As long as the transaction clears, we take it all," Ursula said.

"Perfect." Alex picked up the pen and wrote a bid. He glanced around at everyone watching him. Poe gave a low whistle. Theo shook his head and held up his hands. Lucy's lovely eyes practically popped out of her head.

Ursula took a step back and called out, "One minute."

"No, that's too much. Um—I can't let you do that," Lucy said anxiously, reaching for the pen, but Alex placed his hand over hers. She pulled back gently. He held her hand. Lucy stared at him. He didn't look away, watching her wiggle in his grasp. Playful defiance flickered in her face. She shook her head, but he wasn't budging. This wasn't an act of friendship he could explain away with a casual statement.

This was an act of possession. An act of desire. An act of—he shut down that word. No. He couldn't feel that way about her. Lucy, who he knew was never demure, squeezed his palm, sending a shot of pain through his hand. He grasped her wrist and held it close enough that her charms pressed into his flesh. They fumbled for a moment for the bid clipboard, their limbs becoming entangled with each other's, not leaving any room for daylight. Under the thin fabric of her dress, he felt her generous chest press up on him. He swallowed tightly, trying not to be distracted by the jolt of desire that went over his body.

She was killing him softly with those curves.

"Ten seconds!" Ursula said.

Lucy's breath came in short bursts as she made one final

grab for the sheet. Alex mashed her arms into his chest and wrapped his arms around her. She squirmed. He let out a startled groan at the contact. To the outside world, it looked like two lovebirds having a play fight.

Lucy looked up, a silent plea in her eyes.

Alex gave a small head shake, hoping his face conveyed his own request. *Let me do this for you.*

Finally, Lucy relaxed against him, tucking her head against his chest. He was dimly aware of Ursula counting down, but his senses were consumed with Lucy. Her hair still had a sheen of hair gel, showing off her pen-spring-size curls. Her scent mixed perfectly with spun caramel and vanilla oil. The dress, despite seeming voluminous, was sheer and as thin as a bedsheet, hinting at her body hidden underneath, which instantly turned him on. Tomorrow they'd be the town's biggest source of gossip, but right now this moment was just for them.

"Time's up! The bidding is over."

Alex loosened his arms from around her. Lucy stepped back. He'd won. But what would it cost him?

✳

"I didn't know merfolk liked cake that much!" Sirena said, settling down on the fainting couch. She took a long, dramatic sip from her iced tea, giving Lucy a saucy look. Callie said nothing but stirred her tea while holding back a laugh. They'd gathered for iced tea and gossip, and to discuss the aftermath of the cakewalk drama. Once Lucy summarized the entire event, her sisters gave her twin glares of amazement.

"How do I fix this?" Lucy asked.

"I think it's romantic," Callie cooed, pressing a hand to her heart, fluttering her eyelashes. "It's like he said 'Hey, world, this is my cake, and this is my woman. Back off.'"

Lucy clutched her iced tea, staring down at the ice cubes. "That's what I was afraid of."

The Grove was buzzing with the news of Alex's outrageous cake bid. She'd made a quick friend in Poe, the owner of the yet-to-be-opened Rain or Shine Bookstore, but found herself intrigued by Theodore Duval, Poe's co-owner and friend. He also was a guest professor at Meadowdale College. Lucy had been on the verge of asking him out for drinks when Alex came over with a stormy expression. He'd picked up the pen, scribbled a number, and thrown the cakewalk into chaos.

"You've crushed on Alex forever. It was only a matter of time before you two do something or do each other," Sirena said. She lifted her eyebrow for emphasis.

Lucy groaned. It didn't make any sense. She cast a wish spell and then suddenly her high school crush was into her big-time. She shook her head. Something had to be done about the wish before it wrecked her life and heart. "Has a package come in yet?"

"Nope. No book," Callie said. "I checked the mail."

This moment wasn't real. It was the wish at work, sprinkling excitement in her life like sprinkles on a cupcake. Speaking of which, Poe had already texted the time and date for the next Delectables group meeting. Apparently, next month's theme was blueberries. She would think about baking later.

"Can we please talk about something else?" Lucy asked. "Si, how did your investor meeting go?"

"Eh. My investor got nervous. Apparently, she didn't like the whole witchy thing." Sirena threw her hands up.

"You'll get it next time, Si," Callie said.

"I'm scaring everyone off with my vibe. I can't get an investor. I can't get a date. No one's put a bid on my cake in a *long* time. I wish I had someone to bid on my cake," Sirena mused.

"Felix hasn't put in his bid yet," Callie said sweetly.

"I'm getting really confused. We are talking about sex, right?" Lucy asked, her head still spinning from yesterday's events.

"Keep up, Lucy! Of course, we're taking about doing the deed. The horizontal tango. Knocking boots. Making—"

"Thank you for clarifying," Sirena said loudly, interrupting Callie's growing list of euphemisms. She turned to Lucy with a concerned look. "Have you spoken to Alex yet?"

Lucy shook her head. They hadn't talked, but his touch had stayed with her all night long. He texted and she answered. When she wasn't texting Alex, she was also texting Theo. A small wiggle of guilt nestled in her chest. She shouldn't feel guilty about texting another guy, but there'd been an obvious spark between her and Alex at the cakewalk. He'd picked her. He'd bid on her cake, claimed her cake even when there were plenty of interested buyers.

He didn't do it because he felt sorry for her but because he wanted to show the Grove that...she paused. She mattered to him.

He'd held her tightly to keep her from taking back his bid, and they'd gotten tangled up as one. Even though she could've easily gotten out of his grasp, they'd stayed in their embrace. Then, there was the issue of the vision she had on the boardwalk. It changed how she saw her friendship with Alex. If Ursula hadn't threatened to hex Alex, then things might have ended up differently.

She might have asked Alex to stay the summer with her before she left for college. Instead, she invited him to her graduation party, which he immediately turned down, and he left town that night. Past and present emotions were mixing together, creating a sense of chaos inside her.

Lucy took another sip, crunching the ice cubes she caught in her mouth. There wasn't enough tea to make her forget all the nasty things she'd thought about doing to Alex. She'd had a fevered dream about Alex, their limbs tangled together, but they were buck-ass naked in her bed. She'd run her tongue up and down his body, devouring him like a melting ice cream cone. He'd returned the favor repeatedly. Slowly. Sweetly.

"Did he like your cake?" Callie asked, invading her dirty thoughts.

"Hm?" Lucy responded. Callie and Sirena stared at her, waiting for a response.

Lucy clutched her tea. "He's never had my cake."

"He bid on your cake. He must really like cake." Callie slid Sirena a sly look.

"Can we please stop using the word 'cake'?" Lucy snapped, rubbing her temple.

The front door opened and closed. Ursula entered the room in her usual professional wear. She greeted Callie and Sirena but gave Lucy a nod. Ursula's lips were puckered so tight that it looked as if she'd eaten not just one lemon but an entire lemon tree.

"How are you, cuz? It's been a while," Sirena said.

"I've been busy with wedding planning. I have a nail appointment today. We're finishing up dress alterations, and we're looking at finalizing cake flavors. I like Earl Grey, but Marcus likes mango," Ursula said, doing a little dance of victory.

Sirena raised a brow at Ursula. "Marcus went to the tasting?"

"Lincoln couldn't make it. We're going out for karaoke, though, just to blow off some steam," Ursula said. "You're all invited to come out with us."

"Wait. You haven't told me about your wedding flowers," Lucy said. "I want to have them done in time."

"We have time," Ursula said lightly. "There's no rush. I mean, we're *just* picking out the wedding cake."

"Speaking of cake, how was the cakewalk?" Callie asked.

"It was fine," Ursula said crisply.

"You know what Nana said about being fine?" Callie lowered her voice and took on Nana's classic raspy drawl. "Baby doll, 'fine' is just another way to say 'feelings inside, not expressed.'"

"'Fine' is just another way to say 'I'm about to be upset soon,'" Sirena added with a smile.

"It was more than fine." Ursula took a seat; she studied her nails. "We broke last year's fundraising record."

"That's wonderful!" Lucy sat up. Ursula still didn't look at her. Uh-oh.

"The committee wanted to personally thank Alex for his extreme generosity. I just went over and talked to him." Ursula paused, then sighed. Her words came out in a quick rush, as if she'd run out of air. "He paid a lot of money for a cake made by a home baker and, well...I made him an offer."

Lucy's stomach dropped. "What did you offer?"

"Well, I offered a private afternoon tea reading and tasting with the baker if he pledged to double his donation."

Lucy pointed to herself. "You're talking about me."

"I'm not talking about Betty Crocker! Yes, you." Ursula rolled her eyes. "He guaranteed he'd donate the money if you go today. It would be great for the committee if we could follow through on the offer, and it would look good for me."

"Welp," Sirena said, finishing her drink.

"I don't know." Lucy put her tea down. Stunned and embarrassed after Alex's winning bid, she had cleaned up her table and traded contact information with Poe and Theo, then immediately left.

Ursula's eyes grew round. "Please, Lucy. Mrs. Walker's so impressed with how I ran the fundraiser. This donation is a sure thing. I need you to do this favor."

Lucy stood. Before she did this favor for Ursula they needed to talk about Alex. Sirena and Callie watched from their seats, leaning forward. Lucy didn't want an audience for this conversation, so she decided to move.

"You look thirsty. Let's get you a fresh glass of tea in the kitchen."

Ursula nodded. Once they were alone at the kitchen table, Lucy poured Ursula a glass. She didn't drink it but stared at Lucy.

"Say what you need to say. I'm burning daylight and I have a lot to do."

"Did you threaten to hex Alex?"

Ursula blinked. "Yes, and?"

There wasn't a hint of apology in her voice.

"Seriously?"

"Don't be fooled. He wasn't the sensitive, sweet photography guy back in high school." Ursula tilted her head to the side; her eyes took on a skeptical glint. "He was a player. That merman flirted with all the fish in the sea. You didn't see how he looked at you."

Lucy straightened, interested. "How did he look at me?"

"He looked at you as if you were a whole plate of salmon cakes and seaweed at Sunday dinner," Ursula said.

"I see you've been hanging out with Uncle Leo." Lucy shook her head at the familiar family phrase. Caraways loved their metaphors a little too much.

"I didn't want him using his aquatic wiles on you and leaving you high and dry. What's the point of having magic if you don't use it to protect yourself and those you love?"

"I really liked him, Sula," Lucy said.

Once Ursula heard her family nickname, she sighed and took Lucy's hand. "I wanted to protect you. It was wrong of me to threaten him, but I saw things. If you kept hanging out with Alex, you were going lose a lot more than your panties."

There was a warning tone in her words that set off bells in Lucy's head.

"Wait," Lucy said. "He never even kissed me. Where in your mind did you see him make a move?"

"You're not the only person who can read the leaves," Ursula said cryptically. "I saw what I saw."

Ursula rarely looked into the future, but she had peeked

for her and Alex. Lucy didn't know how to feel about this revelation.

"You're asking me to read for him," Lucy pointed out.

Ursula's lips twisted to the side. "You're grown and I think you know better. You can't stop the tide from coming in. I can't stop you from being with him. Have fun, but don't count on him to stay. A merman can't change his tail."

Lucy thought to herself while Ursula took a long sip from her tea. She didn't want to stop texting Theo, but the more time she spent with Alex, the more her reluctance grew. Was Theo her soul mate? Probably not, but she couldn't just give up because she had this merman on her brain. Alex was as lasting as writing on the sand. She couldn't invest her heart in someone who could disappear within a single wave. Somehow, Lucy felt her heart was already out to sea.

Chapter Thirteen

lex stood in his makeshift bedroom, looking in the crooked mirror he'd managed to find at a thrift store. He frowned at his reflection, unsure. A vintage T-shirt, dark denim, and fresh sneakers were good for an afternoon tea, right? As the full moon approached, he always felt as though he was climbing out of his skin. He'd have to get a midnight swim in.

He went downstairs, taking in the bare-bones furniture: a table, two chairs, and a love seat Horatio had gotten delivered over the last few days. He'd started getting his mail forwarded from his old address, but the mailman had misdelivered his neighbors' mail. If he wasn't getting makeup samples or birthday cards, he was collecting packages for every other house on Summerfield Street.

When Ursula offered him a private tea reading, he'd jumped at the chance to see Lucy in her element. He always wanted to have his leaves read but lacked the courage to get it done.

Lucy came over dressed in shades of pink that popped against her skin, cradling a wooden tea caddy while balancing a bulky tote bag on her shoulder. She, in her bright pink

shirt and pastel pants, looked like a delicious—and furious—
tuft of cotton candy. Her posture was stiff, and her eyes
narrowed slightly as she scanned the living room, then went
into the kitchen.

"If you wanted a tea reading, you could've just asked me,"
Lucy said, clutching the caddy to her chest. "It didn't have to
be a whole thing."

"I agree. I was going to text you, but Ursula came over
and . . . well, she made me an offer I couldn't refuse."

"My cousin would sell sand to a beach." Lucy shook her
head with a smile.

"Ursula knows your worth."

"Do you?" There was a hint of longing in her voice.

He took a step forward. "You know the answer to that."

Lucy's posture eased a fraction. She looked him over and
gestured at his shirt with her chin. "Nice shirt. I love that
Prince album."

"*Sign o' the Times* is a classic."

Lucy nodded. "Do you want to do it here or in the
kitchen?"

"We can do it wherever you'd like."

Lucy tossed him a flirty look, crooked her finger, and went
into the kitchen, twitching her behind in a "come follow
me" sway. He wasn't a fool and joined her immediately.
She made herself comfortable, filling the electric kettle with
water, clicking the button, and setting it to boil. She moved
toward the basic kitchen set he bought last week—a table
and two chairs.

"Can I help?"

"I've got this." Lucy placed her tea caddy on the table.

She pulled two teacups from her tote and set them on the table, then looked around. "Where's the cake? We can have it with our tea."

"Mom said a cake that nice deserves a real kitchen," Alex said with a grin. "She stole it."

Lucy laughed. "Did you even get a taste?"

"I did." The cream puffs had melted in his mouth.

"So, what did you think?"

"You're gifted."

She looked at him. He saw open tenderness in her gaze. It rendered him speechless. He wished she would never stop looking at him this way. "You're too nice."

A lump formed in his throat. "It's the truth."

Lucy opened the tea caddy. It held teaspoons; the top was decorated with printed labels explaining every type of loose tea brew in artfully arranged jars. The top listed the selection in the caddy and what it helped with. Alex scanned the labels, trying to decide whether he wanted to decode his dreams or manage his stress. The scent of sage and leaves hit him, easing his nerves. His attention drifted over the bottle underneath the yellow label that claimed to help him pick the right path.

"What type of tea would you like?"

Alex picked the yellow label. "I'll have the hibiscus and honey brew."

"Hmmm...interesting choice." Lucy picked up a small spoon and doled out dashes of loose leaves into the cup.

"How so?" Alex asked cautiously.

He had never really vibed with herbs and flowers. The fruits of the Earth just made him aware that the ocean was his home. The curve of her lips and the amused gleam in her eyes relaxed him.

"These herbs are aphrodisiacs."

"They make you fall in love?" Alex gave her a side-eye glance. Lucy detached the kettle from the base and poured steaming water into the cups. They settled at the table for the reading. Loose tea leaves and parts of dried flowers bobbed on the water's surface. Steam curled up and evaporated into the air.

She lifted a brow. "There's nothing about this tea that has anything to do with love."

"Really?"

"It's all about lust, desire—yearning. Aphrodisiacs are all about getting the blood moving, the juices flowing. They're about bringing out absolute pleasure."

He was caught off guard by the sudden husky quality to her voice. He noted the tightness of her shirt around her curves. Alex shifted in his chair and hoped that he wouldn't shame himself by getting turned on over tea. Fantastic.

"So, you're not dropping a love potion in my drink?" Alex joked.

Lucy gave a head shake and made a face. "No way. That's a rookie move. If I wanted, you'd be my love zombie. I have many ways."

Alex smiled as his mind thought about all her unlisted ways. "Love zombie?"

Lucy's smile was as intimate as a kiss when she said, "Yes, because my love is so good, you'll crawl out of your grave to have more of me."

Blood drained from his face, traveling southward to other parts, and his mind conjured an image of them. He was covered in graveyard dirt while she was in a lacy, tight night-gown befitting a neo-Gothic romance heroine. He'd dragged himself from the grave just for her flesh. They rolled around underneath the moonlight on the wet grass. His hands dug into her thighs while she pressed herself against him, and he bit the sensitive skin behind her ear. He squeezed her willing body; she threw her head back and screamed his name—

"Alex. Your tea's getting cold." Lucy slid the cup over to him. Alex shifted in his chair again, unable to hide his excitement from this angle. He focused on his tea to cool himself down. All this talk of aphrodisiacs was giving him good ideas of how to be bad in the best way.

Lucy motioned over to the small crystal bowls. "Sugar?"

"Yes, honey?"

Lucy blushed. Oh. It's nice to know that little flirtations and compliments made her blush. She added honey to both their teas. He'd keep that in mind. He drank slowly, enjoying the bright, fragrant taste. There was no reason to rush a good cup of tea. Lucy sipped her cup, finishing her drink much quicker than him.

"How's your drink?"

"It's good—nice and sweet. Just like a certain witch I know."

"Thanks," Lucy muttered.

Alex hid his grimace behind his cup. Maybe he shouldn't say his thoughts out loud, but around her his defenses came down like sandcastles being knocked out by a rushing wave.

"As you finish the tea, leave a little liquid at the bottom," she ordered Alex.

He left enough tea for the leaves to float and bob in. She took the cup from him. A zing went through him at her gentle contact. He was getting hooked on holding her, touching her—just being around her. She swirled the mixture thrice, then dumped the leftover liquid on the saucer. She waited for three seconds, then turned the cup back over. Lucy eased the dish to the side, then cradled the teacup in her hands. Small sighs escaped from her lips. She peered at the teacup. Alex leaned in close to her. The scent of honeysuckle flower and sharp spice radiated from her skin; her body oil invaded his senses. The world spun off its axis momentarily.

For a few precious seconds nothing weighed him down.

"Anchor, Square, Moon," Lucy said clearly.

He crashed back to reality. No way. Where did she see all these things? Alex reached for the teacup; their hands brushed together. Sparks like small fireworks popped from their skin. Whoa. She gasped. He hovered, soaking in energy from their touch. Pleasure rippled in the air. *Take it easy.*

He held the cup out for both to view. "Show me what you see, please."

Lucy scooted closer, until their knees bumped together. He tore his eyes away from her and focused on the teacup. Shapes in the porcelain appeared slowly but surely.

"Tell me what *you* see," she said.

"It's going to sound weird."

"Not to me." Lucy bit her lip, then leaned in. He got close. "Stop trying to shape the leaves and just read what's there. Read what you see, not what you feel."

He narrowed his eyes. "I'll start with the anchor symbol on the rim."

"So, anchors mean good luck in business and a stable love life."

"Are you sure that's my cup?" Alex said without humor. "I don't have a love life. I have a void."

He hadn't been with another woman since Nahla left him.

"Really?" Lucy asked. Her brow wrinkled in thought. She opened her mouth, then closed it. He wanted to tell her what happened and make sense of the last year for himself. He'd moved on from his last relationship, not bothering to talk about what happened.

If he kept moving, then he wouldn't feel the pain.

"I know you saw the post," Alex said. "I got engaged last year."

"I saw."

"She wanted this. My ex-fiancé wanted this place." Alex pointed to the walls, then dropped his hand on the table. "She wanted a home base."

"That's not what you wanted."

He still heard Nahla's soft yet firm voice. *You can work from home. Your job doesn't need you to be there. They need me to be in Denver. I must go to San Francisco. I need you to be my anchor. Be here. I need to know you're here for me, for us.*

There was another bakery she was opening in a city hundreds of miles away, another event she had to attend to help promote her cookbook. He'd been her anchor for a while, but the walls had begun closing in on him. He'd wake up in the middle of the night, aching for the ocean and sea. She accused him of not being serious and only wanting fun times. He hung his head. The truth was he wanted to try to be there for them. He just wasn't strong enough.

"Next symbols, please," he said quietly.

"Squares mean comfort and peace. You're going to get a

sense of order in your life. Things you've planned will come into place," Lucy said, turning the cup in his hand. "Moon, especially the crescent moon, means happiness and success. You're going to have some happy times soon."

Alex returned his cup to the table. "Is it going to be in this house?"

"That depends on you. How's the house design going?"

"It's been going. I have a bed, a table, and chairs."

"That's an improvement," Lucy said with a grin.

"I don't think this house likes me very much."

"You haven't painted anything!"

"I don't know where to start. But I'm thinking of hiring a designer."

"You found a designer?"

"Yes, I did. She's super talented but brand-new. She's self-taught, but she's special."

Alex stared at Lucy. Her eyes widened in understanding. She was picking up what he was putting down.

"No," Lucy said. "I don't know anything about design."

"You know more than me. I saw your face when you started talking about cobalt and tangerine, accent walls, and other stuff," Alex said. "I need this house staged. You have skills I need, and I can afford your price."

"I didn't give a price," Lucy said.

"I'll pay for your time. I know your worth," Alex said.

"Let me think about it," Lucy said, but her eyes glanced around the kitchen. She was probably envisioning sky-blue walls and fancy towels. For some reason, Alex felt a nudge on his shoulder, as though someone was encouraging him to keep talking, to find a way to convince her.

"I think the house would like it if you said yes," Alex said.

"Did it tell you to say that? Is this place talking to you?"

"No, but I'm learning to pay attention."

Lucy held up a hand. "Say no more. Let's work out a schedule. I have my tea reading clients to take care of, but I think we can work something out."

"I'm honored." Alex pressed a hand to his chest in a gesture of gratitude. A sense of hope came over him at the thought of her being in his space.

Lucy started to clean up the teacups. Alex didn't want her to leave just yet, hesitant to let this hopeful feeling fade.

"Our reading isn't over, is it?" He pointed to her empty cup. Leaves were clumped against the sides. "What about you?"

"I don't read my own leaves anymore."

"Okay," Alex said. He took her cup, swirled the dregs, and turned it over on the saucer just like Lucy did. Reading the future couldn't be that hard, right? He flipped it over and peered into the cup. Lucy reached for it, but he pulled back, waiting for the shapes to form. Slowly, they appeared, and he laughed while she playfully tried to cover his eyes. There was a queen's regal crown on the rim, a bird with open wings, and a mushroom-looking shape.

"There's a crown, a bird and...uh..." He narrowed his eyes, then leaned in closer. "A mushroom."

Alex turned to Lucy. She paled and sat back away from him.

He set the cup down and placed a hand on her arm. "Hey, what's up? Talk to me."

"Did you make that up? Is that what you saw?" she demanded, glaring at him.

"Yes." Alex reached up and cupped her cheek. "Talk to me, Lu," he said gently. "What do they mean?"

"A crown means success and, of course, honor. Um...birds can represent good luck and a journey."

"Okay, that doesn't sound so bad."

"The last symbol means a—" Lucy took a steadying breath. "It means a sudden separation of lovers following a fight."

"Well." Alex dropped his hand to her neck. He swallowed thickly.

"Well," she repeated back to him.

"We have nothing to worry about." Alex forced a light tone into his words. "We're not—lovers."

Yet. That unspoken word remained suspended between them. *We're not lovers yet.* Lucy stilled; her pulse kicked under his hand. He dropped his hand away from her. She packed up her tools quickly, rinsing off her cups and discarding the leaves in the trash.

"This is why I don't read my leaves," Lucy said. "You stir things up you have no business knowing."

They were not lovers, yet he wanted them to be soon. If not tonight, by the end of the summer, he'd want to spend time in her company and, if he had the pleasure, in her bed. Being near her felt like bathing on the jetty rock and laying out in sunlight.

He wanted to bathe in her light.

"Lu, you forgot something."

She spun and faced him; her eyes were guarded. "What?"

He wrapped his hands around her waist, and her body leaned into him. He wanted her as much as the ocean yearned for the shore; it was elemental. He captured her lips with his, bringing her into a deep kiss. She responded with a surprised squeak, which turned into a breathy sigh. His mouth did not become softer as he kissed her. He claimed her. He possessed her with every lick, stroke, and nip of her lip. Her tote dropped from her shoulder, crashing down on the ground. They moved together slowly, until their bodies pressed against the wall. Once they made contact, they bumped together, which jarred them for a moment. Their hands grabbed at each other frantically.

He pinned her gently against the wall, pulling her arms above her head with one hand, while the other felt down her body and brought her leg around him. He caressed her thigh, leaning into her so that they were snug together. They fit, chest to chest, sex to sex. She breathed in shallow, quick gasps as he pressed himself against her. A moan slipped through her lips, electrifying him to keep going.

Alex let her hands go. She wrapped her arms around his neck. His imagination went off into dark, dirty directions. He rested his nose against hers, calming himself down. If he didn't, he was going to strip her naked right here and have her on the floor. She deserved moonlight and magic, not awkward fumbling in a half-built house. The tea reading repeated in his head. This was a kiss that led to more things. Dangerous things. Things that broke your heart into a thousand pieces. Things that made you wish for forever. How was he going to let her go? *Can you give her forever? You can't even promise her the entire summer. Let her go for now.* He let out a breath, then pressed a quick smooch to her lips. Lucy let her leg slide down his body.

Alex reluctantly stepped back away from her.

Lucy leaned down to reclaim her tote bag. Her eyes went over to the mail stack they'd scattered in their haste. She stilled. She picked up a soft mailer package. "I didn't know you had this."

Alex briefly explained the mail delivery issue, while Lucy tightly clutched the envelope to her.

"Is it important?" he asked.

She spoke with a quiet firmness. "It might be."

Chapter Fourteen

The display window of Home and Hearth Hardware Store on Main was filled with seasonal gear to celebrate the heart of summer and camping products, including grills, bug spray, and tarps. Summer was in full effect in the Grove with people strolling the sidewalks in bright pastel clothing and shorts. The bell on the front door chimed as Alex and Horatio entered and walked toward the back of the store. Alex clutched Lucy's list in his hand as his sneakers squeaked against the wood floor. The shrill grind of metal being shaped into a key invaded his thoughts. He practically jumped out of his scales. *What are you doing here?* He should've gone across the street, knocked on Lucy's door, and kissed her senseless again. She seemed as spooked as he was once they kissed. No. They didn't just kiss. They damn near knocked down the walls. The counter area of the store was crowded with a key tree, a key-cutting machine, and a wall of paint chips. The kiss only confirmed he needed this house ready for the open house in August.

Horatio pointed toward the wide wall of outdoor power tools.

"I have to check on this tubing. Are you good on your own?"

This cottage was his responsibility.

"I'm good." Alex gave Horatio a thumbs-up. He blinked and Horatio seemed to disappear down the narrow aisles filled with home-repair items and tools.

Alex approached the front counter, addressing the older employee. "Excuse me."

"Is that one of the Dwyer sons?" The man, who had a gray beard and a potbelly and was wearing an old H & H shirt and jeans, looked over the edge of his glasses. His mouth rose into a surprised smile.

"Hi, Mr. Giddings," Alex greeted the bespectacled older gentleman behind the counter. "How are you?"

Horatio used to work here back in high school, and so Alex had ended up hanging out at the store, pretending he knew the difference between a slotted screwdriver and a stubby screwdriver when shoppers came up to him. Mr. Carl Giddings had let him hang around and had given him the chance to decorate the window display.

"I'm good. Just trying to keep these bones from rattling too much." Mr. Giddings patted his back, giving Alex a sly grin. "What can I help you with?"

"I don't know if you know, but I own the Fortunato Cottage."

A light of understanding flashed on his face. "So, you're the Funny House owner!"

"I guess so."

Alex held up the paper list to Mr. Giddings. He felt closer to Lucy just by looking at her handwriting. "I'm looking to get a few paint samples for an accent wall. I also need to find a fabric that is monochromatic or look for a toile de jouy print."

Mr. Giddings scratched his chin. "Kid, all I heard was paint samples."

"I don't know what I'm doing."

"Welcome to the club." Mr. Giddings gave a long sigh. "My advice, do whatever she says and let her do what she wants." He pointed to the paper. "The handwriting. In my years, I've seen a lot of partners being sent to my store with a honey-do list."

"Honey-do list?"

Mr. Giddings rolled his wrist as he spoke. "Honey, do this. Honey, do that. It's a to-do list that spouses write out for things they want done around the home."

"She's not—I'm not—We're not—"

Mr. Giddings held up a hand. "Don't worry. I'm not grilling you about what you kids call it—relationship status. I'm just here to make sure your houses and homes look good and don't fall on your heads. Phoebe knows about all the fancy designer terms and the latest so-called trends."

Mr. Giddings called to the back, "Phoebe! You've got a customer."

A statuesque woman with dark black skin and braided hair in a ponytail on her shoulder strolled out from one of the aisles. She wore a paint-splattered shirt underneath jean overalls and steel-toed boots. They shared the same wide eyes that took in everything.

"Yes, Mr. Giddings."

He rolled his eyes lovingly. "You know you can call me Dad."

"No, sir." She shook her head with a smirk. "Not while we're at work."

"Alex needs help with his honey-do list."

"Do you mind if I take a look?" Phoebe reached for the list, which Alex handed over to her for inspection. Her eyelids closed, and she took in a focusing breath; he could see her eyes moving rapidly underneath the lids. It appeared as if she went into a trance. Her mouth moved, but no sound came out. Then her eyes snapped open, and she smiled at him. "She has good taste. The living room will look great with that orange-gold color, the kitchen should be sky blue, and the bedroom is perfect for that lovely deep ocean blue. I know she'll love the toile wallpaper for the hallway."

Alex's jaw dropped. He looked at Mr. Giddings, who beamed with parental pride, then focused back on Phoebe. "Are you psychic or something?"

Phoebe moved her head back and forth, as if debating about which word to pick. "'Or something' is the best way to describe it."

Horatio came back from the wall, holding tubing in his hand. He stopped and narrowed his eyes at her.

"Phoebe." He tipped his head in her direction.

"Dwyer," she said to him, stiff. "Make sure to double-check your tube size. It might be too big."

"My tube is just fine. It's perfect. Thanks." Horatio ground out the words between his teeth. He went to the cashier. Phoebe gave Alex a "he's hopeless" look.

"I'll get you a sample of those colors, and we'll put in an order for the toile print." Phoebe went to the paint-mixing area.

There was a confident gleam in her eyes. "Trust me, she's going to love it."

Alex rubbed the middle of his forehead as Phoebe went to work on his order. He didn't want to think too hard about why he wanted her to love it. Maybe he wanted her to know that he could follow through on something that mattered.

✳

Wishes might have been fishes, but Lucy had magically pulled in an entire merman. She kissed Alex. She. Kissed. Alex. And it was a freaking great kiss. Frustration burned in her chest. She resisted using magic on Alex in any way, but somehow through some twist of fate, she ended up being thrown in his path.

Lucy dabbed a few drops of orange-blossom oil behind her ears and neck. She did a little spin in the foyer and checked her reflection in the mirror by the front door. A little attraction oil wouldn't hurt her on her lunch date with Theo. She thought about canceling the lunch, but she needed to think about life after Alex. Theo was stable. He worked at Meadowdale College and owned his own condo. He wasn't going anywhere. He wasn't going to come in and out like the tide. She owed it to herself to get to know him.

Then again, Theo wasn't Alex. That kiss kept repeating in her head like a GIF on repeat. Just because she still felt Alex's arms around her while she lay in bed at night didn't mean that they'd stay together. He was leaving as soon as the house was sold. She needed to keep her lips and hands to herself until she figured out what she wanted from Alex. Her phone beeped.

She glanced over at the text:

> Never trust a merman with paint samples. If you're not too busy, I'd love to hear your thoughts. 😉

Lucy's stomach flip-flopped. She couldn't resist paint samples and a good color scheme. It wasn't going to take long. She didn't want to show up too early for lunch with Theo.

Lucy grabbed her purse, left the house, and went over to Alex's. His door was already open for her arrival.

"You shouldn't leave your door open," Lucy said.

"I knew you were coming over. Besides, the door's been acting up. I was fixing the jamb." Alex came over and closed the door with a snap. He glanced over at her and lifted a brow. "You look nice."

A flutter of delight went through her. She did a little twirl, showing off her retro outfit. "I try."

"You didn't get all dressed up for me?" There was a teasing tone in his voice.

"No, I'm meeting a friend for lunch."

Yes, Theo was a friend who could mean more, if she let him become more to her.

Lucy looked him over. *Hello there.* Alex, in his fitted plaid shirt and light-colored denim jeans, looked like the long-lost fourth Property Brother. She wanted to personally thank whoever sold him those jeans because they were making him look too damn good. He held a huge tote bag stamped with HOME AND HEARTH. The jars clicked and clacked together.

Lucy peered at him. "Did you get samples to the entire paint aisle?"

"I got a little carried away."

She leaned into the bag and scanned the jars. "You have more colors in here than a bag of Skittles."

Lucy reached and took out a sample. The pint-size jar was labeled with the name of the paint color. There were numerous samples clacking together in the tote. She kept digging, scanning the titles. She picked up a few items and cradled them in the crook of her arm. "Ice Sculpture. Tropical Hideaway. Vanilla Cream," Lucy said. "This bag is a whole mood."

"Okay? Is that good or bad?"

"It's great."

He'd stuck to the plan. He bought at least half the color shades on her list. There wasn't a color or shade in there that she wouldn't have picked out for herself.

"How many paint samples did you get?"

"I wanted you to have options." Alex looked at her, his eyes warmed. There was a flicker of something more, something that made Lucy feel light-headed. She'd gotten lost in the moment and forgotten that he was picking out paint for a house that he didn't even want. For a house that he wasn't going to keep. This situation was getting a little too familiar. *Stay strong.*

Lucy looked away from him and down at the samples. "You need my opinion."

Alex took the samples from her and laid them out in a row on the living room table. "It's only going to take a few minutes."

"My opinion never takes a few minutes," she said.

"I was thinking about cool colors for upstairs and bright,

active colors for common rooms downstairs. I wanted to match the color to the feeling of the room. Peaceful colors for the bedroom, social colors for the kitchen and living room."

Lucy made a surprised sound. Then she leaned back and smiled at him. "Okay, listen to you sounding like a designer superstar."

"I might have read up on a few blogs." Alex ducked his head, and a bright blush filled his cheeks. Lucy watched him. Ugh. Why did he have to look so freaking cute talking about paint? If she wasn't careful, she might trip, fall, and accidentally kiss him again.

"What theme are you thinking about for the entire cottage?" Lucy asked.

"This place should feel like a seaside hideaway," Alex said.

"That's perfect. That's the title for your mood board."

Alex scratched his chin. "Wow. I don't remember the last time I made a mood board. I'm curious as to where you'd start with yours."

"I like images. You can use objects. Find things in nature that speak to you. What items and images say seaside hideaway to you?" At his blank look, Lucy reached out and closed his eyes. She kept her hand on his eyelids, relishing his warmth. Why was she coming up with different ways to touch him?

"What do you see?"

Alex said nothing for a few seconds. When he spoke, his voice was thoughtful. "Tumbled sea glass, driftwood, dried seaweed, deep blue, shell white. Stones. Sandy brown. Pearl white. Silver coins."

Lucy dropped her hand away from him. "Silver coins?"

Alex gave her a sly look. "Let's just say there's a lot of unclaimed treasure in the ocean."

"Did you claim any for yourself?"

"Finders keepers," Alex said, pressing a finger to his lips. He then pointed to the row of samples. "Which color do you see in the bedroom?"

"You're going to be sleeping and resting most of the time, so you don't want it to be busy." Lucy tapped the sample labeled Ice Sculpture. "This is your bedroom shade."

Alex lifted a brow. "How does your bedroom look?"

"It's pink. I like pink."

"How pink? Like champagne-room pink or sexy-underwear pink?"

"Get your mind out of the gutter."

"Why? It's my favorite place to vacation." Alex waggled his brow playfully. "Thanks for coming over."

Lucy shrugged. "I didn't do much."

"You helped me think out loud. I've been speaking to myself a little too much." Alex made a face. "I started getting worried that I heard the walls talk back."

"It might be the gnomes," Lucy warned in a low voice. "They get angry and rude if they don't eat. You do not want to mess with a hangry gnome."

"I'm not afraid of no gnomes," Alex said.

"You've been watching *Ghostbusters* again."

"Maybe. Listen, only my streaming algorithm can judge me."

"Well, if you want to watch a movie without ghostbusting, then I'm always across the street."

"Thanks," Alex said.

"You've already thanked me."

"Once doesn't seem like enough." Alex smiled. Lucy's insides squealed. *You have a date. You need to remember the date that's waiting for you.* Lucy checked her phone. Eh. She needed to leave like five minutes ago.

"I should head out."

Lucy went to the door. She took the doorknob in her hand and pulled. The door didn't budge. Okay. She yanked again, but it felt like it was sealed shut. Alex watched her, concerned.

"The door's stuck."

"Huh. I thought I fixed the jamb." Alex reached around Lucy, clutched the doorknob, and pulled. Nothing. It didn't go anywhere. "Excuse me." Lucy stepped back, and he yanked again, bracing his feet around the door while leaning back and using his whole size and weight against the door. Nothing happened. Jingling laughter, like tangled sleigh bells, was heard from outside.

Heat flushed Lucy's face. "Oh no." She gently moved him out of the way. It was time for her serious teacher voice. She raised it so they could hear her from outside. "Hey! Herbie! Half-Pint! Jinxie! Stop playing around. Open this door right now."

The laughter increased; jingling sounded out like a box of ornaments. She felt Alex's hand, steady and calm on her forearm.

"Who are you yelling at?" Alex asked.

Lucy motioned angrily at the door. "The gnomes! You left something out for them to eat, right?"

"Uh—"

"They aren't going to let us out if they're hungry. Always feed the gnomes!"

"I thought you said not to leave anything out for the gnomes."

"I said don't leave out treasure for them!" Lucy paused for a moment. She'd told him about the food, hadn't she? Ugh.

"Okay. What do gnomes eat? I hope it's not seafood," Alex said, holding up his hands in defense.

Lucy rubbed her forehead. "They're vegetarians, so they love seeds, mushrooms, and beets. If you're feeling fancy, then you can leave some tea and a little bottle of wine for them."

"They're going to be eating better than me. I don't have anything like that here." Alex glanced around the house. "Do you think they'd like cheesy eggs?"

"You're not cooking them breakfast; you're bribing them." Just perfect. She was possibly being sabotaged by hangry gnomes. Lucy banged on the door with her open palm. "Open. Up. This. Door. Right. Now." She marked each word with a bang. Her hand stung from the repeated impact.

Alex caught her hand in his, cradling it carefully. "Hold up. You're going to break your wrist swinging like that."

He turned her hand over in his; the scales on his palm caressed her skin. The contact wasn't unpleasant, but it was way too thrilling. *You should pull back.*

"You can always climb out the window," Alex suggested.

"Excuse you." Lucy took her hand back and pinched his shoulder. Alex lightly pushed her hand away. Her skin tingled. "I'm not showing up to lunch covered in honey-suckle bush."

"The natural looks good on you. Wear it to your lunch."

"We'll see." Lucy took her phone out of her bag. She sent Theo a quick I'm running late, be there soon text. She owed him a huge apology in the form of mixed drinks and a nice meal. It was going to be fine. Everything was going to be fine. "First we have to solve our gnome problem."

"How are we, trapped in the house, going to get food for them, out there?"

Lucy tapped her phone and opened a delivery app. "Rapunzel's Pizza has a great mushroom pie. Do you want anything?"

"I wouldn't say no to a half-sausage, half-spinach pie. Don't forget my favorite drink."

"I can't forget it. Lemonade and iced tea," Lucy said.

She clicked in their order, turned to the door, shouting again, "I hope you're happy!"

There was a gaggle of squeaking whispers outside in response to her words.

Lucy and Alex settled on the floor on either side of the door. "The order's going to take a while. It's lunchtime, so we have some time to hang out. You know how busy Rapunzel's gets in the afternoon."

"Why feed the gnomes if they do things like this?" Alex asked with a note of irritation. She didn't blame him for getting annoyed.

"It's a habit. Nana taught us to respect all magical crea-tures," Lucy said. She turned to the door, raising her voice again. "No matter how freaking annoying they might be."

A squeaky muttering came through the door in response to her comment. Lucy faced Alex, and he watched her with an interested stare.

"When Nana got sick, she couldn't take care of the garden. I was busy with school, so the gnomes kept it alive for her," Lucy said. "It doesn't take an act of magic to be kind."

Alex nodded. "Nana Ruth was a great one."

"She always asked about you and whether I saw you on the 'Social Book thing.'" Lucy laughed to herself. "I showed her your photos. She told me you had an amazing gift. You captured life."

She heard his sharp intake of breath. Alex sat there amazed and moved at the compliment. *Beep. Beep.*

Lucy looked down at her phone. She read the message, then clicked her teeth.

"Is everything okay?"

"Theo rescheduled our lunch. There was an impromptu department meeting, and he can't make it."

Lucy looked at Alex. His face was blank. Unreadable. He held up a hand. "I get it."

"Do you?" Lucy asked.

"I wish—" Alex interrupted himself.

He looked to her, opened then closed his mouth.

"If wishes were fishes..." Lucy mused, echoing Nana's words but not wanting to finish the second part. The silence seemed to say it all.

"We'd all cast nets," Alex finished for her. Their eyes met. *Kiss me.* The sudden demand sent a shock through her. A truth descended upon her skin like a light mist of rain. She wasn't going to be satisfied with anyone but Alex. Like a fern stretching its roots into soil to draw up water, nothing less than being with him would satiate this want in her chest. They said nothing but sat in companionable silence.

Twenty minutes later, the very confused but helpful delivery person dropped off the pizza on the porch. Lucy groaned at the scent of the bubbly cheese and toppings that wafted through the door. There was high-pitched squeaking and cheering from the other side of the door.

"I think they like it," Alex said. The locks clicked, and the door eased open. Lucy jumped up and yanked it open all the way, letting the sunlight flood the room. Only one pizza box remained on the doorstep. The second one was replaced with a hastily wrapped bouquet of wildflowers. Alex picked it up and handed it to Lucy. She clutched the flowers to her chest. Those gnomes were sweet when they wanted to be.

"No good deed goes unforgotten," Alex said.

"I don't think that's a saying."

"I'm making it a saying." Alex cradled the pizza in his arms. "I can't eat all of this. Stay. Get a slice."

Lucy looked at him again. She could get used to this, being with him bringing a pizza home for dinner along with paint samples. Being here in his house and feeling like she belongs.

I'm going to want more than pizza. I'll want this moment.

Lucy shook her head and left. She needed to take a step back. Once upon a time, she would've followed him into the ocean. If he had asked her, she would've held her breath forever and dived in just to be near him. Now, all those feelings were coming back. No more wishing; it was time to act.

Chapter Fifteen

As Lucy slept, shades of blue, orange, and white shimmered above her bed. The Fortunato Cottage appeared to her like an unfinished watercolor, pulling her forth over the lawn. The dew on the grass left the soles of her feet wet, and the full moon gave her enough light. Her steps faltered, but she continued to the cottage. Someone—or some spirit—stood in the window and beckoned her forth. A phantom touch pulled her out of sleep and woke her. It was minutes to midnight, and Lucy couldn't sleep a wink. Everything from her skin to her toes still tingled from being with Alex only a few hours ago. She hadn't felt this way—the long pull—since high school, and now her body craved it like a sweet treat. Now that she'd gotten the *Wishcraft Made Simple* book from Alex, old fears bubbled within her.

She'd done some light reading before bed, flipping through a few chapters. One line caught her attention so much she stopped on that page.

No matter how hard the wish, you can always wish again.

Lucy closed the book. If she tried to tweak the wish in any way, would it change whatever the hell was happening between her and Alex? Not only was he paying her to design the home of her dreams, but the merman was kissing her senseless. Where was Mr. Sandman when you needed him? Her phone buzzed twice, alerting her to a text message.

U up?

She barked out a laugh and responded.

Maybe.

Good to know. I can't sleep.
Still thinking about earlier.

Same here.

Meet me for a late-night swim?

Lucy paused.

Where?

Grove Lake

✳

Every Caraway witch knows that mischief begins at midnight. Lucy and Alex made their way to a path from the parking lot down into the water. Her steps slowed. The full moon was so bright, they needed little help from their flashlight. Dimmed lights from the nearby houses around the lake were still on, reminding Lucy that they needed to be quiet.

The surface stilled; moonlight and a few wayward stars sparkled. Magic, ancient and old as the earth itself, washed over her skin from Grove Lake. Lucy took it all in. It had a rocky shoreline with colorful gravel in shades of white, brown, and gray. Driftwood, twisty and knobby, lay at the water's edge. Trees bowed over the lake, casting their reflections on the surface.

Before leaving the house, Lucy had changed into a bathing suit, tossing on a skirt and jean jacket over it. She'd brought two big towels for them to sit on by the lake. Lucy laid out the towel while Alex stood at the end of the wooden dock. Uneasiness wedged under her rib cage. She hadn't been to the lake since Alex left town, and seeing it again brought up an unfulfilled desire.

He helped her down onto the towel. She crossed her legs. The soft terry cloth felt good against her skin as she sat on it. She pulled her jacket closer to her body while staring up at the stars. They shimmered like cracked crystals against a wide blue blanket. She looked at Alex.

He paused, glanced up at the sky.

"Do you remember the planetarium trip?" he asked.

"I remember writing the report." Lucy shook her head, annoyed. "Didn't you pick Pisces?"

During their sophomore-year science class, they'd gone to the library together and traced the stars for an astronomy project. They had to pick a constellation and present it to their class. Alex got an A. Lucy got a B. Even after all these years, she was still salty about getting that grade.

He peered at her. "Yeah, I did. The fishes."

He motioned to the surface, his voice distant. "Do you mind?"

"Please. Go ahead."

Alex yanked his shirt over his head in one smooth motion. Lucy swallowed. Mercy. He stripped down to his boxer briefs, which showed off his peach-shaped ass and his impressive size and dropped into the lake. Heat pulsed between her legs.

Alex dunked under the surface. He flung a piece of fabric from the water onto the docks. Wait—were those his boxers? Grove Lake glowed, and his form warped and shifted. He popped up from underneath the surface and met her stare. Water droplets hung from his eyelashes and chin. Scales, iridescent and bright, covered his face, from his chin to his forehead. He swam out away from the dock.

Once he dove under the water, his tail caught the moonlight and his back fin glittered. Ripples bounced off the lake and expanded out. He did a few laps, then came back to the dock. Lucy scooted to the edge. She studied his warped figure underneath the surface, her eyes darting back and forth. He emerged from the water, his hand clutching a hidden item.

Alex pulled himself out of the lake, onto the dock. He sat next to her, flopping gracefully. She moved over, giving him space.

He was still glossy from the lake. She paused, scanning him. Where his legs were once located, there was a tail. What a tail. It was thick and long and took up space on the dock. Whoa. It formed at his upper thighs; the scales blended in with his skin. But above his thighs, he was completely naked and exposed. He'd transformed into a merman. A hundred teenage fantasies came to life in this one glorious night.

Alex waved a hand over her face, breaking her stare. "You've never seen a merman's tail before?"

Her eyes darted away to his face. "Never. You're my first merman."

"Oh." That single word reverberated over her skin and sent a longing throughout her body.

"Don't look so smug," she said.

"I can't help it. I'm honored to be your first." The underlying suggestiveness in his words held her still. In another universe, he would've been her first, her last, and the one who would stay within her heart. Neither of them moved. As she watched him lie on the dock in his merman form, a memory of her going to Jenkinson's Aquarium popped into her head. She'd loved going there when she was young and had been fascinated by how smooth fish scales felt under her fingers. Were his scales smooth or rough? There was only one way to find out. Her skin flushed at the thought.

"You can touch me if you like," he murmured.

"Um...okay." Lucy rubbed her palms together. She dipped her hands in the water quickly, then pressed her hands on him midtail. His quick inhale filled the silence.

She froze. "Did I hurt you?"

"No." Quiet satisfaction rippled over his face as he responded.

As her hands inched up, his eyes sharpened. Every fiber of her being warned her against touching him, but he felt so warm under her hands. Smooth. Alive. His scales mimicked those she saw on fish at the market. They blended from deep aquamarine blue into sea green to pearly white with blue tips. He was still slick and wet from his dip. *Let me be the water on his scales.* A thrill went through Lucy when his eyes turned sharp and blazed.

"How do...? How does it work?" she said.

"Which *it* are you talking about, sugar?"

"If you get wet in the shower, does it appear?"

Alex moved his head from side to side, his eyes slightly unfocused. "The rules work differently for every mer family. Dwyers transform with the phases of the moon. My tail pops up under a full moon and in water," he said. "I have to be submerged. I try to swim as much as I can."

"When you dry off, you get your legs back."

"Yes."

Lucy paused. "Can we stay like this for a little while longer?" She wanted to watch him bathed in moonlight and magic just for a few more minutes. He nodded.

Lucy looked to his hand, noticing he had something inside of it.

"What did you find?"

He held out his palm. There was a collection of shells of different shapes and spirals against his scales.

"These are lovely," she said. Lucy reached over and took them from him. She focused on the shells, tracing the ridges with her fingertips.

"I don't know if you could add them to the mood board."

None of her lovers or boyfriends had even considered her hobbies or designing or thought about her the way Alex did. She seemed to always be on his mind. Just like he was on hers.

Alex peered at her. "Do you like them?"

"I do." She placed the shells on the dock. He saw the magic in her, and he did not shy away from it.

In a frantic tangle, she reached for Alex and ended up straddling him on the dock with a leg on either side of his tail. He yanked down her bathing suit top, exposing her to the night. The air tickled her skin and gave her goose bumps. *Stars above.*

She put her arms around his neck and captured him in a kiss.

Her heart stumbled to a stop before getting its rhythm back. He moved and dipped his head between her breasts and nibbled the sensitive skin. She raked her hand through his hair. His hands explored the outline of her waist and hips until coming to a rest on her ass. A squeak went through her as he squeezed. Her hands went everywhere, taking him in and touching him with a desperation that bordered on senseless. There was too much of him and not enough at the same time. He pressed himself against Lucy. She pressed back tightly. Not even moonlight came between them. Nothing in the world would come between them right now. A mixture of moist and delicious body heat made her glow. She gave in to the sensation of his steady touches and kisses. The time for words was done. She licked lake water from his mirrored scales. The water on his skin tasted divine, and she desired more. He shuddered. Parting her lips, Lucy rose to meet his mouth, eagerly responding.

His kiss hit her again like a wave rushing to shore and knocking her over. She was really going to make out with Alex on the dock. She struggled to regain her inner balance;

his hands roamed over her skin with precision. Craving wrapped around her body and squeezed her like a long-lost lover. Sweet mercy. Her mind skidded to a single, demanding refrain: *Touch me. Touch me. Touch. Me.* She reveled in the delightful jolt of Alex's hand working up the curve of her hip, over her stomach, and cupping her breast. His thumb grazed her nipple with a slow, lazy circle. Multicolored sparks popped up behind her eyes, and she gave a breathy moan. Right then she wanted nothing more than for Alex to explore her body with his fingertips and send her up to the stars above. His hands roamed down her stomach and slipped down between her legs.

He cupped her, waiting for permission to go further. She nodded and opened herself to him. He eased his fingers inside her. Lucy gave in to the delicious sensation, rocking against him, looking up at the stars. He teased and touched her, eliciting moans, the swell of emotion building within. She was almost, almost, almost there—no, she was right there. He increased his motions, and she clutched her hands on his bare shoulders as the sky broke apart.

Lucy embraced Alex. He relaxed against her body and gave in to her touch. Lucy buried her nose in the crook of his neck. His fragrance—cool air, ocean water, and a note of musk—stirred a primal feeling inside her. She wanted to peel away his worries and unburden him from his thoughts. His arms held on to her like she was a life preserver, and he was adrift. The air around them sparked and glowed.

"Lucinda." Alex whispered her name reverently, the way you'd say a desperate spell or a heartfelt prayer. He said her name the way she whispered the wish spell. She shut her eyes and let his warmth touch a part of her that she hid away from the world. This wanting weaved within her soul and stayed there, nestled in her heart until the wish bloomed and came to life.

July 1

Please join your fellow Freya Grove Gladiators for a night of elegance.

Save the Date! Reunion Weekend is August 27–30!

We are counting on you to be a part of this celebration.

If you have any questions, contact me!

Best,
Quentin Jacobson
Class Secretary

July

larkspur and water lily

Chapter Sixteen

he Swan's Nest Bar and Grill, illuminated by blue and purple neon lights, was filled with possibility and mixed drinks. It was karaoke night, which meant the shy librarian who shushed patrons could end up belting out a power ballad or the gruff trucker passing through town could sing a pop song with vigor. Karaoke was held in the back room of the bar so that those customers who didn't want to hear a painfully earnest rendition of "Stay" by Rhianna could enjoy their drinks and snacks in relative peace. The maritime-themed bar was decorated with paintings of eager sailors dancing down the street and busty pin-ups in tight sailor gear. Happy hour drink specials were posted on one of the many chalkboards around the room. The booth Lucy and Ursula had claimed was outfitted with condiments, stuffed wire napkin holders, and laminated menus. Lucy reached over and picked up a menu.

She frowned as she read it over. "I'm pretty sure they misspelled barbecue."

"No one's here to spell-check the menu," Ursula said. "So, are you singing tonight? I hear there's a cash prize for the top three performers."

Lucy gave an uncertain smile. "I signed up."

The bimonthly karaoke contest started after the open mic, which was taking place just then. Lucy heard the squeal of the mic from the back room. Her heart raced. For moral support, she'd invited Poe, Theo, and Alex to hear her karaoke debut. They'd all texted back that they'd try to make it, but she was prepared to sing to a roomful of strangers if it came to that.

"Did your neighborhood merman inspire this?" Ursula asked.

"No. I decided it was time for a risk."

Ursula studied her nails with a twist of her lips. "Mm-hmm."

Lucy cocked her head to the side. Two sounds that expressed a world of doubt and skepticism. "What do you mean by 'mm-hmm'?"

Ursula gave her a concerned look. "All I'm saying is keep your guard up. You've always had a blind spot for him."

"Thanks for looking after me."

"I just don't want you to end up in deep water with Alex, if you get my drift."

Lucy held up her hand in warning. "Please, I can only take so many water puns."

"Witches aren't the only ones who can cast spells," Ursula sang.

Lucy kept replaying the dock encounter in her head. It had been a week since that night. Alex had been swamped with deliveries for the cottage, and since the cakewalk, Lucy had been swamped with tea leaf reading requests. There had been stolen kisses here and there, when they saw each other in passing. They hadn't shared anything as earth-shattering as her riding his hand into bliss by the water. Maybe he wanted to take things slowly, or maybe he wanted to give her some space. Or maybe he was waiting until his bedroom was finished.

Ursula looked past Lucy, and her eyes widened. She gave a welcoming wave. "Be nice," she warned in a low voice.

Why would I need to be nice?

Marcus and Lincoln came over to the booth, holding their drinks. Lucy blinked hard. *Look who crashed the party.* They were identical twins. Marcus was the older of the two, having been born three minutes before Lincoln. They both wore pressed polo shirts and jeans, along with fresh sneakers. Several customers stole glances at Lincoln and Marcus, clicking a few snapshots of them. The Walkers were something like local royalty, with their mom being the mayor and their father being a town councilman. Marcus slid in next to Lucy, giving her a soft smile. Lincoln sat next to Ursula, placing a quick kiss on her lips. He acknowledged Lucy with a curt nod.

"Sorry we're late." Marcus gestured to Lincoln with his drink. "Somebody couldn't decide whether he wanted to smell like hazelnut or cedarwood. They're the same."

"It doesn't matter to me. You look and smell good either way." Ursula's eyes moved up Lincoln's chest, and she gave him an adoring smile.

"So, who's performing tonight?"

"I signed up." Lucy held up her hand.

"What about you?" Lincoln asked, throwing an arm around Ursula. "You can't let your cousin one-up you again."

Ursula smacked Lincoln's arm and shot him a sharp look. Lucy narrowed her eyes at Ursula. "When did I one-up you?"

"You got a lot of attention with the cakewalk," Marcus said. "Mom wouldn't stop talking about your big bid. Some people felt a little left out." He gave Ursula a long look.

"No way. You organized the whole thing!" Lucy said.

Lincoln shot her a withering glance. "You couldn't help yourself. You just had to hog the spotlight."

"That's not what happened. Alex and I—"

"Oh. Of course, you were with a Dwyer." Lincoln snorted dismissively.

Something ugly flared within her at his dismissiveness. "Yes, he was there. His generous bid helped Ursula break her fundraising goal," Lucy said. "Did she share that with you?"

He faltered for a moment, then waved her off. "Whatever. I bet you didn't even bake anything. You probably bippity-bobbity-booed with your magic to get a high bid."

Lucy folded her hands and sat up, meeting his mocking tone.

"How much did you donate to the cakewalk?" she asked. "Since you care so much about bids."

Lincoln jerked back as if slapped, then gave Marcus a pointed stare. Lucy glared at him. Lincoln shook his head, annoyed, and got out of the booth. "Let's get you signed up for karaoke." He held out his hand to Ursula. She took his hand and went with him, flashing a pleading look at Lucy. She hadn't started it, but she was going to end it. Once they left, she faced Marcus.

"What the what was that about?"

"Lincoln's been stressed out. He wants everything to be perfect for the wedding," Marcus said. "He wants to make sure nothing ruins it."

"So, he's coming at my neck about a cake." Lucy held up her hands. "I didn't do anything."

"I hear you. Mom likes you a lot. Ursula feels like she has to live up to your example."

"Your mom didn't like me when we were dating," Lucy pointed out. "It's not my fault Ursula didn't get the credit she deserved, or no one bid on her cake."

"No, she got a bid," Marcus said. "I—I know she got a bid." He snapped his mouth shut. Lucy eyed him. His face flushed, and he peeled off the beer label. Lucy's senses tingled. Something was going on. There was a movement in the crowd as people shifted around and came into the bar.

"You've been acting strange since Alex moved back," Marcus said carefully, as if walking on eggshells.

"Strange how?" Lucy asked. Maybe the wish was making her act a little different.

"I mean, you never baked for me."

Alex approached the table just in time to hear her respond.

"You don't like my sweets," Lucy said.

"I love your sweets. I'll eat them right now," Alex said.

Alex stood there in his jacket, T-shirt, and jeans, watching them. His black hair caught the overhead lights and shimmered against his brown skin. Behind his black-framed glasses, his hazel eyes lit up with a quiet warmth. He jammed his hands into his pockets and leaned back. His solid jaw could cut glass, and those lips of his made her yearn for quick kisses. Lucy wanted to throw her hands out and squeeze him.

"Sorry I'm late," Alex said.

"You're just in time."

Ursula and Lincoln returned to the table. They briefly greeted Alex, then faced Marcus and Lucy. "The contest is starting. All performers need to head to the back room." Ursula clapped excitedly.

"We should head back there," Marcus said. "I want to be able to feel and hear the off-key notes."

The five of them made their way to the back room of the bar. There was a makeshift stage next to a large screen that displayed the words and had a tinsel curtain. Several tables and four booths served as the captive audience for the empty karaoke stage. The group claimed a booth tucked in the corner next to the stage.

Alex eyed the thick binders of laminated paper and the slips of paper on the table. "I completely forgot how this whole situation works. Run it by me again."

Lucy leaned over to Alex. "You find your song number in the binder. Write down your name and number on the slip. Give it to the DJ in the back. You wait until your name and song pop up. Then you go onstage and sing."

Alex glanced around for the DJ. Lucy motioned to the back corner of the room, where a man in an illuminated booth was working on a computer.

"Actually, tonight's contest is a little different," Ursula said. "They'll announce the theme, and then we pick and perform a song based on it."

"Do you know the theme?"

"No. They keep it a secret until the night of. Last month, the theme was One Hit Wonder," Ursula said. "Linc, do you remember the song I sang?"

"Something about Tina," Lincoln said with a laugh.

"'Mambo No. 5,'" Marcus said without looking up from his drink. Lucy shared a look with Alex, who raised a questioning brow. Marcus and Ursula seemed to have become fast friends.

The DJ's booming voice came over the speaker. "Good evening. Tonight's karaoke theme is Heartbreak and Love Songs! All songs must be connected to love, lust, and broken hearts. If you're competing in tonight's karaoke contest, please select your song in the next five minutes. Write down your name and submit your song. Once again, today's theme is Heartbreak and Love Songs. Get those songs in!"

"I've got the perfect one!" Ursula sang happily as she opened the bigger song binder.

"So, you and Alex are dating?" Lincoln asked, pointing between them.

"We're just catching up from our high school days," Lucy said.

"Is that what we're calling it?" Alex asked low enough that only she heard him. Lucy nudged him with her shoulder, causing him to laugh. They were catching up using their mouths and hands, so what? She'd rather have this conversation in private. Lucy threw open the binder and scanned it for the song she wanted to sing. Alex rested his hand on her knee and squeezed. Lucy held back a moan. If knees weren't erogenous zones then for her they were now. She looked to him. He winked at her.

"She didn't say she was seeing anyone when she RSVP'd to the wedding," Lincoln said.

"Things change. Alex is welcome to join us," Ursula responded.

"I'd be honored." Alex put his hand to his chest.

"Come on, bro. It's karaoke night. Wait until she's drunk before you grill her."

Lincoln lifted a shoulder. "I need to know. We're paying for his plate; I'd like to know if this is real."

"I have to pick my song," Lucy said quickly. She didn't need her ex to hear about her—what?—merman-across-the-street friend with benefits.

"If this is just a hookup, we don't have to feed him. We need real couples only." Lincoln took a long pull from his beer bottle and sat back against the booth. "This whole party's getting too expensive."

Lucy bristled at his comment. She really didn't appreciate Lincoln labeling their wedding as a party, especially since Ursula was grinding day and night to make this wedding perfect for his family. Ursula shifted in her seat from side to side. She looked down at the binder, completely invested in writing down her song choice.

"Shit, man," Marcus said. "Tell us how you really feel."

"Don't get mad at me for speaking the truth. I'm keeping it real."

Lucy rolled her tongue in her mouth to keep from snapping at Lincoln. She didn't want to spoil the night. Alex took her hand in his. He didn't give Lincoln a second look when he said, "We're together. It's real."

Lincoln faced Ursula with a nod; Alex's answer seemed

to have appeased him. Lucy wasn't too happy. A song title popped into her head. She hadn't thought of this song since high school but it seemed fitting for the moment. Lucy hummed the first notes to herself. She flipped the binder until she found the song she was looking for. She scribbled down the code and then wrote her name.

Ursula found her song and filled out her slip. Lucy delivered their songs to the DJ. Soon after, the karaoke contest started, shutting down any awkward conversation. Her attention went toward the stage. The first singer of the night, a trucker who earnestly held the glittery mic in his hands, took the stage. He tried and failed to hold the infamous high notes of "I Will Always Love You."

Lucy turned to Alex. He tilted his head toward her to give them a little privacy.

"Are we good?" he asked.

"No, not really." She shook her head. "I'd rather not discuss our relationship while strangers are sing-screaming Whitney Houston."

Right then the trucker's voice cracked again, and a few people covered their ears.

Alex winced, taking in the atmosphere. "My fault. I didn't like his tone."

"Lincoln's always going to have a tone. Are you going to tell everyone who has a tone about us that we're together?"

"I can if you want me to."

Once he was done singing, everyone clapped for him. While the DJ set up the next song, Lucy decided to take advantage of the music break. This wasn't really the place for a relationship talk, but there was no point in delaying.

"So, you meant it." Lucy motioned between the two of them. This wasn't just a fling.

"I do," Alex said. "Is the soul mate search ongoing?"

Eh. Lucy blinked rapidly to collect herself. Welp. They'd been avoiding the topic of soul mates since the boardwalk. She was going to put on her big-girl booty shorts and deal with this conversation.

"Is this your way of asking me if I'm still searching?" she asked back.

"I didn't make any promises or ask you to commit," he said. He tensed up next to her.

"I touched your tail. That's kind of a major commitment," Lucy said through pressed lips, making sure that only he heard her. Alex had the sense to look sheepish, and his cheeks flushed at the memory of that night. She liked that she had this effect on him. He needed to know the truth. "I'm not looking."

The instrumental opening notes to "Someone Like You" played over the speakers. Lucy rolled her eyes. Was the universe throwing her serious shade? She focused back on Alex who watched her. Once their eyes met, the tension eased from his body.

"Are you asking me to be your *girlfriend*? Can I wear your varsity jacket in study hall?" she asked.

Alex grinned to himself. He'd been on the swim team and wore that jacket every single day during the entire season.

"Maybe," Alex said. He pulled her in and kissed her. Her blood pounded and her body grew hot with want.

Throughout the night, they kept finding ways to touch each other. A brush against his thigh. A kiss to the neck. No matter how this night ended, she was going home with him.

Ursula was called to the stage. She sang a Madonna pop ballad that had the room swaying with synth eighties nostalgia. When she was done, Lincoln rewarded her with a sweet kiss. Marcus bowed out early for the evening, wishing them both good luck.

"Do your best, Lu," Alex said, pressing a kiss to the back of her hand. "I'm right here."

The DJ's voice boomed overhead.

"Lucy C, report to the stage! Lucy C, you're our final singer of the night."

Ursula clapped. Alex whooped. Lincoln tapped his finger against his empty bottle. Lucy went to the stage and picked up the mic from the waiting stool. The instrumental track kicked in; Lucy swayed to the soaring piano and bass line. Her eyes darted briefly to the screen. She didn't need the help; she knew the words by heart. She'd listened to this song throughout college; it had been the balm to her bruised heart. The words lit up. She brought the mic to her mouth. Showtime.

Her voice, deep and throaty, came over the audio system.

A few patrons sat up and nodded at her. Suddenly, half-way through the first chorus, the mic went out. Lucy tapped it, but the mic powered down. Panic rolled through her. She noticed a handful of patrons hold up their cell phones, ready to record a viral disaster.

The wish struck again. There was an odd pause as the audience yelled that they couldn't hear. She glanced over to her booth, stunned. Ursula cringed and covered her face. Lincoln smirked and watched with a light of glee in his eyes. Strangers ran out, not wanting to watch her fail.

Alex stood up. *Sing to me*, he mouthed, not breaking eye contact with her.

He wasn't going to leave. Relief, cool like a glass of water, washed through her chest. She wasn't alone. Lucy dropped the dead mic on the floor, her attention on him. She didn't want to break this spell and gestured to the DJ to keep the song playing. The DJ lowered the track volume enough so her voice carried out to the room. She belted out the song. Tomorrow she wouldn't have a voice, but if he heard her tonight, she didn't care.

Lucy heard people cheer for her to keep going and encouraged her, but all she saw was Alex. She sang strong and clear, digging within herself to hit each lyric. She sang for the dreams she'd abandoned and for the wishes she wanted to come true. Tears blurred her vision, but she kept her attention on Alex. He didn't look away once. All the things she wished for with him burst inside of her with every note, every lyric. Lucy sang everything she couldn't say to him without breaking her heart. She wanted him to stay.

The song was winding down, but she kept on singing. Finally, someone handed her a working mic; she brought it to her lips and sang out the last line. The entire room erupted once she finished. Everything happened in a blur. Lucy rushed into Alex's arms, or Alex pulled her to him. He kissed her tears away, cradling her face and whispering words of support.

Yeah, it was real.

Chapter Seventeen

☾

he champ is here," Alex said, holding Lucy's arm up in
the air. She felt like a heavyweight champion of Freya
Grove. Lucy held out the medium-size trophy, a shiny gold
star atop a round base engraved with the words "Third-Place
Winner." It sparkled underneath the streetlights as they
walked down Summerfield Street. The smell of impending
rain was pungent in late-night air.

"I shouldn't be so happy about third place, but I'm pumped."
Lucy tucked the trophy to her side. "I've never won anything."

"You also won the Most Memorable Award." Alex had
watched as the bar patrons chanted her name when asked
to vote for their favorite performance. The DJ gave her the
award and even requested an encore song from Lucy. By that
time, Ursula and Lincoln had gone home, while Lucy led
everyone in a sing-along to the karaoke classic "Piano Man"
by Billy Joel.

"Tomorrow no one will remember the third-place finisher
of a local bar's karaoke contest."

"I will," Alex said. He took her hand in his and squeezed.
"I'm proud of you."

She smiled up at him. "What? You're proud of me for not

shutting up?" Her voice was a little raw, but there was a new strength behind it.

"You didn't give up. I think I would've run off stage and cried in the bathroom."

"I had a song to sing," Lucy said firmly. "I should put this trophy away before the gnomes see it."

They finally reached their houses. He was to the left; she was to the right. He didn't want this night to end. He wanted to stay with her a little longer.

"I have a surprise for you."

"Now?" Lucy laughed. "It's almost midnight."

"I finished the main bedroom."

Her eyes lit up. "It's done?"

Lucy had taken a special interest in the main bedroom right down the hall from the guest bedroom. He'd been late coming to karaoke night because he'd been waiting for one last delivery for that room.

He nodded. "Come check it out."

"I have to check on Shadow," Lucy said. "Give me fifteen minutes. I'll meet you over there."

Lucy raced up to her house and went inside. Alex returned to his space, switching on the porch light for her. It had started raining. The plinking of drops sounded off on the windows and roof. True to her word, Lucy came right over, using the key he left out for her in the stone mushroom by the door. She was covered in a light layer of raindrops. Alex's breath caught in his throat. She'd changed into a dress, draped in shades of blue and green, a water elemental, a mythical being relishing in their power. As she stood in the doorway, keys in hand, a thought came to him. *She belongs here.*

She brushed off the water with a hand and slipped off her shoes. "Sorry. I forgot my umbrella."

"Don't worry."

He showed her upstairs to the master bedroom. Lucy stood at the threshold, taking it in for a moment, then walked inside the room, looked around, and turned to Alex.

"Wow," she breathed.

"Really?"

"Yeah."

He let go of the breath he hadn't known he was holding.

"Wow," she said again, but it was more emotional. "It's everything I could wish for."

Her eyes began to water. She wiped away a tear before it could fall. Alex gathered her into his arms. He didn't like to see her cry. He reached up, wiping away her tears with his thumb. Lucy took a step back from him, looking down at her feet.

"You did a good job for the open house," she said in a distant tone.

Alex shook his head. "I didn't do it for that."

Lucy snapped her head at Alex.

"Stay."

Lucy peered at him. Alex stepped forward. He put his forehead to hers and said, "Stay the night."

He wanted to wake up with her. Nothing more, nothing less. He'd kissed plenty of women, but standing in this room he'd made for her, she mattered. She reached out; her right arm went to his side to give her support. On tiptoe, she touched her lips ever so softly to his. Once they kissed, it was as if he'd been submerged in cold water, his system shocked into awareness. Here she was—the undiscovered ocean he'd desired to explore and revel in—and he was being invited to explore. He would not waste this time. More. Every cell in his body demanded more. He moved his hand from his side, ran his hand up her forearm, touching her bare skin, over her shoulder, tracing the lines of her body. She trembled with eagerness as he lifted her chin and deepened the kiss further.

They moved together farther into the room, until they knocked into the bed. He lifted her onto it. His hands ran down her back and gave a playful squeeze of her behind. She laughed and nipped his lip. Alex continued kissing her with a careful savagery that tested his patience. She responded by pressing herself against him, closing the gap between them.

They crashed into each other with the same elemental force as when a wave met the shore. There was no telling where she started and he ended with their desperate touches.

He'd wanted this ever since the night by the lake, but he was waiting until the room was ready for her. Alex brushed another gentle kiss over her skin, lingering to breathe in her scent—sweet honeysuckle, earthiness, and crushed black pepper. She moaned and arched against him. All he wanted was to taste the rain on her skin.

His senses heightened. Alex's blood stirred as he moved and searched out all her pleasure points with his mouth and hands. *What does she like? How can I pleasure her?* He nuzzled her neck, kissing away the raindrops nestled in the hollow of her throat. The sound of her panting sent all his blood downward, and by the time he licked her neck and cleavage, he was stiff and throbbing with need.

"Alex, please," Lucy pleaded. He wanted her so much.

Alex tucked a finger under her chin and lifted her head so that he could see her eyes. He paused. There was no turning back after tonight. She deserved more than a rain-soaked seduction. She deserved a husband who came home safe every evening, a garden where she'd tend to her blooming honeysuckle bushes, and a chubby-cheeked baby who would chase after butterflies. He tensed. She reached up and cradled his face in her hands. She kissed his eyes and face, whispering softly between kisses, "It's okay. It's okay."

"Tell me what you want from me," Alex said.

Lucy sat up and shimmied out of her dress, tossing it on the floor.

Alex scanned her body. The rain had made the lace bra and underwear nearly invisible. They clung to her body and showed off every delicious curve and her delta, the apex of her thighs. A ragged sigh tore from him.

"I want you," she said. "I want everything."

"You don't have to tell me twice," he responded.

"Yes," she said. There was a note of surrender in her voice. After all this time, they were giving in to desire. He wouldn't rush tonight.

He moved in and yanked her panties down, tossing them to the side. He pressed a quick kiss to her sensitive skin, relishing her natural scent. Lucy gasped. Alex kissed his way up from her thighs, her stomach, the valley between her breasts, and then he captured her mouth again. She held on to him, her hands grasping and bunching up his shirt so that she could touch more of him. His hand slipped down and felt her slick wet folds under his fingertips. She arched against his hand. He kept his hand moving with delicate, thoughtful strokes. He increased his tempo with his fingers. Her breathing came in short, steady breaths, and then he touched her, the core of her pleasure, and stroked.

She went on in a guttural voice, saying "yes, yes, yes; oh right there; yes, yes, yes," and then, after several long strokes and kisses, she came against his hand. The storm raged outside and raged within him at the sight of her orgasm overtaking her. Her head went back, and a long, luscious scream escaped her lips. Through the lace fabric of her bra, he took a nipple into his mouth and licked slow, deliberate circles until she was hard against his tongue.

"Alex," she cried.

Alex looked up and watched as her head lolled back and her eyes pinched shut. If he didn't thrust inside her heat soon, he'd come right here. She took in ragged, panting breaths and gave him a dazed, delighted smile. His heart spun in response.

Alex eased her down onto the bed. He stripped off his T-shirt and pants, leaving himself bare. She bit his lip and gave his body a raking gaze as soft as a caress. Desire, raw and exposed, shined in her eyes. Gods, he adored this woman. He went over to the dresser, pulled out a foil packet, and dropped it on the bed. They studied each other silently. She leaned down and gave him one long lick. The broad side of her tongue sent a deep shudder that hit him from the tip of his toes to the back of his balls.

He laid his head back on the pillow. "You can keep doing that. I don't mind at all."

Lucy gave him a sexy smirk. "Don't tempt me." She took him into her hands and stroked.

He couldn't take this torture anymore. "Lucy, please."

Lucy took the package. "Let me do the honors."

She sat up, opening the foil packet. Lucy sheathed him and then straddled him, lowering herself inch by inch upon him until they were joined, flesh to flesh. Alex moved underneath her, pushing upward into her warmth. She rode him, and he met her thrust for thrust, their moans mixing into a duet. Tonight was a song Alex's soul would never forget. He rolled her over onto her back and drove into her again and again. Lucy hooked her legs over his and allowed him to go in deeper. The world spun on its center. Lucy writhed under him. Her words blended into frantic pleas: "Yes, yes, please, yes, yes, right there, right there, don't stop, don't stop," turned into a long, desperate whimper. Alex felt the stars gather within him, his release building, building, and then the stars shattered and their light exploded—bright and blinding. He came with a rough yell and pressed his face to her neck.

I could stay here forever. He stilled at the observation. *I want to stay here.*

Lucy buried herself deeper in the bed. Alex stood up and strode over to the bathroom to clean up and collect himself. He caught his reflection in the mirror. His hair was mussed, and the bright flare of desire remained. Was once ever going to be enough? No. Alex returned to the bedroom. Lucy was now wrapped up in the flat sheet like a burrito.

"That was…" Lucy trailed off into silence. Rain pitter-pattered against the window.

"Yeah, I know." Things were way past serious with them.

He looked at her. Her skin glowed and shined. She was enchanting, and it had nothing to do with the wish. They, bare naked and radiating with satisfaction, were beyond words right then.

✷

This early-morning air smelled of raw magic—of freshly uncovered earth and cracked seashells. The moon, still aglow, hung in the rapidly lightening sky. Daylight and darkness shared the air. Lucy loved this time of day even more now because she saw Alex sleeping in the morning light. He lay in bed, his face burrowed, clutching the pillows to his large body. The blending light-blue and burning-orange shades of the sky eased her nerves. She counted off the charms on her bracelet, collecting her thoughts. One question kept repeating in her brain like a software update on her computer.

Was this night because of you or the wish?

She had sung to him, but the wish had forced her to use her voice. She'd baked the cake, but Alex had stepped in and helped her. Alex slumbered as the last of the night trickled down through the bedroom window. Morning was coming soon, and she'd have to figure out what to do with the rest of her summer and what to do with the merman in question. *You know what you'd like to do with him.* The promise of love brought the most powerful humans to their knees and made them willingly sacrifice their power. What would Alex demand from her?

The answer to the question stole her peace of mind. She stood at the window, looking outside.

A cool breeze tickled her skin as she adjusted his borrowed shirt over her behind. Lucy took a generous inch of her skin, twisted it between her thumb and forefinger, and pinched. Ouch. She wasn't dreaming. She turned to the bed and faced him. The blanket cradled his body. He clutched the pillow to his sleeping face. She'd lost count at how many times they'd reached for each other throughout the night. Two? Five? A dozen? A worried thought raced through her mind. Dread worked within her chest and stayed there. What would happen when he sold the cottage? Once he got rid of the cottage, there wasn't anything keeping him here but...her. Would the wish be enough?

Alex stirred and woke. He blinked sleepily at Lucy, and in a dazed, sleep-filled voice said, "Come back to bed, honey."

The gentle plea in his voice pulled her forward and into Alex's arms. She burrowed herself into his chest, feeling the steady beating of his heart against her back.

He nestled his face against her neck; his breath tickled her skin. "What's on your mind?"

"Nothing much."

Alex made a disbelieving sound. "Never play poker. You are a terrible liar."

He readjusted his hold on her so that they were face-to-face. His eyes scanned her. She settled comfortably into his arms. "I heard you thinking from across the room. You're regretting last night."

"No," Lucy said. "I don't regret the first or fourth time with you."

"Then what's got you thinking?"

"Are you a mind reader, or what?"

"Call it a merman's intuition. Talk to me."

Lucy held back a smile. "This thing might get messy."

His hands wrapped tighter around her body. "This thing might be fun."

A small hope buoyed in her chest. They had the rest of July and August to figure out what was going on between them. She wanted this fleeting time with him. Lucy wanted the perfect summer she was denied when Alex walked away from the Grove immediately after graduation. For once she wanted to be completely selfish and have this moment with him for as long as she could hold on to Alex. She'd somehow caught this merman, and she wasn't letting him out of her grasp. *Let the wish work for you.*

He kissed her nose, then her eyes, and then captured her lips again. He whispered against her skin words as ancient as the Earth's waters. She sighed blissfully.

"So, what's next?"

"Well, I was thinking about touring the Grove. Checking out the Medusa carousel. Maybe head over to Bruce's Arcade. I'd like some company."

"Okay. It's a date."

"You wish."

"I do. I really do." Alex ran a finger along her cheek. "I'll make you some tea in a while. We've got to take care of that voice." He kissed her forehead and held her tight. Lucy nestled into him, capturing his scent, the brine and salt of the endless ocean.

Chapter Eighteen

uess who just went viral!" Callie thrust her phone in Lucy's face. A witch didn't make the front page of the *Freya Grove Press* website without really, really trying. And Lucy did it by accident.

"I am not drunk enough to deal with this right now." Lucy peered at the photo of her and Alex kissing on the phone screen. She pushed it away. They were caught offstage mid-embrace, his hands firmly planted on her ass. If she wasn't so embarrassed, she would admit that they looked good together. Sirena refilled her flute from the pitcher of mimosa mix on the table, then slid it back to her. "Drink up."

"You made the Precious Moments page," Callie sang.

Lucy snatched up the glass. *Bottoms up.* She emptied it in four gulps, then held it out. "More. Please."

Sirena filled her glass again. Lucy downed the second glass even faster. The bubbles tickled like popping stars cascading down her throat into her stomach. Mimi's Diner, a mainstay of Freya Grove, was rolling out their Sunday Brunch Special. Since Ursula was swamped with wedding planning for the summer, they'd made plans to treat themselves to their bottomless brunch.

By the time their French toast and bacon arrived, Lucy was going to be passed out. Oh well. Callie could feed her brunch like they gave Shadow treats underneath the table. Lucy groaned. When was the last time she'd fed their cat? The wish had taken up so much time in her life that she didn't even have time to take care of her familiar.

"It's not that bad." Callie enhanced the image and then turned the screen toward her. Lucy pushed it away. She didn't need to see her behind in HD.

"Everyone's going to see it," Lucy countered. "Everyone's going to ask about Alex."

"Why is that a bad thing?"

Everyone would ask the question she was scared to answer. *Is he going to stay?*

Lucy lowered her voice. "It's not real. It's my wish."

"You don't know that. A wish only works but so far," Sirena said. "You don't know where the wish ends and you start."

Being with Alex was a fantasy from her wildest thoughts. The way he fell apart in her arms and pulled her down into the depths of pleasure haunted her. Mercy. She didn't want this wish to end too quickly.

"Speaking of wishes, how's everything going with you two? Is anything happening?" Lucy asked.

Sirena finished her drink, looking over at other tables. Callie held up her phone, scrolling with her thumb. Were they really ignoring her? Lucy waved her hand in front of them. "Hello. I know I'm not speaking Klingon! What's going on with you two?"

"I've been going to the wrong class for the last two weeks,"

Callie said. "Before you say anything, it wasn't my fault. They switched the times on me."

"So, I may have hooked up with a kitchen god," Sirena said slowly. "I don't know. I have to check my mythology book. He might just be a demigod."

Lucy blinked. She looked at Callie, who shrugged and toasted her sister.

"We're going to have to talk about this picture," Callie said. "You can't hold out on us."

"I don't want to talk about it."

"It could be worse," Sirena said. "You could be in your underwear."

Argh. Leave it to Sirena to find the bright side. Callie flicked through the online gallery with her thumb. "Whoever took these did a great job. Oh. Nice. I just found my new background photo!" Callie held up her phone, waving it in her face. Lucy held up her hand.

"Stop. I'm trying to get my money's worth in mimosas right now."

"Not until you really look at it!"

Fine. Lucy snatched the phone from Callie. Her jaw dropped. Whoa. Who was that lady?

"Tell me you don't look gorgeous. Those jeans make your butt look good."

"Not from that angle," Lucy muttered.

"Those are my jeans. Thank you very much," Sirena said.

"So, when is the wedding?"

"Please don't mention the word 'wedding' to me."

She sipped the dregs of her mimosa while holding Callie's phone. Despite herself, she clicked through to the photo series. They looked good. Like a Shutterstock photo that she used on her personal Instagram post to show what the best version of love could be. They were wannabe #couplegoals. In another world, these pictures could've been their engagement shoot. Her heart hoped. Lucy handed Callie back her phone. *No*, she ordered herself, *don't wish for anything that can break you.*

Ursula swept into Mimi's Diner.

"Who picked this place? The parking is terrible." Ursula sat down in the booth.

"Look who's gone viral." Callie held up her phone.

Ursula glanced at the photo with passing interest. "I heard. Mrs. Walker showed me the video."

"There's a video! I have to see this." Now it was Sirena's turn to pick up her phone.

"She was very surprised I won first place instead of you." Ursula made a face. Lucy sipped from her flute even though it was almost empty. "I said that it was a singing contest, not a performance, but—oh." She lifted a shoulder. "She adores it. She won't stop talking about it." Ursula poured herself a drink. She studied her nails, not looking at Lucy. Lucy's stomach dropped. Uh-oh.

"She wants to know if you'll consider singing at the wedding."

Lucy felt the familiar tingling on her tongue. Callie peered over her phone. Sirena looked from Ursula to Lucy. She didn't want to say yes, but the wish compelled her not to say no. Enough was enough. Her wish wasn't going to ruin Ursula's wedding. She wasn't seeking excitement at the cost of Ursula's happiness.

"It's your day."

"It's not a big deal."

"It's a big deal to me."

"Are you saying no?"

Lucy let the silence speak for her. Ursula chugged the glass in one swallow. She dabbed her mouth with a napkin from the table, then faced Lucy.

"Rethink your answer. Mrs. Walker said it would be perfect," Ursula said, her voice sounding robotic. "I can't tell her no. She really thinks that it would be perfect. You can't say no, because I need you to say yes. Because if you say no, I have to tell her—I can't tell her no."

Ursula clenched her mouth shut. The table grew silent.

"Do you want me to sing at your wedding?" Lucy asked.

Ursula's face fell. A shadow of grief crossed over her face. "It doesn't matter what I want."

"It does to us," Lucy said. This wish wasn't worth it. Nothing, no contest or spell, was worth hurting her. Ursula looked away from the table. She pulled a pair of sunglasses out of her bag and put them on, then faced them. Her chin trembled, and she took in a sharp breath. Tears fell from behind her glasses and dropped onto the table. Callie reached out to Ursula, but Ursula held up a hand.

"I'm fine. I'm fine," she said shakily. She stood up. "You know, I forgot I have an appointment. I'll call you later."

Ursula left. They sat there wordlessly staring at each other. Their magic was getting out of control.

Sirena called over the waiter. "Keep the drinks coming. We're going to need them."

Callie looked to Lucy, her brow furrowed. "When was the last time we fed Shadow?"

"Don't ask. I wouldn't be surprised if Shadow ran away," Lucy said. "We've got to get our lives together."

✳

It was time to invoke the ancestors. Their wishes were pulling apart their bond.

Lucy cradled the lit candle. She cupped her hand around the flame as she padded down the hallway toward the back room. The Caraway ancestral altar was set up on a long table against the wall, covered by a crisp white tablecloth. There were over two dozen photos and mementos of the Caraway ancestors going back more than a hundred years on the table. The most recent addition to the altar was the silver gilded frame of Nana. As Lucy stood before the table, a deep and familiar ache throbbed underneath her heart. Her nana's spirit was at peace. Lucy reached out and touched the frame of her grandparents' photo. James and Ruth Caraway caught together at a family cookout—Ruth had whispered a joke to James, whose face crinkled in mid-smile—their eyes were alive and captured in a private moment.

I wonder what they wished for. Did their wishes ever come true?

White tea light candles were arranged at the four corners, and fresh-cut flowers were placed in small crystal vases. Lucy set the candle down on the table next to the water bowl on the side and reached over to the pile of incense, picked up a stick, and lit it. She waved a smoke trail around the altar to purify the air, then, with her other hand, dipped her fingers into the bowl and sprinkled water over the items. She returned the incense to its holder. This space was where Caraways gave tribute to those who came before them and asked for their guidance. She bowed her head, letting the incense smoke touch her skin. Prayers for Sirena, Callie, and Ursula fell out of her mouth and went out into the air, where they were embraced by those who had come before her. A whisper, as light as angelica oil, touched her ear.

You are what we've always wished for.

"Blood of my blood. Aid us. Stand by our side. Guide our way."

August 3

Please join your fellow Freya Grove Gladiators for a night of glamour and elegance as we end our reunion weekend with dinner and dancing.

Grove Pavilion August 30, at six o'clock in the evening

Attire: red carpet chic

Please book your tickets by emailing Quentin Jacobson.

Congratulations, Lucy Caraway!

You've been awarded by your classmates the Class Cup—Most Transformed! Your achievements since graduation have impressed your fellow former Grove Gladiators, and we'd love to honor your life! Please respond to this email within the next two weeks if you are able to attend the ceremony.

Best,
The Freya Grove Alumni Committee

August

gladiolus and poppy

Chapter Nineteen

Whenever Lucy went into a Jersey Shore arcade, she felt like she was trapped inside a circus tent. There was a sense of delightful chaos that thrilled her. The musical trill of the machines and flashing lights played around her and Alex. Shouts and screams filled the space as beachgoers won and lost points and prizes with the flick of a button. There were at least half a dozen people wearing animal print or muscle tees that showed off overly tanned arms. Alex clutched his camera, scanning the space but not taking any pictures.

"You said you needed inspiration," Lucy said, stretching her arms. "Take it all in."

Alex made a face at the prize booth. "Bruce's hasn't changed in years. I don't know how much inspiration I can get from a Ferris wheel shot glass."

"Give it time. You'd be shocked where you find your muse."

An early-evening breeze came from the ocean, bringing in the scent of salty air and fried food. They wandered around the arcade, checking out all the games.

"Do you have anything for your gallery showing?" Lucy asked.

"Not yet. I managed to get a few photos I like. I'm trying to come up with a theme." Alex took a few random pictures of the Skee-Ball display. He checked his screen and sighed. "Nothing is speaking to me right now. So far I'm taking it easy. You're helping me with my project. Is there anything I can help you with?"

"I don't know. I was thinking about applying for a program."

"Do it. You're talented. You'll get in."

"I didn't even tell you what it was about."

"I know you. That's all I need to know."

Lucy clicked open her phone. She pulled up the website and went to the teachers' page. Even though she knew the requirements from memory, she needed someone outside her family to talk to about it.

"The program's called the Teacher in Residence Program at the Library of Congress." Lucy showed him the program page. Alex silently read over the information. In addition to working side by side with the nation's top librarians and researchers, she'd create materials and resources to help time-crunched teachers who needed a quick "do now" or a picture. Not to mention, she'd be able to sit and study in the glorious main reading room for hours upon hours.

Once he was done reading, he looked at her.

"What are you waiting for? This program is made for you."

"I missed my chance to apply." She'd been too nervous to submit last year. By the time she'd gotten up the courage to submit, they weren't taking any more applications.

"Wait, it's opening up again in the fall," Alex said. "Did you see that notice at the bottom of the page?"

Lucy looked again. "I didn't see that." The wish was always finding a way to sneak up on her when she wasn't expecting it.

"I'll personally call you up and ask you if you've applied yet."

"You can't do that."

"Why? Do you plan on changing your number anytime soon?"

"No, but—you don't have to check up on me when you leave."

Lucy bit her tongue. They were having a nice time, and she had gone and brought up his impending departure. She didn't want to be that person—jumping to her phone whenever there was a text or call hoping that it was Alex. Wanting it to be him. Then her heart being crushed that it wasn't him and feeling like a fool for wishing for him to call. She wasn't eighteen waiting for him to reach out and connect with her. If she wanted something from Alex, she needed to open her mouth and be honest. Alex said nothing. He snapped a few pictures of the neon lights above the pinball machine before turning his camera on Lucy. She didn't look away from him. He took a few pictures of her, then looked at his LCD screen. He made a small, excited sound.

"You look nice under neon. You're very photogenic."

"You're going to spoil me with all these compliments."

"Good."

"I don't know if you're busy this weekend."

"What's up?"

"Auntie Niesha's having a cookout at the house," Lucy said. "She wanted me to invite the cute merman from the picture. She's calling us the Karaoke Cuties."

Laughter floated up from his throat. "I like it. That picture's gotten me into so much trouble."

"How so?"

"Mom and Pop keep asking me to invite you over for dinner."

"I like your parents." The Dwyers were nice merfolk who she always waved to whenever she saw them at the local supermarket.

"Oh, they like you, too. I think they like you better than me."

"Well, they didn't buy me a house."

"True." Another laugh, less cheerful, bubbled up from Alex. When he laughed, the years melted away and he was Alex from English class, the new kid all over again. Her own smile deepened. A warning rang out in her head whenever she leaned in too close and smiled too widely at him. The warning went *whoop, whoop* in her head like a klaxon siren every time he returned her smile. *"Merman. Merman. Whoop. Whoop. Don't get too close."* She didn't like this siren.

"Should I bring anything to the cookout?" Alex offered.

"Just bring your cute self."

"I can do that," Alex said smoothly. Then his eyes dimmed. He stilled for a moment and faced her.

"Do you mind if I check up on you when I leave?" Alex asked, playing with the camera lens between his thumb and forefinger.

"Friends usually check up on friends. I wouldn't mind it, but we're more than friends," Lucy said. "We never defined what's happening between us. Is anything happening between us other than—really good sex?"

Alex peered at his camera, then at Lucy. She pushed on. Things were getting heavy, but she could handle it.

"The sex is *only* really good," Alex said. He gave her a too-sexy-for-the-daytime smile that hit Lucy right at the base of her back and made her wobbly. *Keep it together, girl.*

"What are we to each other?" Lucy asked. Alex stepped forward to be closer to her. She wasn't done talking to him. "I'd like to believe that we're seeing where things go for the summer. Defining what we are now might set up expectations and keep us from getting hurt."

"We should've talked about this before," Alex said.

"Well, last time we were uh—busy. I was using my mouth for something other than talking."

"Oh," Alex said huskily. "I remember."

His mouth dipped into a small frown, and his forehead wrinkled in concern. Alex opened and closed his mouth like a fish gasping for air. He was practically walking on seashells, trying to keep from hurting her. She took a deep breath and gave him her full attention. He didn't have to do this alone.

"Okay, let's define it. Right here, right now," Lucy said. "'Companion'?"

"No. It sounds like we're in a Jules Verne novel, racing around the world in eighty days."

"Okay. What about 'lover'?" Lucy offered with a growl.

Alex slashed a hand over his throat. "Nope. We're not in the 1980s, getting freaky in a hot tub."

"Okay." Lucy ticked off her fingers as she said each word. "Partner? Sweetheart? Flame? Intimate?"

"No. Too cutesy. Too odd. And did you really say 'intimate'?"

"I don't know. I'm trying."

His expression was tight with strain. "I know. I just want to get it right."

"What is it about one word that freaks you out?" Lucy threw up her hands. She'd probably run through all the entries in Dictionary.com and still not come up with a word that worked for Alex. "You jumped off a cliff into the Pacific Ocean, but you can't jump on a word."

"I knew what I was jumping into then. I don't know what I'm doing with you now," Alex said. He twisted his mouth to the side, then turned to her fully, his expression warm. "I've known every ocean, lake, and river, but you're deeper than any water I've leaped into—ever. It's the waters within you that scare me."

"I won't let you get swept away," Lucy said. *Goddess, please let me keep this promise.*

"Lu, that's not up to you. This word needs to mean something for us."

Lucy scanned the arcade. Her eye spotted a plush starfish displayed over the prize booth. It had a goofy smile on its face, an extended spread eagle next to a collection of the most recent popular video game characters.

She clapped her hands. "There we go. What about starfish?"

"Okay," Alex said, uncertain but not dismissive.

"I mean, it works. Who doesn't like a starfish? I know they're called sea stars, but I think for what we want, it works. No surprises. No pressure."

His face brightened at the suggestion. "You're my starfish?"

Lucy nodded. Then it happened. His expression changed from one of confusion to absolute confidence. He looked at her with wonder, as if he'd seen an undiscovered ocean meant only for him to explore. Right then, she made another wish. *I wish this was real.* She wanted him to stay in the Grove just a little longer, but that was just too much pressure on him. He'd already spent so much money and time getting the cottage ready for the open house at the end of the month.

If she told him what she really wanted, it might push him away.

She didn't want to share the true wish of her heart just yet.

So, they were each other's starfish. A voice whispered in her ear, *A soul mate by any other name is still a soul mate.*

Chapter Twenty

*L*ucy watched the paper star decorations that littered the Caraway backyard cookout spin in the balmy afternoon air. Her cousins, aunts and uncles, and various friends had gathered to enjoy the weather and eat until they were stuffed. Several young ones of various ages lumbered past Lucy, carrying two filled buckets of water balloons.

Aunt Niesha, tending to the snack table, said, "No way! If you're going to have your water balloon nonsense, go out front," she ordered. "Don't hit any cars! Stay out of the street! If you hit any guests, I'll ground you until Thanksgiving! No Halloween!"

"Yes, Auntie!" they called out faithfully.

They did as they were told and went to the front of the house. Lucy gave Aunt Niesha a dubious stare, which she returned. "Those kids are going to give me more gray hairs."

"I'm glad we weren't like that," Lucy said.

"Ha. You think you weren't, but I put parsley sachets in all your book bags to keep you safe," Aunt Niesha said. "I doused myself in lavender oil every morning. I needed to stay as calm as possible when you four got together during a full moon."

"We've grown up. We won't get into trouble."

Aunt Niesha narrowed her eyes at Lucy. "Are you sure about that?"

Lucy held the stare. *Ursula didn't say anything about the wish spell, did she?*

Uncle Leo called Aunt Niesha over. "Hey, sis! Sit in with me. I need a spades partner."

"You don't need a partner. You need a miracle worker," Aunt Niesha responded with a wink. She went over to the table and joined the game. Lucy shook her head. The last time she'd played spades with Aunt Niesha, she'd been temporarily kicked out of the family for cutting books and costing them the game.

Lucy stood by the snack table, holding her red drink cup, scanning the crowd. Alex had said he'd stop by, and so far, he hadn't shown up. Their adventures over the last month had brought them closer, but she was holding back. As soon as Alex sold the cottage, he'd be on his way and out of her life. Lucy tamped down her disappointment. She peered into her cup, hoping that somehow her iced tea had magically gained a shot of bourbon or vodka. Liquor always made disappointment a little less bitter.

"I hope there's no rum in that cup," Sirena said.

"I wish." Lucy bit her lip at the slip of her tongue. "You know what? I'm done with wishes for the next decade."

"I hear you." Sirena sighed. Then she lowered her voice and said, "How is everything going with that?"

"Honestly, I'm doing my best with this wish. The race is next week. I'm still helping Alex with the cottage."

If helping meant having her way with him in every single

room, then she was helping him to the best of her ability. Sometimes, she helped Alex twice a day.

"Yes, you're helping Alex." Sirena gave her long, knowing look. "It sounds like you have it all handled. What about the whole soul mate issue?"

"I'm putting that on pause."

"A little love charm of raw honey and red candles might move things along and help you out," Sirena said softly.

"No, magic isn't needed in this situation," Lucy said quickly.

"Okay." Sirena glanced down at her phone, flinching at the time. "I should head out soon."

"Where are you going?"

"I'm working the lunch and dinner shifts tonight."

Lucy made a dismayed sound. "Seriously, Si? You've worked every night for the last two weeks. Take one night off."

"My perfect investor might come in. I might be one plate away from making my wish real." Sirena gave her a pointed stare. "Wishes don't come true if you're standing still."

"Don't remind me," Lucy grumbled into her cup, then took a long sip.

"I'm already late." Sirena blew her a kiss. "Save me a plate."

Lucy nodded in agreement as Sirena rushed out of the backyard.

She'd fumbled her way through her wishes over the summer, but one wish had led to more problems. The cakewalk had led to social invitations to hangouts, read tea leaves, and get up to magical mayhem.

The Delectables, Poe's home-bakers' social group, was a collection of witches, wizards, and other enchanting folks who loved their brown sugar and baking delicious treats. They'd welcomed Lucy with open arms and put her to work when she joined them for their blueberry pie baking session. For their next project, the Delectables were hoping to win a visit from a famous food truck traveling around the country handing out cupcakes.

If she was real with herself, this exciting life was becoming a little exhausting.

A certain merman is keeping you up at night.

As if stepping out of her thoughts, Alex strolled into the backyard through the gate. He wore a light-blue linen shirt that fit over his sinewy body and brown khakis that encased his muscular, toned legs. She watched him scan the backyard then find her. A spark of an indefinable emotion flickered in those hazel-brown eyes, and a smile tugged at the corner of his lips. His gaze went over her body with the gentle, surprising caress of a summer breeze. She held her cup tightly against her chest as eagerness rushed through her blood. *What was in this cup?* He approached her.

"Sorry I'm late. I was waiting for a delivery." He leaned in. "Your wallpaper came in early."

"Keep talking dirty to me."

"Do you need a refill?"

"Sure. I'll have an iced tea."

"Of course."

A sudden crush of people and laughter from Aunt Niesha at the card table caused her to step closer to Alex. She found herself taking in his profile as he wordlessly refilled her drink. Today there were touches of his shimmery scales around his eyebrows, highlighting his eyes. Remembering what he said about his scales and ocean water, she decided to ask a few questions.

"You went swimming this morning."

Alex shook his head. "The ocean was calling me. I assume you got in a run."

"I did a few laps around the neighborhood. I just want to finish this 10K race without embarrassing myself."

"You'll get it. The first mile is always the hardest."

"Why am I not surprised that you run?"

"I have to do something for leg day."

Her attention focused on his legs. Some people had a thing for asses. Lucy had a thing for legs. His dress khakis were tailored to his thick thighs, showing off his impressive physique. Those thighs begged to be straddled morning, noon, and night by a willing and able volunteer. She'd been pleased to do the job. The tingle of want inside her was neither unpleasant nor welcomed. Sure, it was fun to let her imagination run away with the idea of Alex, but lately she'd toyed with the belief that he'd stay for good this time. As Alex handed back her cup, their fingers brushed. She took the drink with a murmured thanks and angled toward him, tilting her face upward.

"How's the wish thing?"

Lucy made an annoyed zombielike noise. Alex groaned sympathetically. "It's that bad?"

"More wishes, more problems."

"What do you keep wishing for?"

I keep wishing that you'd stay.

Lucy leaned in close, brushing up against his shoulder so

that only he could hear her. "I need someone to tend to my secret garden."

Alex moved back and studied her face. "Okay." His voice took on an inviting timbre that she felt in her stomach. "Keep going and don't spare any details."

Mermen are a trip. Lucy playfully slapped his arm. "Get your mind out of the dirt."

"But you said—"

Lucy took Alex by the arm out of the backyard. "I'll show you."

She brought him to the front of the house, where two of her younger cousins raced by, each cradling armfuls of balloons. They gave orders to each other and continued looking for their enemies hiding around the house. Lucy gestured to the porch railing, at the collection of small plants snaking out of terra-cotta pots. She touched the wilting leaves of the rosemary, lemon balm, and the other herbs, then faced Alex. He watched her without saying a word.

"I can't keep them in the house. Shadow will chew them up."

He stood next to her. "You need help taking care of it."

"Nana left them for me. I give them sun, air, and water, but they haven't thrived the way I'd like them to." Lucy let frustration bleed into her voice. She'd done everything she could for the little group, but the herbs were quite stubborn. Just like every Caraway witch, they had no quit in them, as Nana said.

"Why is it secret?" he asked her. He took a step closer, closing the space. There were a few inches of daylight between them. She needed to make something grow and heal her heart after another dating disappointment. Lucy tried to find the words, but she couldn't say them. *If I can trust someone with my plants, I can trust them with my heart.* She heard the little cousins buzzing around, but she was too preoccupied with the merman next to her.

"If I told you, I'd have to kill you," she teased.

He held eye contact with her. "I'll take the hit."

Another Caraway cousin, Sage, ran up the stairs and darted behind them. A warrior princess scream went through the air. There was a series of rapid pops and an explosion of water between them. Freezing-cold water hit Lucy right in the chest and ran down between her breasts. She let out a startled cry as the water dripped down. Alex's eyes and chin were also dripping wet. His linen shirt clung to his skin like tissue paper, and his khakis looked like he had peed himself. Remnants of water balloons were scattered all over them. Everything they wore was completely soaked. Lucy looked down. Her dress was plastered against her skin, revealing her bra and panties. She met Alex's eyes and noticed that his attention was directed squarely on her body as if he was trying to trace her curves through the fabric. *Hey. Now.* She dragged her attention from Alex and focused on the trio of cousins hovering around them.

"Oh, man," Lucy's cousin Daphne wailed. "Auntie's going to get you."

"I didn't mean it! I'm sorry!" Juniper shouted in self-defense. "I was aiming for Sage!"

"You're too slow," Sage mocked. Lucy gave Sage a warning glare, effectively silencing her. Everyone focused on

Juniper, who rubbed her face, trying to physically pull the tears away.

"I'm going to miss Halloween!" Juniper wailed, tears welling in her eyes.

Lucy reached out and held the girl by the shoulders. "Juniper, look at me. Listen. You won't get in trouble if she doesn't see us. Caraway cousins stick together."

It wasn't just a saying; it was a promise.

"Yeah?" she asked hopefully.

"We can keep this between all of us. We've had our fun; we're done with the water balloons. Right. Right?" Lucy gave each cousin a pointed stare, eliciting silent nods. "Now, tell Aunt Niesha I'm showing Alex around." Lucy looked at Alex. He nodded. "I'll be right back."

"Okay," Daphne said.

Lucy gently nudged Alex into the house. Shadow watched them with big eyes, tracking them as they rushed past where he lounged on the mantel. He flicked Lucy an "oooh, you're being so bad, it's good" look. Ugh, her cat was so annoying. Voices boomed from the kitchen. Lucy took Alex by the hand and led him upstairs to her bedroom. She closed the door behind them and locked it.

"So, this is where the magic happens," Alex mused.

"The magic happens downstairs or in the attic."

Lucy peered around, trying to see if she'd accidentally left her raggedy yet comfortable high-waisted underwear on the floor. She couldn't wear the cute stuff all the time. She glanced around trying to put herself in Alex's place. There were pops of champagne pink and cream accents that made the room have a quiet, sensual vibe. It was a basic bedroom, littered with secondhand books, witchy treasures of crystals and natural items, and typical furniture: a dresser, a bed, and a privacy screen she'd fallen in love with at an estate sale.

"We have about seven minutes before Auntie calls me back down," Lucy said. "Five minutes if Uncle Leo makes a bad bid."

She threw him her stars- and moon-covered robe. "Get undressed."

"You don't have to tell me twice." He took off his shirt and slipped out of his khakis, showing off his toned body and boxer briefs. She stumbled to a stop. The water had soaked through the clothing and his skin was wet. All the way down. Her mind repeated the plea *Let me be the water on his skin.* Lucy scooped up his clothes and put them on a hanger to distract herself from following through and tasting the water on his stomach.

"I have a pair of basketball shorts that might fit," Lucy said. She studied his flank, unable to look away. How did he get that perfect bubble butt swimming in the Atlantic? There weren't enough squats to give her behind that look, but he had it naturally.

"Lucy," he said, breaking her out of a daze.

"Uh. I don't think they'll get up your thighs," Lucy responded. She turned away, heat rising up her neck. His laugh echoed inside the room. When she looked back at Alex, he'd belted the robe around his solid form. The wide bed was a splurge, and she'd decorated it with a floral comforter, which seemed lush against his body. *Why does he look so good on my bed? Maybe he belongs there.*

She pushed that thought away.

"You really like candles." He pointed to the nightstand, which was littered with soy candles, each labeled with their scent, surrounding an antique lamp.

"I like ambiance."

"You read in bed."

"Of course. It's the best place to use your imagination."

"I bet." A beat passed between them. "What do you like to imagine?"

Oh. Don't go there. "Winning the lottery. Buying my dream home. Collecting first editions."

"Hold up. If you win the lottery, you're not going on vacation?"

"I wouldn't know where to go."

"Imagine."

That one word he said conjured up a single image of the cerulean-blue ocean that stretched out until it touched the sky. Out of the corner of her eye, she caught sight of the postcard on her corkboard, kept safe for more than seven years.

"I'd go back to the Indian Ocean."

"You've been there before?"

"Yeah." Lucy looked over at her corkboard on top of the dresser.

"Don't leave me hanging, Caraway."

"I did a summer study abroad with Meadowdale College. I spent the summer before my junior year in East Africa, researching and writing the history of the Swahili Coast. I've never been in an ocean that…blue or warm before."

She couldn't bring herself to get rid of the postcards or the kangas—the folded colorful fabric she'd brought back from her travels. The longest time she'd ever left home was the last time she'd taken a risk and had an adventure. Back then, she'd sought excitement. She'd been brave and foolish. Since then she'd been so careful about what she did and where she went. Life was safe. It was comfortable. It was fine.

"I'd love to go with you." The promise in Alex's voice sent a shiver through her body.

No. She was letting herself want an adventure that she couldn't have. She needed to stop fooling around and get back to the cookout. "We should get back."

"I don't think Auntie Niesha will appreciate my outfit change." Alex gestured to the fluffy robe that barely reached his mid-thigh. "I hope you found something other than this."

She went over to the dresser, yanked it open, and tossed several items onto the bed for them to change into. He looked over the clothes, sorting through the pile.

Alex held up a bedazzled shirt. "I think this matches my scales."

"Wear it if you want," Lucy muttered. This wet dress clung to everything.

"No, I don't want to stretch it out."

He put the shirt down, then held up a black lace bra. "Why haven't I seen you in this yet?"

Lucy snatched it from him. "Let's go."

Alex held a gray shirt with the purple logo of the Freya Grove Gladiators.

"Is this mine? You've kept it all these years."

"It is, and I did." Lucy glared at Alex, willing herself not to let him see how much a scrap of fabric meant to her. It had been his and that fact made it valuable. He was her starfish, nothing else. *Play it off. It's nothing.* "It's a good sleep shirt. I wear it and nothing else."

He watched for a heated moment, then licked his lips at her. Pleasure pulsated deep between her legs. Yeah. Nothing else. Lucy found basketball shorts and placed them on the bed.

"I should change."

Lucy picked out a pair of leggings, a tunic shirt, and panties. She darted behind the privacy screen and undressed until she was naked. Her nipples hardened and her body turned taut. He was right next to the screen. Less than two inches separated them. The throbbing within became pleasurably painful.

"Lucy."

"Yes?"

He didn't look over the screen but held up her bra, then draped it over the side. Lucy reached out, and their hands touched. Everything froze. The roughness of his scales sent goose bumps racing over her skin. They could've been getting dressed after stripping off their clothes and tumbling into bed together. He'd be the type of boyfriend or lover to sneak away from the party just to steal a moment alone with her away from the world. He'd also help her get dressed, handing her back her clothes while watching her with a loving gaze. The music from the backyard would muffle them and any noise they'd make. They were going to make noise.

"Yes or no, Lu?" The words sounded raw.

"Yes."

Alex pushed the screen aside. His eyes were hooded with lust. He tore the comforter from the bed, grabbed a few pillows, and draped it all on the floor. Lucy went to the dresser. She took out a few condoms and tossed them. Alex lowered her down onto the soft comforter, crushing his body to hers. He was unashamed. As was she. She was left bare. She lay on her back.

Wantonly, Lucy spread her legs and revealed herself to him. He placed a hand on each of her knees and made slow circles on her skin. Alex nestled his face between her legs, the nearness of him overwhelming and captivating her. Delicious heat raced through her, setting everything aglow. She was so close. His mouth brushed against her sensitive, aching skin. Then she gripped the back of his hair and guided him to right...there...right there...right...there.

She moaned. Hands dug into her flesh, teeth nipping and tasting the hidden geometry of her body. She didn't want to get there without him joining her. Lucy pulled him to her and captured Alex into a kiss. She tasted herself on his lips. They both turned over. She rose above him, kissing a trail down his chest, his stomach. She nipped at his waist, eliciting a startled laugh from him.

"I couldn't help it. You look delicious," she said. Her hand caressed the skin of his thigh. Then she took his sex into her palm. He lay panting, chest heaving under her attention. She lowered her nose and breathed in. Sea brine enveloped her and stole her thoughts. Desperate, she took his full, thick length into her mouth and hummed pleasurably. He writhed underneath her. She traced circles and triangles with her tongue on places on Alex where she'd only fantasized in her dreams.

"Please. I need you."

She sheathed Alex. He gasped as she lowered herself onto

him, letting him inside every part of her. As she rocked back and forth, he leaned up on his forearms to meet her. They joined together. His lips and tongue licked up and tasted the water of her skin. Their fevered breaths fueled their frantic, eager movements. The world spun on its center, their bodies in delicious harmony. She felt the sparks gather within her—the release building, building up, rising into the open sky... then shattering, and light exploded inside them both.

Chapter Twenty-One

☾

The kettle whistled as Lucy opened the jar of tea and scooped the tea blend into the mug. The smell of sage, crushed rose petals, peppermint, and jasmine flowers wafted up while she poured boiling-hot water. Lucy twirled the spoon in the teacup. There wasn't enough tea in the house to get the image of Alex worshipping every inch of her with his tongue. Every. Single. Inch. She still tingled from his contact even all these days later. *Think about him later. You've got work to do.* She settled at the table with Sirena and Callie, who had their own drinks.

"How are we doing?" Lucy asked. "Did everyone see Mom's latest email?"

Sirena groaned.

"Please don't remind me. I can't even deal with her and Dad walking on those white sandy beaches. She has a sixth sense for making everyone feel jealous."

"Next time, I'm wishing for a fully paid vacation."

All three sisters nodded.

"Mom forwarded me job listings again," Callie said. She held up her phone and showed Lucy the email. "I feel so unqualified just looking at these postings!"

Lucy sat up when she saw the first job title. "Hey, can you forward this email to me?"

"Sure."

Lucy's phone beeped with Callie's forwarded email. She just stared at the subject line.

FW: Photography-Guest Faculty Position Meadow-dale College

Could it be this easy? Alex would be perfect for this job. He could stay in the Grove. It was a flexible position, and he could travel but he could come home to— Lucy clicked her phone off.

The Grove wasn't his home. The wish wasn't going to give up on him so easily.

"I got kicked out of class," Callie sighed. "Professor Analog didn't like me texting."

"You do know you're paying to be in class, right?" Lucy explained. "Try not to get kicked out."

Sirena shook her head. "I agree."

"Listen, I have moves to make," Callie said sharply. "I can't pay my tuition if I don't make money! I can't run my business while my phone is on mute. Sirena, say something about your job."

"I messed up. I made the wrong weekly special." Sirena winced. "I thought we had enough fish, but—nope. The fish stew is just stew. What about you, Lucy?"

She had her 10K race on Saturday, but she wasn't feeling too confident about how well she would do on the day. Unable to think of anything else, she said the first thing on her mind.

"I slept with Alex," she blurted out.

"Finally! Where did his tail go?" Sirena asked.

"So that's where you were! I thought you were going to get ice," Callie said.

"He didn't have his tail that time."

"You've done it more than once. Enjoy yourself. Get him out of your system." Callie narrowed her eyes. "No. He's probably fantastic. You'll want to keep him for good."

"You know you get a wish if you catch a merman," Sirena said with a sly wink.

"Don't remind me. Besides, Alex isn't sticking around to get caught. I'm done with wishes for a while," Lucy said.

"I could only imagine what he could do with his tail," Sirena said.

Lucy collapsed on the table, *thunk*ing her forehead on the edge. "I'm so screwed."

"Only if you ask him nicely," Callie sang. Lucy raised her head, picked up her teaspoon, and threw it in Callie's direction.

She dodged it. "Okay, let's get serious. What's the worst thing that could happen?" she asked.

Lucy looked up at the ceiling, going over the options. "He could leave again."

"Or he could stay," Callie said. "If you asked him to stay."

"I don't want to pressure him."

"Maybe he's waiting for you to ask him. How does that sound?"

Lucy frowned at the thought. Well, that was a plot twist. They'd agreed to be each other's starfishes, but what happened when she wanted more? What if he wanted more? There was only one way to find out, but the feeling of failure felt like a heavy hand pressing on her back.

"It's the wish," Lucy moaned.

"You keep saying that, but I don't know. Wishes only last for so long," Callie said.

"I think Alex is realizing what he's missed out on for all these years," Sirena said. "You, the shy duckling, are now a fierce swan. He's enchanted by your beauty. Enchant him back."

"Speak on it," Callie said, snapping her fingers in support. The front door opened, and Ursula's voice called out, "Hey, y'all, hey."

"We're in here," Sirena responded.

Ursula rushed into the kitchen, clutching her bag to her side. Her pearls were missing, and her hair, tucked beneath a crocheted hat, poked out like purple crinkle-cut fries from the oven. Her eyes appeared bright and wild.

"Why is your hair purple?" Callie asked.

Sirena gestured to her neck. "Where are your pearls?"

"There was an accident at the salon. I don't want to talk about it," Ursula said. "We have to cast another wish spell."

"Good morning to you," Lucy said. She studied the bags underneath Ursula's eyes and her dazed appearance. "What's going on?"

"Get the spell book."

Uh-oh. Lucy's ears burned as if an invisible person held a lit match by them. Even though her sixth sense was not nearly as strong as Auntie Niesha's or Callie's, she knew—she just knew—big things were going to happen very, very soon.

"Tell us what's going on."

"First, I need to hear this hair story," Callie said.

"I wanted to go blond, okay?" Ursula sniped. "I just need another wish spell."

"My wish hasn't even come true yet," Sirena said sharply.

"Maybe you didn't do it right. That sounds like a you problem."

"At least I'm not wishing again," Sirena pointed out.

Lucy held up a hand. "Everyone, pump your brakes. Let's chill out, drink some tea, and talk about our next steps."

"There's no need to talk. I don't want tea," Ursula said. "Let's get the book and make this wish happen correctly this time."

"A second wish couldn't hurt," Callie said, biting her lip in thought.

The burning in Lucy's ears intensified. This wasn't the right step. She'd finished reading the *Wishcraft Made Simple* book recently. She had to have faith and trust the process. The wish was going to work out. "You can't call it off," Lucy warned. "It'll be worse if we stop cold turkey. The second spell could backfire and make everything worse."

"I don't like the sound of that," Sirena said. "Let's just let it ride."

Ursula closed her eyes, took in a deep breath, then snapped them open. There was a dangerous determination in her eyes that made Lucy lean back against the table.

"I'm going to do this with or without your help. You can either help me or get out of my way."

"Lucy might be right." Callie walked out of the room, shaking her head. "I'll be right back."

"We're not making another wish," Lucy said. "Just let it play out."

"Let it play out." Ursula bit off each word. She practically shrieked. Sirena glared. Lucy stood still. "My future is on the line, but you're too busy trying to get with Alex."

"How is that relevant?" Lucy demanded.

"The only way you could ever get Alex is because of the spell." Ursula crossed her arms over her chest, rolling her tongue in her mouth. "Tell me that isn't true."

Sirena cut Ursula a sharp look. Lucy clicked her back teeth to keep from snapping at her.

Lucy faced her cousin head-on. "You don't throw bad magic after good."

Callie returned, cradling the family spell book. "I found something. Nana left a note."

"I—I didn't see a note. Did you see it?" Lucy stood next to Callie. Ursula joined them and looked over her shoulder to read the note.

Callie read it out loud. "'Remember, once the wish is made, it can't be taken back until it is done. It might take days; it might take years. Wish well and with a wise heart, my darlings. Love, Nana.'"

"This isn't happening," Ursula huffed. She rushed out of the kitchen. Neither Callie nor Sirena moved. Lucy rushed after her. It was too easy to get a spell from a neighbor or a friend. Someone had to keep Ursula from burning the Grove down with chaotic magic.

"Hold on. Wait," Lucy called. Ursula kept going. She reached for the door handle and yanked the door open. Lucy shoved her hand against the door and shut it.

"Don't try to stop me," Ursula said.

"He wasn't my wish," Lucy snapped. "I didn't wish for Alex."

Ursula studied Lucy with a skeptical glare. "But I saw you. You wrote—"

"I told you not to look. I asked for excitement in my life," Lucy said.

"What happens when the spell ends? This whole thing isn't you," Ursula said, waving her hand dismissively. "Making cream-puff towers, singing karaoke, and designing houses. It's all been the wish. You think he likes you? He likes what the spell makes you do!"

"That's not fair. He's changed."

"Oh okay. Why haven't you asked him to stay yet?" Ursula asked.

Lucy said nothing, Ursula's question hitting its intended mark. She didn't ask him because she didn't want to know his answer.

Ursula's voice went low, turned nasty. Fire flashed in her eyes.

"Wishes end. Then he'll leave again. What will you do then?"

Ursula pushed past Lucy. She slammed the door as she left. *All spells end.*

Chapter Twenty-Two

$\smile$

Summer was in full swing in the Grove. Technicolor-bathing-suit-clad citizens walked up and down the sidewalk with terry-cloth towels over their shoulders. Alex took aim with his camera capturing the scene before him. Several storefronts were open and teeming with customers holding plastic bags filled with heavy purchases. Passersby devoured french fries from paper bowls and licked dripping ice cream cones. However, there were nasty-looking dark clouds on the horizon that hinted at an impending rain. Maybe the sunshine would hold out until the afternoon.

The large display window of Home and Hearth Hardware Store on Main was being changed out from summer grills to fall gear like leaf blowers and coolers. Alex peered at the items in the window. He snapped a few pictures of the display, making sure to capture the feeling of the impending autumn season. Phoebe came out of the store, waving to Alex.

"Good morning, Dwyer," Phoebe said. "We're having an end-of-summer sale if you're interested in buying more paint."

"No, I'm good. The house is almost done. I have the guest room left and then it's finished."

"Someone's moving in soon."

"It's more complicated than that," Alex said.

"We've got more goods inside," Phoebe said. She went back inside the store, and he followed. Bags of home and gardening supplies were stacked near the entrance next to the pop-up display of different seed packets. Alex looked over the colorful packets that displayed blooming wildflowers and instructions.

"We're having a seed sale. Buy two packs, get two packs free. Do you know anyone who likes to grow things?"

Alex looked to Phoebe. She gave him a questioning glance, waiting for his response. She looked at him as if his head was made of crystal and she could see into his brain. A rapid series of thoughts popped his mind like text notifications.

Lucy loves seeds. Get her some.

"I'll have to think about it," Alex said carefully. Phoebe nodded. The chime of the bell on the front door rang when three customers came in asking questions about flashlights and tarps. She helped them while Alex went down one of the narrow rows.

He found the red and white plastic Open House sign next to the citronella candles. It was smaller than he expected. He reached out to grab it and then hesitated. *Was it necessary to have a lawn sign? Maybe it was overkill.* Horatio did ask him to make a good impression for the potential buyers.

The open house was happening within the next two weeks, and he still hadn't gotten the sign. He'd been delaying picking it up. If he wasn't hanging out at Lucy's house, then he was putting finishing touches on the house and snapping up images of the Grove. They'd texted about getting together soon, but his impromptu meetings and her last-minute tea-reading clients often left them unable to meet up. Instead, they texted and left each other silly, fun messages. Whenever his phone buzzed or beeped, his heart kicked up a little. He put off getting the sign, telling himself there was always tomorrow. *Get the sign later*, he'd say to himself, then forget to go by the hardware store. Enough with all that noise. He needed it today.

Alex went to the cashier stand where Phoebe was working. He placed the red and white plastic Open House sign on the counter.

"You're selling your house," Phoebe said. Alex peered at her. Why did she sound so surprised?

"I wasn't planning on keeping it."

"You still believe that," Phoebe said. She shook her head sadly and smirked at him. "Why are the cute ones so stubborn? I think it might run in your family."

Alex didn't want to read too much into that comment.

"I think I need a bigger sign. Will people be able to see it from the street? I should get some balloons so cars can see it."

"The sign isn't the problem. I don't want you wasting money on a sign that's going to collect dust."

"You know something I don't know," he said.

Phoebe blinked slowly, then focused her gaze on him. A smug glint appeared in her eyes.

"I know everything that you're trying to hide."

His body tensed in astonishment. He spoke quickly, trying to douse the rising shock within his body. No one knew. He couldn't let anyone know that he was having second thoughts.

That he wanted to keep the cottage.

"Having a home is too much responsibility. Unexpected maintenance. Septic tank issues. Basement flooding." He wasn't even making sense, he was moving his mouth and hoping his words made sense.

"Do you have a basement?" Phoebe asked.

"No, but the attic can flood." Alex fumbled for his wallet. He pulled out a few bills and placed them on the counter.

"All those things can be fixed." Phoebe counted out the money, opened the register, and made change. "I guess you don't like the neighborhood."

"I love the neighborhood. I don't feel like I'm a good fit."

He didn't take his change. Alex thanked her and left the store. A tumble of confused thoughts and feelings overcame him. It was the truth—he loved the neighborhood. The sights and sounds played out inside of his mind. Kids stayed out until the streetlights came on and then ran home, shouting goodbyes. Families returned home from vacations and day trips, carrying their sleeping children in their arms. Ms. Shirley chatted about the gnomes digging up her yard. Lucy tended to her porch garden every other day, whispering encouragements to the smallest plants. They, he assumed, like her students bloomed under her rapt attention. This summer he'd watched the neighborhood from a distance, and he'd fallen for this place.

He'd been asked by the Neighborhood Block Association about what dish he was making for the block party for Labor Day weekend. He'd looked at his calendar, checked, and felt his stomach sink. Labor Day was after the open house. He wouldn't be around to bring a dish. He was going to sell the house. He didn't want to stick around long enough to let anyone down.

Alex dropped his sign into his car. His phone beeped with a text notification. He checked it.

I'm at the starting line. Wish me luck. Meet you afterward back at the house. 👟

He'd texted her GIFs of Wonder Woman being a badass superhero lady to show what he thought of her. She responded back with hugs and kisses emojis. Maybe he should've gotten her the seeds. He didn't even know what seeds she liked. He smiled at the thought of her opening a gift box stuffed with flat seed packets. He'd even buy her extra pots and soil. The things you do for—Alex pumped the brakes on that word. Nope. Not now. Not ever.

"Hey, brother," Horatio called out. He came over to him from Little Red Hen Bakery, holding a four-cup carrier filled with iced tea, wearing his usual shirt, jeans, and work boot outfit. "There's only one reason someone smiles that big. You've got a special lady."

"I don't—I don't know what you're talking about." Alex tucked his phone away.

"Please, everyone knows about Lucy. It's about time." Horatio went over to his pickup truck and placed the drinks on the front seat. "Well, it can't be too serious."

"Why do you say that?"

"She hasn't seen your tail."

Alex froze. Blood rushed to his face. Merfolk couldn't become invisible, but he was damn well trying to disappear.

Horatio's mouth dropped open. He lowered his voice to a stunned whisper. "She's seen your tail?"

"It just happened! She was careful. It didn't hurt."

"She touched your tail!" Horatio said in a high-pitched voice. Did he have to sound like a Jersey Shore Steve Urkel?

Alex punched Horatio in the arm. "Can you calm down?"

"I mean sex is sex, but it's your tail."

"Don't start."

He'd never, ever let anyone touch his tail. Mom always taught them to protect their tails from any human. It was too personal, like someone cracking his chest open and tapping his heart with their fingertips. But Lucy had been so careful with him, and he could tell from her bright smile that she'd been satisfied by what she saw. He was laid bare on the dock under the moon and by the water, under her delicate touch. She'd seen him, and she hadn't looked away or flinched. For one moment, holding her willing body against him and his soaked scales—the risk had been worth it. So what? *She saw you. It wasn't a big deal.* He'd tried to show Nahla his tail, but she wasn't around during the full moon. There was always another culinary experience she had to attend, or he had another photo assignment. Once Nahla asked him to stay home to save their relationship, to be her anchor, he struggled. They hadn't stayed in the same place long enough to get to know each other. This realization settled heavily on his shoulders.

Horatio cackled. "Don't let Mom find out. She'll start planning the wedding."

A swift terror gripped Alex. *Who said anything about marriage?*

They were only starfishes to each other. That was enough.

"I'm not staying," Alex snapped. "I'm also not getting married."

He'd barely been engaged. He had no business even thinking about getting married.

Horatio rubbed his palms together as if summoning the right words. He faced Alex; his eyes became serious. "Does Lucy know that?"

Alex lifted his shoulders to his neck. "Eh…we haven't really talked about it."

"Maybe you should," Horatio said. Alex wanted to hide from Horatio's concerned glare.

Lucy knew that this was just a fling. Nothing had to change. The cottage was still going up for sale. He was leaving at the end of the summer. That was the plan. He was sticking to the plan. Dread filled him at the thought of leaving the Grove and Lucy, but he knew it would be worse if he stayed. History had taught him that lesson. It was better for him to deal with the tides he knew rather than swim into the unknown.

✳

Run a race, they said. It will be fun, they said. Well, there wasn't a real "they" or a person who'd encouraged her to run, but she'd been the one with the bright idea that she'd run a 10K race. It was only six miles, she thought. Only six miles in the rain. Only six miles in the stinging, sideways rain in her thin racing gear. Thank Goddess she was wearing her black top. Otherwise strangers would've seen the entire outline of her sports bra.

Lucy limped up the stairs to her porch, favoring her left leg. Her rain-soaked racing medal *thunk*ed against her chest as she took it one step at a time. She'd been less than a mile from the finish line when her ankle rolled. Her leg went out from underneath her, and she'd hit the ground hard, scratching her arm, hand, and knee. She'd lain there on the wet muddy pavement, wanting to give up. She'd wanted to give in, but something happened. Something she didn't want to think about just yet. Lucy took a calming breath and made her way to the porch landing. There was Alex sitting on one of the porch chairs. He had a gift bag on his lap.

Alex looked her over, his brow rising as he clocked her dirty racing gear. He stood up, holding the bag. "Are you alright?"

He came over and cradled her face with his hand. "You look like you've had quite a day."

Lucy leaned into him. His touch was the balm she needed to ease her aches and pains.

"Don't worry. I left some mud on the ground. I didn't bring it all home."

Lucy dug into her racing pouch and pulled out her keys. She let them into the house, toeing off her muddy sneakers at the threshold. Alex closed the door behind her, and they went into the living room.

"Lu, you should get out of those wet clothes. You'll get a cold."

Lucy took a step forward, closing the space between them. They were close enough to touch but far apart enough that she didn't get him muddy.

"I should've been there at the finish line."

"You would've been waiting for a long time," she muttered. It was clear that having Alex there would just have added to the pressure she felt standing at the starting line.

Alex stared at the medal dangling from her neck. "You finished."

"Barely," she whispered. A thin layer of shame covered her, along with the rain.

She didn't just come in last; she'd come in dead freaking last, the last person to cross the finish line in the entire race. The Freya Grove Fire Department had sounded out the sirens for her, and all the firefighters in their gear clapped her very late arrival. It was kind of them, but she couldn't look them in the eye. The race director personally gave her the medal as the crew cleaned up the finish mat. Lucy had held back tears as she drove home. Failure felt like she'd swallowed a fistful of sand that made her mouth dry.

"You didn't give up."

"I was last. I was *the* last person to finish," Lucy said. "I should've been better; I should've been faster. What will people think?"

The people who read the class notes would probably laugh at her once the race results were posted online. *What type of runner am I? I could barely finish six miles.* There was a certain unspoken expectation that came with being the woman she wished to be. It seemed like there wasn't enough room or space to mess up because of the image she projected.

"Hey," Alex said softly, breaking her out of her spiraling thoughts. She looked at him. His eyes turned warm, momentarily lifting the chill from her body. "They're going to think, 'Look at this amazing woman giving everything she got. She didn't walk away. She kept going. She gave it all she got because she has no quit in her.'"

"Yeah," she said. Her breath caught in her throat. Nana would've said the same thing to her. Maybe she was speaking through Alex in some way.

"Yeah," he echoed. "Think back to the finish line. Tell me what you saw."

"Strangers were cheering for me. They didn't even know my name and they were so...proud." Lucy lowered her head. The truth humbled her. She touched her bracelet, and her mind flashed back to the moment when she'd considered stopping the race.

"When I was all alone out there, bruised and banged up on the course, I wanted to quit."

Alex waited for her. He listened.

"I heard Nana. It was like she was standing right there with me. She was cheering me on," Lucy said. "Once I heard her voice, I felt like I could've run the New York City Marathon."

Alex stayed silent. He waited for her to finish.

Lucy paused, emotions stealing her voice for a moment. She hadn't run a race since Nana died, unable to bring herself to lace up her racing sneakers. Today, covered in rain, she felt it, the feeling that she could do beautiful things, that she was capable of lasting magic.

"There's always next year," Alex said with a grin.

"Let's handle one wish at a time," Lucy said. She noticed the bag in his hand. "What's this?"

Alex reached into the bag and took out the gift. A soft gasp escaped her lips.

It was an arrangement of tea bags in the shape of a flower bouquet. Each tea package was attached to a stick like a stem. Rather than a vase, the bouquet was presented in a huge tea mug. It was purple and covered in white spots. A glow of appreciation flowed through her as she looked closer at it. Suddenly, Lucy didn't feel so cold anymore.

Alex shrugged. "I don't know your favorite flowers yet, but I know you like tea."

"That's true."

He held out the gift to her. "If you don't like the mug, you can return it."

Lucy shook her head. "I couldn't think of a better gift."

She didn't like it. She loved it. She flung herself against him. The thoughtfulness of his action had rendered her speechless. He rocked her back and forth in his arms. He took her breath; she was dragged under the water, but she did not drown.

Chapter Twenty-Three

☾

*E*veryone in Freya Grove was trying to get in their last bit of summer by attending the Freya Flea Market. The Funky Flea, as everyone called it around the Grove, consisted of vendors from all over the state who came to sell their goods to customers fearless enough to search through piles of junk to find possible treasure. Red and white pop-up tents created a makeshift maze that filled the parking lot of Ocean Avenue and Grand. Local artists laid out their wares of jewelry, arts, and crafts on blue and black blankets. Rows of antiques, collectibles, and vintage items were neatly scattered underneath wide umbrellas. Every merman in his family couldn't get enough junk, found treasure, and supposed trash. Horatio loved refurbishing old technology, Pop kept coins from all over the world. Alex was all about cameras. He scanned over the collection in front of him, his eyes darting among compact, bridge, and mirrorless cameras.

"I don't know if it works, but I want it," Alex said, staring down at a vintage instant film camera. It, with a black and silver striped design, looked right out of the box brand-new. His palms itched to hold it.

"Get it," Lucy said. She looked at the camera and checked

out the sticker tag. "That's not a bad price. I'll buy it for you." Lucy reached for her purse.

Alex placed his hand on hers, stopping her from moving. "I don't need it."

"You obviously want it." She peered at him confused. Of course, he wanted it, but where was he going to keep it? With a sudden pang of awareness, he realized he wanted to take this camera home. A thread of yearning pulled through him. He wanted to put it on the mantel and take instant pictures. *No. Keep only what you can carry.* Alex gave an easy laugh, trying to hide the fact he had an epiphany next to an artisanal hot-dog stand.

"Don't spend any money on me," Alex said. "Besides, I don't have any room in my bag, or it might get broken in the move."

Lucy said nothing but stared at him for a long instant. He felt himself becoming uneasy under her attention.

"Okay," Lucy said, but her unconvinced tone told him another story. She'd probably bring it up later tonight. They walked away from the camera tables. Alex looked her over, trying to get his thoughts off even thinking about home.

She wore jean overalls with a tank top that proudly declared TOWN WITCH.

He relished seeing a flash of smooth skin whenever she moved around the flea market. "I didn't know you could look so cute in overalls."

"Please. Don't lie to me." Lucy grinned. "I feel like I'm going apple picking."

"That can be arranged," Alex said. He ran his hand down her arm and took her hand in his as they walked through the market. Their hands interlocked with each other, and she just fit right here next to him. They went over to another seller right across from the camera stand.

"So, you said you had some big news."

"Quentin contacted me about the alumni awards. Apparently, there was an error, and I won an award."

"Which award did you win? Most Photogenic?"

Lucy didn't meet his eye. "I won the Class Cup."

Alex reeled back. Okay now. According to his social media posts, the Freya Grove Class Cup was awarded to alumni who'd been on international magazine covers, won Oscars, and made an impression on the world. He absolutely adored Lucy, but her current accomplishments didn't qualify her for the award. She'd earn the award in her own time, not because of the spell.

"I can feel you thinking. Trust me, I'm freaking out."

"So, you're going to turn it down."

Lucy squeezed his hand.

"I can't. They already took the award from another person. I'd look like a fool. I can't tell them about the spell. I don't know what will happen to me if I break it. I'll figure it out."

Alex opened his mouth, then shut it. She'd figure it out on her own without his help. Lucy didn't ask or want his opinion about the reunion. Besides, he'd be riding out of town at the same time she'd be giving her speech. A swift sadness stole his breath for a long second. He really was leaving.

Lucy dropped his hand and gasped. "I can't believe it!"

Alex watched as Lucy made a beeline right for a pair of lamps nestled next to a massive ship in a bottle.

"May I?" Lucy asked the vendor. The woman in a

short-sleeve shirt covered in orange slices, a safari hat, and jean shorts nodded.

Carefully, Lucy picked up one lamp and showed him. It wasn't anything too special, but it did have that simple seaside vibe he was going for with the house.

"We can't leave without getting these. I put them on our mood board. I manifested these lamps." Lucy waved a hand over it as if she were showing off a grand prize on a game show. Alex just listened to her talk. He could listen to her read from a weather app; it didn't matter. "Recycled wood banister with distressed white paint. We can replace the shade, but they'd be perfect for the living room."

Alex checked out the price tag. Whoa. He blinked rapidly, hoping that maybe he added on an extra zero. "For that price, a genie needs to come out both of them."

The vendor perked up. "If you're looking for a genie lamp, I know someone who can help."

Alex held up a hand. "No thank you, ma'am."

"These are perfect for the end tables. You can't put a price on perfection. It'll tie the living room together."

Lucy bounced on her toes doing a little cute dance, cradling the lamp. He wanted to make her happy, but that price was bending the budget. The house didn't need it, but maybe they could find a compromise.

"Let's look around and if we can't find anything better, then we'll be back."

"Okay," Lucy said, giving him a pout. She patted the lamp and returned it to the vendor. "You're the boss. It's your home."

Lucy made an *oop* face. He froze. Her words played in a loop in his head. The world spun around him as if he were on a carousel. *It's your home.* It *was* his home. Lucy reached up and placed a hand to his forehead. Her hand felt so soft and cool against his skin.

"Hey, you look a little pale."

"I'm fine. I should get some water," Alex said. He patted her hand and stepped back. If he touched her again, he'd want to hold on and not let go. *We accidentally hurt our lovers by taking them underwater for too long. We forget to let them go.*

"Stay here. I'll get us something to cool us off."

Lucy went off toward the row of food trucks.

He looked over his shoulder at the camera table down the way. That instant film camera was still there waiting for him, taunting him to take it. To want. He wanted to *stay.* Alex stopped and a took a deep breath. He wanted to stay, keep this house, and make it into his home. Their home. He wanted Lucy to stay with him. This mistake wasn't supposed to happen again.

Alex looked around until he found her. Lucy was walking back toward him, cradling two drinks in her hands. One cup was just iced tea, but the other was mixed lemonade and iced tea. Such a small detail to some people meant so much to Alex. It meant a lot to the merman who had never found his place to know that he had this temporary safe space with her. He couldn't keep his eyes off her even though she wasn't looking at him. She was joined by two people.

Poe stood on one side, while Lucy chatted with Theo. Joy radiated from her entire self.

When you gave your heart and soul to a place or a person, you gave it the power to shatter your heart and tear apart your soul. You can't lose what you don't carry. If your hands are always empty, you can't leave anything behind. This cottage wasn't supposed to complicate his life. She had to understand that a merman couldn't be kept in a fishbowl. The world was waiting for him. *You knew better than to believe in the Grove; you were always going to leave.* He couldn't stay. If he stayed, he'd eventually let her down and disappoint everyone. His heart dropped to his stomach.

We forget humans need air, land, and sunshine.

Lucy belonged here. He didn't belong, even though he wanted to with every ounce of ocean water in his veins. Alex couldn't ask her to go with him. He didn't even know where he was going to stay. She had her students, her coven, and her life in the Grove. If he stayed, she'd stay and give up everything she wanted just to make him feel secure. She'd get into the residency program because she was brilliant and deserved to do amazing things. Grounded. Safe. He had no right after all this time to ask her to change her plans, her dreams, because he decided to stay for now. He watched her laugh at something Poe said.

He didn't want to get in the way of her wish.

✳

Lucy wished she had a sock so she could stuff it into her big mouth. She'd seen the blood drain from his face when she slipped up and said the word "home" to Alex. The one time she wanted her mouth not to work, it did without a problem and completely derailed the day. He didn't even want her to touch him.

She rushed off to get them drinks from the Refresh Hut truck, thinking of ways to ease his nerves. Lucy didn't mean to rattle him, but it was clear as day that he didn't want to leave. He hadn't packed up his clothes from the bedroom. His cameras were all over the table. Evidence of his life was scattered all over his home, but he acted like he was just visiting.

Lucy wished to not so gently shake some sense into him and say, "You're home. Stay."

On her way back to Alex, Lucy ran into Poe and Theo, who were shopping for the grand opening of Rain or Shine Bookstore.

"We're looking at decorations for the store," Poe said. "We're thinking a cozy book nook house feel."

"Why would people want to leave their house to sit in a place that feels like a house?" Theo pointed out.

"Eh," Lucy said, smiling. "He does have a point."

"Well, help us design and plan the store. We'd love to have your help."

Lucy agreed to meet up with them early next month. Hopefully, the wish would hold out long enough that she'd be able to help them. When she returned to Alex, he thanked her for the drink and barely said three words out loud. He didn't reach for her hand but stayed close to her side.

A vendor wearing a shirt that boldly stated COLLECT MEMORIES standing by a massive jewelry kiosk called out to Alex. He got his attention with a high whistle and a wave.

"Hey, bro. Buy your lady something nice."

Alex looked to Lucy. She nodded. "I could use a little sparkle for the wedding."

They went over to the booth. Necklaces of every length and jewelry of different sizes and shapes were displayed before her.

"This is you." Alex pointed to one of the rings displayed on a large porcelain dish. "It'll match your earrings. Try it on."

"It's a little much for a wedding." It was a classic princess-cut platinum ring that could've been in an upscale jewelry boutique. Alex took the ring out of the holder. Lucy held out her hand and he slipped it on her finger. The emerald ring flanked by two small diamonds fit perfectly.

The vendor nodded with a smile. "Look at that. It's made for you."

She wiggled it, getting used to the weight. Her heart squealed in glee. It would go nicely with her earrings. She looked up at Alex. He placed an arm around Lucy and pressed his head next to hers in a supportive side hug. She breathed in his clean, sea-salt scent, and her body fit against his. He kissed her temple and whispered against her hair. *Click.* Every muscle in her body tensed. *Click.* He was hers. Even if he were on the other side of the solar system, he belonged to her and no other. She was overcome with the urge to fall to her knees and sob. *Click.*

She leaned away from him and shook her head. "This is too much."

"It's just enough," Alex said. He paid the vendor.

"Do you want to wear it or hold it?" the vendor asked.

Lucy slid it off her finger and cradled it. "Um—I'll hold it."

Why could he give her something meaningful, but she couldn't? It wasn't fair.

"So, you can buy me a gift, but I can't buy you anything."

"You have a place to keep it."

"So do you," she snapped. "You have a whole home—wait, my fault. You have a *house*. For a second, I thought that maybe you might have changed your mind. That you'd—" She snapped her mouth before the truth slipped out. *Wish for me. Wish for us.* Every moment she spent with Alex felt as if she were grasping at sand—time slipped and spilled through her fingers, and what was left were haunting memories. She'd be in the shop or running errands, and she'd recall the rough stubble against her thighs or his hands teasing and stroking her until she cried out in release.

Lucy gave him back the ring. He stared at it then put it in his pocket. She could feel the hurt flash in his face.

She couldn't wear it and not wish for him to be there. It was too much and not enough at the same time. She didn't want the ring; she wanted him, body and soul.

"It looks like an engagement ring!" she exclaimed. "People are going to start asking when we're getting married," she said.

"We know the truth. You're marrying your soul mate," Alex said, a little too peppy for Lucy's liking. "That's what you wished for."

"You don't need to remind me. I know."

A tense moment passed between them.

"I'll meet you at the wedding?" Alex asked.

"I can go alone."

"I promised I would go with you. If you don't want me to go now, then tell me. You don't have to worry about my feelings."

She cared too much about his feelings. His heart. He

didn't want to stay. She was letting him go because she loved him enough to give more than the Grove. *Nana, I get it now. You can't keep a merman in a fishbowl, because he deserves the ocean.* Alex looked at her, waiting for her to respond.

"I know you have a lot to do with the open house," Lucy said. "I mean, there's going to be a lot of people there, and you know how it goes. It'll make it hard to explain what happened to us when"—she paused to breathe—"when you leave. I'll still be here being asked, 'Where's Alex? Where did he run off to now?' Meanwhile, you're sunbathing in Bali."

"It's none of their business." Alex waved off those questions.

"The Grove makes everything their business," Lucy countered.

"So do you want me to stay so that they don't talk about you?"

"Stay because you want to stay. Stay because I..." Lucy faltered. *I want you. I need you. I love you.* She let out a sharp sigh.

"Come with me," Alex said. Fate had terrible timing. She had wished to hear those three words years ago. Now, they terrified her.

"I can't."

"I'm not staying," Alex said, his tone final.

Something snapped within Lucy. This wasn't the time to hold back but to put it all on the table.

"You've said it enough times. I believe you. Do you believe it yourself? All this talk and you haven't packed anything. You want to stay. I can see it." Lucy gave him a side-eye look.

"I knew better than to come back," Alex said, his shoulders dropping.

"Why? Because people might have the nerve to depend on you?" Lucy asked. Alex said nothing. "I thought that maybe, just maybe, you'd fall in love with the Grove again. You never lied to me about who you were, but it still hurts to know you're leaving."

"I said I couldn't stay," he said.

"You didn't even try," she said, dropping her head to her chest.

"The Grove will always be here," Alex said, his voice sounding hollow.

Lucy gave him a stiff smile. "Yeah. I guess it will be, but I won't."

"If you could wish for me to stay, would you?" he asked. "I just want to know."

Well, damn. Lucy drew her lips into her mouth. Of course, she wanted to wish for him, but what if she failed to keep his heart? If the wish worked on Alex, it would never be real. She could never trust that he'd stayed in the Grove because he wanted to and not because her words compelled him to stay.

"I don't see the point in wishing for that," she finally said. She wasn't going to guilt him into staying where he didn't want to be. He didn't fall for her before the wish, but only after it came true. Her soul called out to him, *I can't keep you here. You have to want to stay here.*

"You're going to get an offer at the open house," Lucy said.

"I'll turn it down," he said, but there was a note of uncertainty.

"What if someone offers you a million dollars?" she blurted out.

It wasn't uncommon for houses at the Jersey Shore to sell for as low as fifty thousand to into the tens of millions. There wasn't a number on a check that could ever make her give up the Caraway house. She hoped that he knew that his home was priceless.

"For a million dollars, anywhere can be home," Alex said.

He didn't even hesitate with his answer. Her stomach dropped. She had heard enough. It wasn't the answer she wanted, but at least it was honest. Alex closed his eyes, then opened them. It was clear from the dimmed light she saw in there that he regretted his response.

"Wait, let's talk about this." Alex reached out for Lucy, but she held up her hands.

This was her cue to bow out. She was taking it.

"We had fun. Let's not leave on a sad note," Lucy said. Alex stiffened. She mustered up enough cheeriness to fake her way through her breaking heart. "Safe travels, Alex."

She turned and walked away, willing herself not to look back.

The wish would end, and she'd go back to being boring Lucy. Whatever spark she'd captured over the summer would fizzle out, and then it would be back to her old life. She didn't want him to resent her for asking him to stay when he didn't want it. He'd get bored with her and the Grove. The world waited for Alex. She loved him enough to let him go.

You don't need to complicate his life. This is why you don't give your heart away. It can be broken. People can be thoughtless and careless with your heart. He hadn't asked for her heart and soul, but she'd given them to him anyway without realizing it. *Silly witch.*

Chapter Twenty-Four

☾

The Berkeley Hotel, built in the year of Freya Grove's founding, was the meeting place of those who mattered and those who had power in the community. Local people often saved for months, even years, to afford an evening of Berkeley luxury. Inside the ballroom, paper and foil stars dangled from the ceiling; the slightest breeze sent them moving to and fro. The ballroom was packed with people and mystic beings decked out in suits and dresses, cradling and clutching their half-empty champagne flutes and making hushed conversation. The live band played music made for ignoring, making enough noise that people could speak over it without shouting. Lucy adjusted her dress, a cocktail gown the color of sunshine, to keep it from slipping down. She didn't want to accidentally flash her cousin's future in-laws. All night Lucy was given openly curious looks from many of the members, who whispered behind their glasses and hands. Apparently not everyone was used to seeing a Caraway woman in evening wear. Her family usually leaned into more natural clothing that mirrored their connection to the elements. The Walkers were splurging for the good stuff for the wedding rehearsal dinner.

"Hey, Caraway." Marcus came over to her. He wore a sharp pin-striped suit that molded to his body. He looked her over. "You look lovely."

"Thank you. You clean up nicely," Lucy said.

He gave her a narrowed, glinting glance. "How's that merman of yours?"

Her breath caught in her throat as she felt her entire body ache. Even days later, it pained her to think of him and how things ended between them. She thought about calling Alex and just talking it out, but she couldn't bring herself to even open his contact page. It wasn't fair to ask him to give her what he couldn't give yet. Marcus waited expectantly for an answer.

"He's good," she said with a note of finality.

"Do you want to take a walk outside?"

Lucy nodded. They went outside through the ballroom door, to the patio. The ocean waves in the near distance crashed against the shore. Seagulls squawked and flew around the lights.

"How's your maid of honor speech?" Marcus asked.

"I wrote that months ago. Please tell me you've at least started yours."

Uncertainty crept into his expression. He took out his phone and opened what looked like a Notes app. "I jotted down a few things here. Do you mind if I read it to you?"

"Let's go."

Marcus took a deep breath, then began reading his speech out loud. Some sixth sense brought her fully awake with every word he said. The nagging in the back of her mind refused to be stilled as he talked about love. He wasn't talking only about marriage and unity, but the preciousness of love.

"You really love Ursula."

Marcus's head snapped up from his screen, and he leaned away from her. "W-what? I don't—can't believe you just said that." His lips thinned in anger, and he pocketed his phone quickly, as though she'd caught him looking at it in class. "Ursula was right. You like causing drama."

Lucy stood in his way, stopping his retreat through the ballroom's double doors.

"Hold on. Let's talk about this."

Marcus backed away from Lucy. "There's nothing to talk about. Just because you're sprung over Alex doesn't mean you have to pair everyone off. What kind of man would I be to—" Marcus interrupted himself. He wiped a hand over his face. "He loves her. She loves him. Point. Blank."

"Are you sure?"

"Don't go there," he replied sharply. She steeled herself against his harsh tone. He wasn't going to bully her into being quiet. "We're going to stand up with her the day after tomorrow and be there. Nothing else."

"We're supposed to be there for her, but is Lincoln there for her? Be real."

Marcus just glared at Lucy; his nostrils flared. Their mutual silence spoke volumes.

She kept going. "Think about it. He hasn't picked out a wedding song or even a color, but you did it all. I think you enjoy being the stand-in groom."

"Leave it alone, Lucy. This is everything that she wants. She wished for this day." He said these words with a tone of inevitability. Marcus glowered at her. He turned away, facing the waves.

"She told you about the spell."

"She didn't have to," he said. "She's easy to read when you notice the signs."

Lucy took a deep breath and decided to relax. *How did I miss it?* She replayed the karaoke night and the wedding preparations in her mind. Marcus had always been there, by Ursula's side, helping her make the day happen. With a pang, she realized that Ursula had fallen for the wrong Walker man. She'd been asked to be the maid of honor, but at what cost? Everyone was so excited about the wedding, the first one in ten years and the biggest celebration since Nana's passing. Was her responsibility to the bride or to the wedding? Marcus studied Lucy. The scrutiny in his eyes sharpened. She saw the unspoken question in his eyes. *What are you going to do?* There was no choice.

"I want her to be happy. What do you want?" Lucy asked.

"I want her to get what she wants." He licked his lips, clearly trying to accept the weak response he'd given her. No, she wasn't going to let him get away with that answer.

"And what if what she wants makes her miserable? What then? What happens then?" she asked, holding back a scream of frustration. His face, clouded in uneasiness, said nothing. Marcus walked around her and went back into the ballroom.

Lucy fought to control the emotions reeling inside her. She didn't want to use any spells or charms. Magic couldn't get her out of this hot-buttered mess, but an honest conversation might work. Marcus needed to find the courage to tell Ursula on his own. She wasn't going to share his secrets or do his dirty work for him.

Lucy opened the door, but someone stood in her way. Her stomach twisted, but she forced herself to put on a polite smile. "Hey, cousin, I was just looking for you."

Ursula's stare drilled into Lucy, her bejeweled cousin holding her evening purse out like a sword.

"I bet you were," she whispered, boxing out Lucy from the doorway. Ursula pushed them both onto the patio, slamming the door. It rattled as she closed it with a bang. Lucy took a huge step back from her. They stared at each other across the space, neither of them talking.

She crossed her arms and pointedly looked away. "Marcus told me your little plan."

"What plan?"

"You're going to object to my wedding. You're ruining my day," Ursula said. "I knew you were jealous. The best part of your life is because of a spell. My spell. If it weren't for me, you'd be dealing with your sad, boring life."

"Watch it," Lucy warned.

"Truth hurts. I'm sorry you can't handle it. You can't deal with yourself, so you screw with me," Ursula replied. "I have enough to worry about. I don't need to worry about you objecting. I'm fine. I don't want you to rescue me." Her voice rose to a hysterical pitch. "Do you know how much money this wedding cost? All the time and energy we've spent getting ready for this day? This wedding is happening whether you want it to or not, whether I'm okay or not."

Ursula choked out that last word. Her breath came out in sharp, unsteady pants.

Lucy pressed her hands together. "Listen to yourself."

"I can't," Ursula said harshly, as if what Lucy suggested was the wildest thing in the world.

"It's okay not to be okay," Lucy said. "You don't have to do this. You have a *choice*."

Those words seemed to penetrate the fog that Ursula was in. She blinked, then refocused on Lucy. Suddenly her shoulders slumped. "I can't."

Lucy reached out to Ursula, but she snapped back. She held up her hands, stepping away from Lucy, widening the gap between them. "You can't come in here and...stop my wish. You can't do it. You can't be my maid of honor. Don't come to the wedding. If you show up, you'll be removed. Don't test me. I'll curse you myself. I swear." A thin chill hung on the edge of her words. Fear and anger knotted inside Lucy's chest, nearly rendering her speechless. She faced Ursula. She wasn't done, not yet.

"Caraways stick together," Lucy said. It was a vow. It was a pledge. It was an oath.

"I'm not a Caraway anymore; I'm a Walker," Ursula said in a low voice, taut with fury. "I have something for you." Ursula dug into her purse. A small hope flared in Lucy, but it was soon snuffed out. Ursula pulled out a coin and shoved it at her.

Lucy didn't look down, but her heart already knew it was Nana's dime. She blinked hard, but tears came anyway. Everything she'd feared had come true, and no spell or charm could fix what was broken between them. "I thought you needed this."

Ursula snapped her purse closed. She shot Lucy a cold look. "I'm good. I have everything I need."

Chapter Twenty-Five

There was nothing that could cure her heartache like a Mimi's milkshake. She didn't mean to hurt anyone, but it seemed that every time she opened her mouth, she said something that changed her relationship. In less than a week, Lucy had managed to alienate Ursula, piss off an entire wedding party, and scare off Alex. She'd become the woman she'd always wished to be, and she didn't like it very much. Lucy settled in the booth in the back, unable to even look at the waitress who took her order. Her level of screw-up deserved at least a large peanut-butter-cup milkshake and an order of sweet potato fries. If she was going to throw herself a pity party, then she was going to eat whatever she wanted. Halfway through her milkshake, Lucy saw Sirena and Callie shuffle into the diner. Sirena was still dressed in her chef's whites. Callie was in her Meadowdale College sweatshirt and a pair of stretch pants. Lucy took in her younger sisters in awe. They were living out their wishes and making strides. She couldn't help but feel pride in them. They settled into the booth with her.

"How did you find me?" Lucy asked.

She'd deliberately left her phone off, unable to deal with

calls and texts from Auntie Niesha as she left. Auntie was the peacekeeper of the family. She'd want to know what happened and how she was going to fix it immediately.

"We scried for you," Callie said. "Niesha told us what happened."

Lucy recapped the evening with Ursula, leaving out the conversation with Marcus. Callie stared down at her hands. Sirena clenched and unclenched her fists. Once Lucy finished sharing what happened, her sisters were silent, but they looked at her.

Sirena gave her an incredulous look. "I can't believe she said that to you."

Callie turned away, unable to look at Lucy. "We're supposed to be family."

"Our wishes started all this nonsense. We need to fix it," Sirena said. Her eyes flashed with determination.

"No," Lucy said. "This separation was starting long before what we wished for. We just sped it up. I don't regret anything; I just wish it didn't go down like this." She blew out a sharp breath. It didn't matter if she won awards or gained clout if she didn't have family and friends to celebrate with. She'd lost so much in the last few days that what she'd gained wasn't worth it.

"Let's talk about something else. How's school going?"

"Well, I didn't fail my class," Callie said proudly. "I'm enrolling for the fall semester."

"That's great. You're doing the damn thing, Cal." Callie brightened. Lucy faced Sirena. "How's the restaurant going, Si? Did you get any investors?"

"Maybe. I'll check in with Felix. It's fine. Everything's okay." Sirena waved her hand dismissively. "No, wait. It's not okay. I can't stop thinking about this—spell. Ursula's wrong."

Sirena's voice rose. A few dining patrons turned their heads in her direction. She continued talking while ignoring everyone. "I'm not going to the wedding if you can't. She can't kick you out. If you don't go, we all don't go."

"All for one, one for all," Callie said.

Lucy teared up. Her heart swelled at their absolute loyalty, but it wasn't worth breaking up the entire family. "She's still family."

"I think she's forgotten."

"No." Lucy lowered her voice, playing with the fork and spoon. "It's her wish. She's getting what she wants, so let her get what she wants."

Callie looked from Lucy to Sirena. "What if what she wants sucks?"

"I don't know if I can watch this train wreck," Sirena said.

"Sirena," Lucy said. "I can't reach her, not if she's under the spell. It's grown too powerful."

"How long will that last? Two days. Two months? Two years?" Callie shook her head. Unshed tears made her eyes wet and glossy. "There has to be a way to stop it."

"We can't. I consulted the *Wishcraft* book. If we try to stop the wishes, then . . . it's going to be worse for all of us," Lucy said.

"How?" Sirena demanded.

Lucy took a deep breath. "Think about stopping a train instantly—you need three or four times the force to stop it. We need a spell four times as strong to end it, and we don't have one. Even if we brought other Caraway witches in to help us reverse it, she'll always remember we stopped her wish. She'd never trust us again. We have to let it play out. No matter what happens."

"What if we lose her for good?" Callie asked, her voice so small Lucy strained to hear it. Sirena paled. "What if we lose each other?"

"We won't. I'm not going to let that happen," Lucy swore. She held out her hands to her sisters. Callie took her hand and squeezed. Sirena grasped her hand tightly. "Caraways stick together. Always. We're blood. We've got magic in our veins. We're the ones our ancestors wished for. We're divine. We're bound together no matter the distance."

Lucy had to trust the blood would bring Ursula back home one day. She might take Lincoln's name, but the magic would keep her connected to the Caraways. Blood would bring her home one day. The more she repeated it, the more she willed herself to believe it.

"We never should've cast the spell. We were better before," Sirena said. Lucy opened her mouth to disagree, but Callie scoffed. She held on tighter.

"Let's be real," Callie admitted. There was a meditative shimmer in her eyes, rimmed with unshed tears. "We weren't doing anything special before. What did Nana used to say? The worst things you could do with your magic is misuse it, refute it, and waste it."

"I remember," Sirena said wistfully.

"I completely forgot," Lucy said.

"We wasted our magic just trying to get by day by day. We weren't thriving, we're just surviving. It was enough, but not anymore. This spell was the kick in the ass we needed to start living our best lives," Callie said. The tears fell from her eyes, pooling underneath her chin. Lucy went to wipe them away, but Callie stopped her. "I'm finally back in school,

Sirena's searching for restaurant investors, and you—" Callie gave Lucy a watery smile. "You've transformed."

Sirena nodded in agreement. Lucy looked down at their hands. Interlocked. Together. United.

"It's all the wish. It's not me."

Callie coughed, unconvinced. "So the wish made you make the cake? The wish made you go after Alex? No, you said the words, but you've acted. The wish may have thrust you into the spotlight, but you didn't run. You shined. You've grown into who you're meant to be."

"When did you get so wise?"

"I learned from the best." Callie squeezed her hand.

"We'll see this spell to the end. We're all in," Lucy said.

"All in," Sirena and Callie echoed.

A calm washed over her like a slow wave. Lucy turned her thoughts inward. It was never the wish. It was her finding the courage to pursue the life she'd only dreamed about. She'd been sleepwalking through her life, but now she'd forced her eyes open to see the world and all its splendor. She'd been wading in puddles, safe from harm, but she was unsatisfied with shallow living. There was no way she could go back to living her life in fear.

She could sing. She could fail. Or she could live with a courageous heart.

If she admitted to making the wish, would she lose her nerve?

Would she lose the nerve to love Alex? There was only one way to find out, and she had one chance to be brave. She'd have to come clean with everyone in the Grove and herself.

Chapter Twenty-Six

Alex watched from the living room, arms crossed and jaw clenched, as potential buyers went in and out of his house. He felt like ants were crawling all over his skin, and he couldn't knock them off. A single thought kept running through his mind. *I don't like strangers in my house.* This morning he'd woken up and pressed his hand to the wall. It was cool to the touch, but there was a pulse of energy there that forced him to stand back. He should have canceled the open house visit, but he'd made a commitment to at least show off the cottage. Visitors tracked dirt in from outside. They touched his couch. They even scoffed at Lucy's colors. Annoyance set fire to his blood at people giggling behind their pamphlets. One potential buyer, a pale man wearing a black turtleneck and wire-rimmed glasses, came and scanned the living room.

"Blue and orange," he said with a slight sneer. He showed his fangs. "How sporty."

Alex cleared his throat. The turtlenecked man snapped a sharp look at him.

"It's tangerine and cobalt. It's complementary," Alex said forcefully. No one was going to diss their color scheme. They wanted to make it feel...like home. Alex glared at him.

The glasses man jolted, nodded to him, and went off into another room, shaking his head. Pop and Mom came into the house, wiping their feet on the mat. They shared the same look of displeasure as they took in the people moving throughout the house like ants on a hill. Horatio followed them, giving him a guarded look.

"Do I smell cookies?" Pop asked. He sniffed deeply and made a happy sound.

"The real estate agent put out some cookies," Alex said.

"They're free, right?"

"Pop, I guess so," Alex said, suddenly tired. He wanted to get this whole thing over with and spend time alone in his— home. Why did he keep using that word?

"It looks good, Alex." Horatio glanced around. He took out his cell phone and snapped a few pictures. "You did good."

"Yeah. It was all Lucy," Alex mused. There wasn't a single room that she hadn't touched with her personal influence. She'd been there to pick out the coral-colored pillows, the secondhand lamps she'd showed him at the flea market, and the paint samples. She'd given this cottage another chance at life. He'd gotten the second chance he wished for. Now, he was on the verge of walking away.

Mom shook her head side to side. "This isn't right. This isn't how it's supposed to be."

"Kia, please," Pop warned under his breath.

"You can't sell your cottage! Where will you live?"

"I'll find a place. I'll be fine."

He had to be fine. The cottage was going to be better off without him. Lucy would be better off without him.

"It's not fine. Where will my grandbaby live?"

Alex's face burned. *Say what now?* He stared down Mom. She slapped a hand over her mouth and slid a wide-eyed glance to Pop. He heard Horatio groan next to him.

"Excuse me. Repeat that again," Alex said.

"Uh..." Mom looked to Pop for help.

"Leave me out of this. I'm going to get a snack," Pop said. He gave a salute and went into the kitchen. Horatio followed him silently.

"Start from the top and keep talking." Alex rubbed his forehead to keep the growing headache at bay.

Mom pouted. "I had a vision."

Alex stilled. "You haven't had a vision since—" His voice broke off.

Mom nodded sagely. "I haven't had a vision since we moved here all those years ago. Then weeks before your twenty-ninth birthday, the vision came to me like a dream. Oh, it was so real. I saw you and Lucy living here. I saw my granddaughter learning how to walk on these floors. I saw you making a home here."

His head spun like a runaway carousel. "How could you see me here when I didn't own this house?" he asked.

"I saw it," Mom said fiercely. "It was meant to be."

"You believe I can do it? You believe I can keep this place." Alex kept that hope at bay. He couldn't believe it could be that simple.

"You have. She's been here with you, making this place into a home. She's your missing piece," Mom pressed.

"She's my soul mate," Alex said. The words felt odd in his mouth. His heart jumped, wanting to believe in those words. "You believe she's my soul mate?"

"I believe she's what your soul needs," Mom said. Alex felt it. Something clicked within him like the right key turning a lock and opening a door. All the hopes and fears he'd been holding on to were let out and set free. This was his home.

Pop and Horatio came back over to them. Alex turned to Pop, who had at least two cookies in his hand. "You knew about this?"

"Mom figured you needed a push," Pop said. "I'm not a knucklehead. I know what people think about me. Those same folks still trust me with their taxes and money, right? I can't be too much of a fool." Pop winked at him, then took a big bite of his cookie.

"I mean—" Alex waved his hand. "From the outside looking in, it does look a little wacky when you guys do random stuff like this."

"So what?" Mom threw up her hands. "We love risks. We love surprises."

"This place isn't a push; it's a shove," Alex said. He lowered his voice so only his family heard him. "I tried this home thing before. I didn't tell you, but I was engaged last year."

Alex waited. Pop kept chewing. Mom cocked her head to the side.

"Where have you been? Pop and I knew," Mom said.

Say what? Alex, speechless, turned to Horatio.

"I didn't know Mom knew how to find you online," Horatio said. "She still gives out her Hotmail email to people."

"I'm one of your ghost followers." Mom beamed at Alex, using the term to describe inactive Instagram accounts that followed his page. He wanted to give her the biggest hug and tell her how much he appreciated her and her shine.

"It wasn't a big secret," Mom said softly. "We figured you'd tell us when you were ready to share. I was hoping you'd bring it up, but you didn't."

He couldn't hold back anymore. It was time to say out loud what he feared to those who mattered so much to him.

"I was embarrassed," Alex said, his voice faltered. He took a breath and pushed on. "I failed. I knew better, but I tried anyway. Domestic life isn't our strength. It sure isn't mine."

Mom stood tall with every inch of her five-foot frame. "No, but love is our strength. Joy is our strength. You must work to keep this life, but it's good work. It's worthwhile," Mom said. "Even though we weren't good at this doesn't mean you can't try. All we ask is that you try to make this place your home."

It was scary to try. To try and feel like you were going to fail. He hadn't truly tried with Nahla, because then he'd be crushed if it didn't work out. He'd tried more with Lucy than he'd ever done in the past but backed out when he'd fallen for her. Alex glanced around at the crochet throws and mismatched chairs. His chest swelled with emotion, and he nodded, unable to speak. This place wasn't part of the plan, but it was home. A sense of peace came over him. He'd made a home, but he wanted Lucy here with him forever. For always. He turned back to Mom.

"Where's Lucy?" She glanced around the living room. "I know she doesn't want people to bring dirt inside her house."

She turned and faced him with a hopeful smile. He felt his face fall. "I messed up."

"Whatever happened, it's not too late to tell her how you

feel," Mom said. "You just look to the horizon and take a big leap."

Alex looked around his house. He cleared his throat and called everyone's attention. "I'm afraid this house is off the market. The owner changed their mind. I don't mean to be rude, but you don't have to go home, but you can't stay here."

Disappointed groans and grumbles erupted from buyers. He sighed; all the tension left his body. Goddess, it felt good to say that out loud. Mom clapped. Pop gave him a slap on the shoulder. Horatio gave him a fist bump.

The man in the turtleneck came up to him. "What happened? Did you lose your nerve?" he sneered.

Alex smiled. Nothing was going to ruin his good mood. "No, sir, I wised up."

Chapter Twenty-Seven

☾

The Grove Pavilion, a landmark building, was where all anniversaries, reunions, and other celebrations were held for all local shore towns. The pavilion had seen its share of scandalous and exciting events over the last hundred years and continued to be a gathering place for all the Grove. Now the graduates of Freya Grove High School gathered here to brag or forget their collective memories. The main room was decorated for the Class of '12 with purple and gray balloon arcs around every entrance. It was packed with people decked out in suits and dresses, clutching their half-empty champagne flutes, making hushed conversation. A portable DJ booth played a mix of one-hit wonders and popular songs from their high school years to get everyone in a nostalgic and jovial mood. Flashes of cell phones went off like exploding stars, making Lucy shield her eyes from the bright lights.

People approached her throughout the evening. They came up to her with outstretched arms and big smiles, hugging her. Classmates approached her, and their words troubled her thoughts.

"Your class notes update made me feel so lazy. I need to get my life together."

"You're who I want to be when I grow up."

"I wish I had your life. You deserve the Class Cup!"

They envied a life that wasn't real. Their compliments, sweet and thoughtful, lowered her spirits but confirmed that she was making the right choice. She hoped everyone had enough space on their phones to record what was going to happen next. It was time for the wish to end. Technicolor lights flashed on the dance floor, while various tables had been abandoned and clutch purses were ditched on the plush seats. Classmates went back and forth between the dance floor and the bar, cradling drinks and bopping to the throwback music. Purple and gray tulle artfully decorated pillars around the ballroom.

The centerpieces were vases filled to the brim with pink and purple stargazer lilies in full bloom. Lucy clutched her phone, focusing on the task to come. She opened her email and read the real class notes. Mixed feelings surged through her, but one feeling stood out. Love. She loved herself enough to be honest about her life with everyone. She was done with feeling afraid and ashamed of the life she'd worked to create. It was time to tell the Grove. The music was turned down. The DJ called for everyone to return to their seats. Once everyone was seated, Quentin made his way to the stage. He stood in front of a table lined up with different trophies and awards.

"Welcome to the Freya Grove Class Reunion Awards. We'd like to say hello to everyone here in person and hello to those joining us on our livestream—"

Did he say livestream? Lucy blinked away the rising hysteria in her chest. *Great.* Now her downfall was going to be broadcast all over the internet. She prayed that she wouldn't be turned into a GIF or—worse—a meme.

"It's time for the event you've all been waiting for! Let's hand out our awards."

For the next twenty minutes, Lucy watched as person after person went up to the stage to claim their award. She slipped her phone into her dress pocket and patted it.

"The Freya Grove Alumni Committee would like to present Lucy Caraway with the Class Cup." Quentin held out the award.

Lucy took a calm breath. Applause erupted from the crowd. She got onstage, thanked Quentin, and took the brass cup from him. It felt hollow and empty. She approached the podium and spoke into the microphone.

"Thank you for this honor," Lucy said. "I know many of you probably saw my class notes earlier this summer."

A knowing murmur went through the crowd. "The note I sent Quentin was what I wished my life was. It was every wish I had for my life but didn't have the courage to make come true. I had never cooked a croquembouche or designed a house or finished a race or fallen head over heels in love with my soul mate—or my starfish—but since making that wish, I did. I made a wish, and somehow it all came true, despite me getting in my own way. It was wishful thinking that made me into the person I've always dreamed of being."

There was absolute silence. Lucy placed the award back on the podium.

"I'd like to make a late correction." She took out her phone and opened her email. "'The last ten years have been kind of busy for basic home witch Lucy Caraway. She's had the pleasure of teaching history and economics at Freya Grove High School for the past seven years to great, amazing students, occasionally finding sticky notes in the oddest places.'"

Light laughter bubbled from the crowd. She continued reading, keeping her eyes on the class notes.

"'She loves her porch plants, tries not to burn down her kitchen baking desserts, and plans to get up the energy for a weekend run one day soon. When she isn't reading tea leaves for neighbors or organizing her tea closet, she's buying more tea in bulk.'"

There were light chuckles, but no one interrupted or yelled. *Keep going, Lucy. Keep going.*

"'She does her best to be a good sister, daughter, and friend, but sometimes she messes up. Nothing's changed much, but she sees her life as it is and knows that she's beyond blessed to be loved and cared for.'"

Her voice broke. She thought of Callie and Sirena. Of Ursula and of all her family and friends who were always on her side. She couldn't have wished for a better family. Lucy opened her mouth, but her voice failed her. Shouts of encouragement came from the crowd. "You've got this!" "We've got your back, sis!" were repeated. She pushed through and picked up where she'd left off.

"'She's going to take more risks, make wonderful mistakes, and not let fear hold her back from living. She hasn't claimed her soul mate yet, but she knows she's one wish from finding her happily-ever-after or happy-for-now ending.'"

Lucy looked out at the audience. Eyes shone with unshed

tears. Heads were lowered in thought. Hands were pressed to lips.

"If you have the courage to wish, you have the courage to act. I've found it, but I found it a little too late. That's why I'm respectfully turning down the Class Cup. I'll earn it one day, but I haven't earned it yet. Thank you for making me want to be better and do better."

Lucy stepped away from the podium. She walked offstage and walked out of the pavilion.

With every step she took, she felt the wish wash away from her skin. Once she was outside in the warm summer air, she was exactly who she wanted to be.

Lucinda Ruth Caraway was all she could ever wish for.

✳

Alex received the video recording from an old classmate who'd attended the reunion. He clicked on the link and heard Lucy's voice, a little wobbly but clear, as it came through his phone's speaker. He listened to her words, his heart aching with every single line. He wanted nothing but to pull her into his arms and hold her. She'd done it. She'd given up the image of the person she showed the Grove and instead had become who she was. She'd done it for them. He looked around the house.

Love had the power to break your heart. Everything else paled in comparison to what he had here at Summerfield Street. His life before, with Nahla, didn't have enough space for anything that mattered. He didn't make room because, ultimately, he was too scared to make it matter. Lucy mattered. Their love mattered. What they made here in the cottage mattered. Hopefully he had enough paint left for what he needed to do. He couldn't make her wish come true, but he could give her a sign. He needed help. He wondered if the gnomes could do him a quick favor. He had to be the brave one this time.

Chapter Twenty-Eight

ucy took the long way home.

She turned off her phone, wanting a break from the calls and texts from her classmates and neighbors. Her body was still buzzing. Apparently, her speech was going viral. Callie was going to love it. Everyone in their own way was casting out their nets and hoping to make their secret wishes real. She parked her car down the street. As Lucy closed the driver's side door, she glanced over at Alex's house. She didn't see the sign on Alex's lawn at first, but the blocky blue and orange lettering caught her attention. The For Sale sign was gone. It was replaced with another sign. *What did the gnomes do now?* She'd have to speak to Herbie and Jinxie about cutting down on their tricks before the new buyers moved in. Lucy crossed the street to get a closer look. On Alex's front lawn, propped up by a crooked and quickly made easel, was a large sign. Her steps faltered when she read it. *No way.* She pressed a hand to her chest, barely able to control her gasp of shock.

YOU'RE MY WISH COME TRUE.

The cottage door opened. Alex came out holding a long wooden sign under his arm. He set down the sign, then approached her, smiling softly. *Damn, it hurts to see him.* Lucy wrapped her arms around her body. If she touched him, then she wasn't going to be able to stop.

"I figured the gnomes owed me a favor. Jinxie thinks you can do better, but Herbie and Half-Pint are on my side."

Lucy swallowed. She wanted to reach out and touch him, but she couldn't. Not yet. She needed to know where this was leading. "I don't know what to say."

"Well, I'm staying," Alex said. Her mouth dropped open. He held up a hand. "Please let me explain."

She moved her head from side to side, not really believing him. "What happened at the open house?"

"I told everyone, you don't have to go home, but you can't stay here."

"Alexander."

"Lucinda," Alex said, his voice raw. "I couldn't sell our home."

Lucy felt rooted to the ground. "I didn't ask you not to sell it. Maybe you can still get a few buyers."

"I don't want to sell."

"What makes this place home? Any place can be your home for a million dollars," she echoed his words back to him.

"You can buy a house. But you make a home. It's home because you're here." Alex pointed to the door. "Be my starfish. Be my soul mate. Be with me."

There was a light-blue wooden sign by the door, reading A SHORE THING. It was the name of their dream home, which they'd thought of years ago. It was everything she could've wished for.

"Phoebe helped me with a rush job," Alex explained.

Her soul spoke to her right then. *Open your heart to the possibilities of love. There are countless reasons to walk away. Find the reasons to stay.*

They faced each other less than a foot apart.

"I want you to stay. No wishes. No charms. No spells. Just love," Alex said. "I didn't keep anything because I didn't want to lose it. A merman knows about treasure. We know when we have something precious and rare. I didn't want to keep you because I didn't want to lose you."

"I'm here. Always here." Lucy reached up. She pressed her hand to his chest, over his heart. It quickened under her touch.

He closed his eyes and placed his hand on top of hers. "There's nothing in the world as lovely and beautiful as what we can build here." Alex held her. "I want you to apply for the residency in the fall."

"Are you sure? I don't have to—" Her voice broke off in midsentence.

Alex placed a hand on her shoulder. "I'll be here. I'll be waiting at home for you. I love you."

"I love you, too," Lucy said.

He wove his fingers through hers. Home. This was home. They fit together like the last two pieces of a jigsaw puzzle. It had taken them years to get to this point, but everything clicked together. They clicked. Her soul rejoiced. He wrapped her in his arms, then pulled back; love shone in his eyes deeper than any part of the ocean.

"Do you know what happened to the merman who fell in love with a witch?" Alex asked.

"I have no clue, but I can't wait to find out," Lucy said, bringing him back into her arms.

He spoke against her forehead. "I've heard that if you catch a merman, you get a wish."

"No need. I have it all."

September 1

Dear Freya Grove Gladiators,

Thank you for an incredible and memorable re-union weekend. It was a celebration ten years in the making!

If you have any pictures or memories that you'd like to share, please forward them to me!

See you next year. Be well.

Best,
Quentin Jacobson
Class Secretary

Epilogue

The Following May

☾

*M*ake a wish." Lucy placed the funnel cake with a single candle in front of Alex. He peered down at the cake with a raised brow. They sat at the picnic tables adjacent to the Madame Zora booth, beneath the Ferris wheel lights.

"I thought you were baking me a cake," Alex said with a grin.

"I figured your sweet tooth wouldn't mind something different," Lucy said.

"I still want your sweet cream." The underlying silkiness in his voice captivated her.

"Well, I do take special requests." Lucy winked, waggling her brows at him. Alex gave her a long, lustful look, then blew out his candle. Lucy clapped. Alex tore the funnel cake into large chunks and handed her a piece. They ate, talking about which rides they wanted to go on and which games they wanted to play. She licked the sugar from her fingers while he watched her with a secretive smile.

"What did you wish for?" she asked.

His eyes sparkled under the festival lights. "I can't tell you or it won't come true."

Clever merman. His birthday gift arrived yesterday, but she hadn't had time to wrap it. She'd been too busy unwrapping him in their bedroom. Everything squealed at that thought. They had a home together. Lucy studied him; her chest burst at the sight of Alex. Her heart lifted. Everything was in its right place.

"If you keep staring at me like that, I might think you love me," Alex teased.

"I do. I absolutely do." She meant every word.

"Did you get Quentin's email?" Alex asked, cleaning the sugar from his hands with a napkin.

"I did. I'm skipping the class notes this year." Lucy ate another piece of funnel cake. If people wanted to know what was new with her, they could check in on her with a text. Otherwise, she didn't need to update people about her life. Her life was golden.

"Too bad. I'm submitting my note this time around," Alex said.

"Oh?" Lucy asked. She couldn't keep the surprise from her voice.

"Something tells me I'm going to have good news to share with the Grove." Alex tilted his head to the side. "Can I get your opinion on it? I'll give you a private reading."

"If you wanted to see me naked, all you had to do was ask."

A bright flare of desire sprang into his eyes. "I will do that."

Alex wore a threadbare Home and Hearth T-shirt, dark-wash jeans, and boots, but he wore the outfit like a designer suit. He was no longer the merman eager to explore other horizons. There was a sense of contentment in his soul that she recognized in him. He'd traveled down to Washington, DC, to visit her during her residency, and they'd called, video-chatted, and texted all the time just to keep, as the elders say, "the home fire burning."

Lucy returned to her home baker roots and continued to make treats for all the neighbors after her adventures in baking last summer. She kept in touch with the Delectables and even signed up for a culinary class. For Lucy's thirtieth birthday, Callie and Sirena bought an online class pass to Interior Design Basics. She learned more about design trends, fabrics, and color theory. Anything was possible if she tried with a fearless spirit and a gutsy heart. She'd let go of fear and held this life she'd made with Alex.

What a difference a year made. Life was filled with possibilities rather than limitations. Her teacup runneth over with blessings. Now there wasn't a day that they didn't share their hopes and dreams. Lucy had shared the job posting with Alex. He applied the next day. Alex, when he wasn't working on his gallery showing, taught photography classes at Meadowdale College to eager students looking to capture the world around them. He worked with Horatio to improve his social media presence and even helped him sign up for an Instagram profile to show off his renovations. Meanwhile, Lucy had recently finished up her work with the Library of Congress just last month. With her principal's support, she took a teaching sabbatical from her school to attend the residency program. She spent the spring studying priceless documents, creating lessons, and getting back that creative spark she'd lost over the last two years.

She'd booked the earliest train home right after the farewell dinner.

Alex had been there at the train station holding a sign reading WELCOME HOME.

Yes, she was home. They stood up from the table, gathered their trash and tossed it into the nearest can. When Lucy held Alex, it was as if the ocean met the shore, and she was in the right place. He pressed a kiss to the top of her head.

"How are the Caraway sisters?"

"Sirena practically sleeps at Ad Astra." Lucy felt herself frown. "I barely see Callie."

"Going back to college is no joke," Alex said, pride in his voice. Even though he wasn't blood yet, he treated her sisters and the Caraways as if they were his own. Aunt Niesha had adopted him as her nephew, and Uncle Leo made Alex his spades partner for every major holiday. Mom and Pop Dwyer spent Yuletide with them at the cottage.

Lucy sighed. Her gut rioted. "I'm proud, but I'm worried."

Alex wrapped a hand around her shoulder, settling her fears. "She's a Caraway, so she can do anything if she has magic on her side."

The magic was always with them. If she wasn't spending every other night at the cottage, then she was casting spells and helping her sisters whenever she saw them. They'd agreed to see the spell to the end, but things changed so rapidly. Sirena woke up before dawn to set up and prep the restaurant. Callie commuted to campus every other day, coming home well after dark, having opted to take night classes. They made time for tea, but their dreams and lives were taking them in new directions.

"I hope so, but something's changed." Lucy closed her eyes and breathed in the air. Everything pulsated with an invisible magic that was unknown. If people thought the Grove was strange, they hadn't seen anything yet. She snapped her eyes open and peered at Alex.

He watched her, concerned. "What do you mean?"

"Our wishes changed everything. I can feel it," Lucy said. "I don't think we've seen everything yet."

"Have you spoken to Ursula?"

Lucy shook her head sadly. They hadn't spoken since the rehearsal dinner. She had been unable to reach Ursula through the power of her wish. Lucy thought about texting and calling, but she couldn't bring herself to do it yet. Time healed old hurts. She hoped. She wished.

"Hey." Alex squeezed her hand. "I'm here when you want to talk."

"Thank you, love. Today we're celebrating you."

"We've celebrated all day—in bed, on the table, in the kitchen." Alex waggled his brow. "You know what I really want for my birthday?" He lowered his voice into a seductive whisper. *Mercy.* He held her flush against him. A familiar shiver of want went through her at his touch, and she wrapped her hands around his waist, settling into their embrace and shielding them from the world.

"I can imagine," Lucy said.

Softly, his breath fanned her face. "A paper fortune from Madame Zora."

Lucy groaned. She dropped her hands away from him. He gave a playful smile, then pointed over to the Madame Zora booth.

"That's not what I was expecting, but okay."

"I never got mine last year. I was too distracted by your beauty."

"Always the merman."

"I can't help it." Alex stood and held out his hand to

328

her. They fit together, her missing puzzle piece. They strolled over to the booth. Alex kept looking around as if something exciting was about to happen. Maybe they were going to get kettle corn and lemonade. Lucy stood in front of the electric-light sign of Madame Zora's Mystic Fortune Booth. Déjà vu rushed through her.

"Why don't you go first?" Alex suggested. "It worked out so well last time."

Lucy fed the money slot and pressed the button. Bells chimed, and a bright light emitted from the machine. The crystal ball glowed, and the robot-puppet waved her be-jeweled hand. The machinery whirled, clicking on the inside. She watched the fortune dispenser slot for the yellow paper. The machine grunted, then beeped. The paper dropped down. Lucy cheered.

She took the fortune and read it. She read it again.

Madame Zora says:
Say yes
Lucky numbers
1, 4, 3, 7, 10, 23

"What does it say?" Alex asked.

"It says 'say yes,'" Lucy said. She fought to control her worry. Usually, the fortunes were not so vague. Had she forgotten something about her wish?

"Hm. Madame Zora is never wrong," he responded, his voice sounding odd, as if he was low to the ground. Lucy heard movement behind her, but she paid it no mind. He'd probably dropped his keys.

"I mean, yeah, she's never wrong, but what am I saying yes to?" Lucy asked.

"Turn around and find out."

Lucy faced Alex, who was now on bended knee. He held out a ring. The same ring they'd picked out during the Funky Flea. The platinum emerald ring glittered under the neon lights of the Ferris wheel. Brilliant green sparks shimmered over the ground. She bit back tears, and she met his open, loving stare.

"I think you know what I wished for," Alex said. "Will you marry me?"

Pure love and affection shone in his eyes and brightened his face. Her future took shape before her eyes within the glittering gem. Holidays filled with joy and laughter. Mornings in the garden eating breakfast together and talking to each other about their life. Long afternoons filled with earth-shattering lovemaking. She chased after a hazel-eyed baby with curly hair at the beach while collecting seashells for their bucket. Alex met her eyes, and at that moment she knew. There was no other universe or world she wanted to be in but this one, here with him.

Lucy managed through her happy tears to give a breathless but steady "Yes."

He exhaled and slipped the ring on her finger. He kissed her hands, then looked up at her. "I can't wait to love you for the rest of our lives."

Alex stood, pressing sweet frantic kisses all over her face. Lucy laughed and held on to him. He captured her lips in his and embraced her. Could someone burst from too much joy?

Much later, when Lucy and Alex were alone back in Alex's bed, naked and satiated from bouts of frenzied lovemaking, they made plans. They wished together. Plans to get married at the festival. Plans to paint the guest room a pastel shade. Plans to grow and thrive in their home. She held up the engagement ring to be blessed by moonlight. Her heart sang. A sense of wonder filled her as she drifted off to sleep, safe in his arms.

She had everything she could ever wish for.

About the Author

A native of New Jersey, **Celestine Martin** writes whimsical romance that celebrates the beauty of everyday magic. She's inspired to write happily-ever-afters and happy-for-now endings starring the people and places close to her heart. When she's not drinking herbal tea and researching her next project, Celestine, with her husband, spoils their daughter in New York on a daily basis.

You can learn more at:

Website: CelestineMartin.com
Twitter @JellybeanRae
Instagram @CelestineMartinWrites